Who the Hell is Rachel Wells?

Meet

...Ermina and Dante, two fierce drag queens who teach a runaway teenager to sashay like RuPaul

...Anna Folanna, a one-time burlesque star held hostage wearing men's boxer shorts

...David Stoner, who still regrets his mother tossing away his collection of Barbie dolls

...Victor, a campus professor haunted by a funky jockstrap

...Greg and Erica, a normal suburban couple who inherit an unusual chair formerly owned by Paul Lynde

...and Daphne, the almost-winning drag queen whose ultimate goal is to emerge from the waves of Daytona Beach like Ursula Andress

...but who the hell is Rachel Wells?

Full of snappy and sharp Southern characters, *Who the Hell is Rachel Wells?* by J.R. Greenwell is a debut collection of clever, big-hearted tales of spunky souls and damaged hearts. Both serious and silly, bittersweet and joyous, these unique eleven short stories introduce a wise and wonderful new author.

"J.R. Greenwell does a lovely job of relaying the comic as well as tragicomic aspects of the over-the-top dramatic world of drag queens, and he nails it exactly."

—Felice Picano, author of *20th Century Un-limited* and *True Stories*

In the 1970's, J.R. Greenwell was a premiere headliner for many years at the Sweet Gum Head in Atlanta, GA, and performed as a female illusionist across the country. He later earned a Masters of Education at the University of Louisville, and now devotes his time as a queer writer creating plays and prose at his home in central Kentucky.

WHO THE HELL IS RACHEL WELLS?

STORIES

J.R. GREENWELL

CHELSEA STATION EDITIONS
NEW YORK

Cover photo by Jack Shelman
Cover and book design by Peachnoy Distillery and Designs

Published by Chelsea Station Editions
362 West 36th Street, Suite 2R
New York, NY 10018
www.chelseastationeditions.com
info@chelseastationeditions.com

ISBN: 978-1-937627-12-6
Library of Congress Control Number: 2013944784
First U.S. edition, 2013

These stories appeared, in slightly different form, in the following publications: "Who the Hell is Rachel Wells?" in *Saints and Sinners: New Fiction from the Festival 2011*; "The Scent of Honeysuckle," *Saints and Sinners: New Fiction from the Festival 2012*; "Silver Pumps and a Loose Nut," *Saints and Sinners: New Fiction from the Festival 2013*.

CONTENTS

Who the Hell is Rachel Wells?   9

Silver Pumps and a Loose Nut   29

The Scent of Honeysuckle   49

Spaghetti Kisses   69

A Colony of Barbies   75

Duplicity   97

Learning to Sashay Like RuPaul   135

Starting Rumors   157

Watch Me Walk   173

Out of the Closet   185

Virgil's Eulogy   201

WHO THE HELL
IS
RACHEL WELLS?

Who the Hell is Rachel Wells?

"It is the secret of the world that all things subsist and do not die, but only retire a little from sight and afterwards return again."
  Ralph Waldo Emerson.

The drive north on Interstate-65 was a long one for Linda and her two kids, but it was a route that they knew well. They often visited Linda's mother in Indianapolis, at least twice a year. Linda wanted to move near her mother and get out of Mobile altogether, especially after the unexpected death of her husband in an automobile accident three years earlier, but she could never muster up the money and nerve to just get up and go. She had a network of good friends and she'd built her cleaning business from the ground up and even had acquired staff to work so that she could take these little trips back home. *Maybe one day*, she often thought to herself, *she could start all over near her mom's, or she could create a cleaning franchise and have the home office in Indianapolis*. Of course, her mom could be overbearing and they'd always had a rocky relationship, and living too near to her mother for a long period of time might not be the right thing to do. *One day*, she thought as she shifted her weight in her seat to lean away from the sun coming through the window, *she would be ready for the move, but not now*. Not just yet.

The left side of her face was warm from the western sun. It was late afternoon on that October day. She was just nearing the

Kentucky state line when Debbie let her mother know that she had to pee. There didn't seem to be enough rest stops in Tennessee, and even if there were, it still wouldn't be enough for Debbie's small bladder.

"There's a rest area just past the Kentucky state line, honey. Try and hold it," Linda said calmly. She looked back at her daughter through the rear view mirror. Debbie looked anxious, but Linda knew the seven-year-olds' routine. She knew Debbie had at least twenty minutes left before she entered the danger zone. There should be plenty of time to get to the rest stop, where Debbie could run like hell to the lady's room.

Danny, Linda's son, was quiet, looking through some old magazines and catalogues. For some reason, he enjoyed looking through J.C. Penney's the most, but even newspaper inserts from Target and Wal-Mart intrigued the five-year-old. He seemed totally engaged at looking at the models' faces and with what they were wearing. He was an odd child, but a very pleasant one. Unlike his older, more demanding sister, Danny was always one to comply and never threw fits, even as a two-year-old as most children do. Linda even worried about his behavior, or lack of it, feeling he might be autistic or something, but the doctors reassured her that he was just a bit withdrawn and even-keeled. It was a contrast with Debbie and her outgoing and assertive behavior, but nonetheless, the two children got along brilliantly, Danny always following his big sister's lead.

It wasn't long before they reached the rest area just north of the state line and south of Bowling Green. They had stopped there before on previous trips. It was usually busy and well attended. As usual, before Linda could put the car into park, Debbie was out the car door and running to the restroom. Linda rolled her eyes and a smile came over her face. Though she feared for Debbie's safety as she darted through the people standing near the vending machines, she couldn't help to detect the humor in the whole situation. Imagine if Debbie were sixteen and really had to go that bad. She's be knocking innocent people down just to get to a stall and relieve herself. "Maybe it'll be something she'll outgrow," Linda whispered to herself.

"Come on Danny, let's go to the restroom with mommy," Linda said leaning over the front seat looking at her second born. Danny was already undoing his seatbelt and was ready to get out of the car. As they headed to the restroom, Debbie was exiting through the door.

"I've told you not to run in public places," Linda said in a stern motherly voice as she grabbed her daughter's arm as to catch her before she could get away.

"But, Mama, I had to go!" Debbie winced back.

"Let's stay together. Come with me," Linda said as they entered the restroom.

A few minutes later, on the way back to the car, Linda noticed the picnic tables in the wooded area next to the main building. They had always been there, but for some reason they looked very appealing on this October afternoon. The kids could use a little exercise and she could benefit from a small catnap, especially with another four hours or so of driving ahead of her.

The kids were delighted to have some time outside. Linda rummaged through the cooler in the trunk and brought out chips and drinks. It would almost be like going on a picnic. They ate for a few minutes and the children wanted to play on the edge of the woods. Debbie was interested in the bugs that were scurrying about. Danny was interested in the leaves and the patterns that they cast on the ground. The kids were so different, but so complimentary of each other.

Linda felt that she just needed five minutes to rejuvenate herself. The table in the shade was inviting, and the kids were fine. She laid her head down on the table and slowly drifted off into a quiet sleep.

"Mama. Mama, wake up." It was Debbie's voice. "Mama, wake up and look at Danny."

Linda looked at her watch. She had dozed off for about twenty minutes, enough she thought to herself, to neglectfully leave her children unattended. Adrenaline rushed through her body as she raised her head, wiping her eyes.

"What's wrong, honey?" she asked.

"Nothing, Mama. Look at Danny. He looks like a girl," Debbie replied, pointing to her little brother standing a few feet behind her. Danny was standing there with a wide grin on his face.

"Look, Mommy. I'm a model out of the magazine."

"Danny...Debbie, what's that on his face?" Linda asked.

"Makeup. I put makeup on his face."

"And where did you find makeup?" Linda demanded.

"Over there in that bag. We found it in the woods. It's got all kinds of stuff in it."

"Debbie, you know better than to go through trash."

"But, Mama, it's not trash. There's jewelry, makeup, CD's, clothes, and there's even a wig in there, or at least I think it's a wig."

Linda rose from the picnic bench and headed over to the bag. It was blue and quite nice. A traveling bag. A fishing tackle box was lying next to it, the top opened with makeup and other accessories on display.

"Look, Mama. See the hair?" said Debbie standing next to her mother, pointing to the blond hair hanging over the edge of the bag.

"Debbie, get back. Stand over there with your brother." Linda was apprehensive about even touching the bag and its contents. What if this was part of a crime scene or something even worse? What if there were body parts in the bag that Debbie didn't see, or contaminated needles that could have infected the children as they rummaged through the mysterious piece of luggage. She slowly filtered through the items. A dress. *Beautiful fabric*, she thought. And a big blond wig. There were Barbra Streisand and Melissa Manchester CD's and others, all female singers, and even a Diana Ross Greatest Hits CD. Linda loved Diana Ross. Her mother would sing Motown songs to her as she was growing up. She uncovered pantyhose and shoes—big shoes— and a note. She gently pulled the folded piece of paper out with her thumb and forefinger, and then opened it up.

The contents of this bag belong to Rachel Wells.
Make sure that you take care of these items and
give them a good home. Thanks.

She put the note on the ground and began to feel around the bottom of the bag. She pulled out a few rolled up dollar bills. Money. Wadded up ones. That was odd.

Linda suddenly looked around to see if anyone was looking at her as she was leaning over the bag. Cars were pulling in and out, but no one was paying any attention to her. She quickly started putting the items back in the bag, even pushing the makeup box in and zipping up the contents. She picked up the note, folded it, and put in her pocket. She really didn't want to take the bag with her, but she also didn't want to leave it there. She put it in the trunk of the car, thinking she would go through the things later when she was alone.

She headed north on I-65, her mind racing about where the bag came from and who it belonged to. She pulled the note out of her pocket. She kept glancing at it as it sat next to her on the passenger side of the seat. Who was Rachel Wells? An actress, a hooker, a singer, or was she even alive or dead? And maybe the dress was just some kind of Halloween costume. Maybe she would never know. She looked back through the rearview mirror. Debbie was listening to music with her headset on, mouthing the words, unaware that her mother was looking at her. She adjusted the mirror to see Danny rummaging through his catalogues. He still had the makeup on his face. *He was a pretty boy*, she thought, *with or without the makeup on. Why did Debbie put so much blue eye shadow on him?*

"Oh my god!" Linda hollered as she pulled off the road into the emergency lane. She put the car in park and opened the glove compartment and pulled out a box of wipes. She ran to the passenger side of the car and opened the back door. She began to clean Danny's face.

"Your grandmother would have a fit if she saw this makeup on you."

"I want it on!" he screamed, pulling back from her. She stopped and stared at him. This was the first time in five years that Danny had rejected his mother's request.

"But Danny, Grandma won't like makeup on your face. She'll

think it's..." She was searching for words. She was still in shock about his reaction. If it were Debbie she would just tell her to "get it off and get it off now!" *Why was he so adamant on wearing the blue eye shadow and lipstick?* He was just five, and she didn't want to impose the girl thing or boy thing on him. But regardless, her mother would have a fit if she saw him like this.

"Debbie," she said. "Take off those earphones. I need your help. Danny doesn't want to take the makeup off."

"So? It looks good on him."

"Yes, of course it does, but it needs to come off."

"But I don't want to take it off," Danny said, raising his voice.

"Mama, he thinks he's a model and they all wear makeup."

"But they don't wear it all the time," Linda quipped back.

"You're right," Debbie said. She turned to Danny. "Danny, models have to have perfect skin and you can't wear makeup all the time and still have perfect skin. You should only wear makeup when you get your picture taken. Right now, your skin should be resting."

"Resting..." Linda agreed, in awe of how Debbie was controlling the situation. "Yeah, resting your skin."

Danny looked at Debbie and then his mother. Debbie took the wipes from Linda and began to gently stroke his face, wiping the makeup off, then running the wipe on her own face, leaving the makeup residue on her cheeks. He laughed and took a wipe and rubbed it over his lips, wiping off his lipstick and then pressing it on to his mother's face. Linda in turn took a wipe of her own and began to clean Danny's face. As the car shook from each passing semi truck and car heading north, the three sat in the back seat and laughed at each other while they made silly faces, all looking like clowns with bad face paint.

"Let's go to Grandma's looking like circus clowns," said Debbie.

"Let's not put her through that," Linda said as she finished cleaning her children's faces. "Look at that, Danny. You now have perfect skin. Clean as a whistle," she said as she polished the tip of his nose.

"I'm a model," he said proudly.

"Yes you are," Linda replied, giving him a hug.

She returned to the front seat and then merged into the traffic. A little while later, she glanced at the two in the back seat. Debbie was still listening to music, her eyes taking in the landscape through the window. Danny was snoozing, his head tilted back against the car door. He had the face of an angel. *He's pretty*, Linda thought to herself. *So very pretty, almost too pretty to be a boy.* And then she started to think about the bag that they found at the rest area. Again, why was it there and who, just who is or was Rachel Wells?

Linda was nearing Bowling Green when she began to worry about the bag and its contents. What if the person who found or possessed the bag was suddenly cast under some weird and dangerous spell? What if the bag were associated with a crime? What if she were to hear on the news, *"Rachel Wells is missing, but was last seen on I-65."* Or even worse, *"Rachel Wells found dead on I-65. Detectives are looking for clues on who could have committed such a heinous crime."* She had enough to worry about without adding some unknown entity to an already busy and complicated life.

She glanced at the rearview mirror and saw that Debbie had just dozed off. Spotting a huge truck stop sign hovering over the interstate, Linda turned onto the first Bowling Green exit. The truck stop appeared busy as she made the right turn and drove to the back of the building. She slowed down and put the car into park. She gently opened her car door, then reached down to release the latch on the trunk. The kids were sound asleep. She quickly got out of the car, opened the trunk and pulled out the blue bag. With the mysterious message in hand, she tucked the note right next to the makeup case, then zipped the bag up, and tossed it to the curb. It landed next to a few tall canisters stacked neatly against the building. Without looking back, she drove forward and got back onto the interstate.

*

"Henry, did you see that?" Gail by nature was an inquisitive person who never missed a move. Inspired by the flood of criminal and forensic television shows, she had once aspired to being a detective, but instead, found herself married to a truck driver and living most of her days with him on the road, sleeping at night in the back of the rig.

"See what?" he replied.

"That woman just took a bag out her trunk and threw it right over there, and then just drove off. Right there next to those canisters," she said, pointing.

"Maybe she didn't want it anymore," Henry said as he took another bite out of his bologna sandwich. Henry and Gail had pulled to the side of the truck stop to use the facilities and to eat. They had the perfect view of the back of the building. "You put too much mayonnaise on the sandwich."

"Shut up and eat it anyway," Gail snapped back. "You'd complain if there's too much or not enough, so just eat it."

Gail and Henry were in their forties and had been married for fifteen years, the second for each of them. They lived primarily from day to day, with their rig as their main residence except for the short stays between runs where they parked the semi in Gail's mother's driveway in Shepherdsville, and spent the nights in a small camper nestled in the back yard. They didn't want much, just wanting to see the world and spend their time together as much as possible. They didn't care about dressing up either. She even wore Henry's old flannel shirts most of the time, and with her short cropped hair always tucked under her Reds baseball cap, along with old torn jeans, the two looked like a set of matching Seventies truck-driving lesbians. Gail's voice was raspy and deep, and people would often mistake her for a man when she spoke. They looked so similar in their appearance, except that Henry carried around a mid-sized paunch around his waistline.

Henry had a slow wit about him. Gail always said that he was a day late and a dollar short, a statement that confused Henry because he always made it a point to have a dollar in his pocket. In contrast, Gail was the adventurous type, often creating her own thrills. When she was a bit bored, it was nothing for her to flash her small naked breasts through the window at the driver in the next vehicle that was passing by. She didn't care if it were a single male driver, a car full of family members, or a van full of Amish workers. She just loved the expressions of shock and disbelief on their faces when they caught a glimpse of her snow white and freckled bosom. The act would embarrass Henry, but deep down he loved her carefree and daring attitude.

"I'm gonna see what's in it," Gail said as she folded a paper towel around her sandwich, putting it down on the seat.

"Gail, don't…" Before Henry could even finish his sentence, Gail was already out of the rig, racing toward the bag. She picked it up like it belonged to her, and quickly walked back to the truck. She threw it up onto the floor, then climbed up the side of the rig, and closed the door behind her.

"Gail, that bag doesn't belong to you."

"Aren't you just a little bit curious to know what's in it?" she said, trying to make eye contact with Henry.

"Not one bit."

"Well, I am." Gail lifted the bag and set it between her and Henry.

"You just flattened your sandwich," Henry said in an easy manner as he rolled his eyes.

"Flat or fluffy, a bologna sandwich is a bologna sandwich," she responded. "And anyway, I'll be the one eating it so don't you worry about it."

"I'm not worried about it. I just don't want you to forget where you put it and claim in the next thirty minutes that I ate it."

"Oh, hush Henry. Look." While Henry was conversing with Gail, she had unzipped the mysterious blue bag and was cautiously rummaging through the items.

"What the hell?" Henry asked as he watched Gail pull out what he thought was a ball of yellow hair.

"It's a wig. It looks like a Dolly Parton wig. I'll be. And there's a dress, a long dress. And shoes, and a makeup box."

"Do you think whoever threw this stuff away was a hooker?"

"For god's sake Henry, it probably belongs to a Hollywood actress or even a country singer. I mean this could really be one of Dolly's wigs. I wonder why that woman had it. Think it was hers?"

"By the size of that dress, I'd say it doesn't belong to her or Dolly." He pulled the dress out. "I'd say this gal was well over six feet tall or maybe even taller than that. I saw a six-foot hooker once."

"Yeah, in your dreams. Look, here's a note." She read it to herself. "Well, there you are. This shit belongs to a Rachel Wells, and it says that whoever finds these items has to take good care of it, to give it a good home. Who in the hell is Rachel Wells? And look here. Music CD's." She began to thumb through the collection of CD's. Gail was a country music fan and any other genre of music was foreign to her. "I think I saw this Barbra Streisand person in a movie. I didn't care for her much. And, Melissa Manchester? She probably sings behind a piano, maybe torch music and love songs. You like love songs, don't you Henry?"

"I hate love songs."

She paused, looking at the contents. "And what in the hell are we going to do with this stuff?"

"I told you not to pick it up," Henry said finishing his sandwich.

"Hey, there's a couple of dollars in here. We can sure use a couple of extra bucks."

"I say you put it back where you found it."

"Not yet. I have an idea."

"Oh lord. I hate it when you say 'I have an idea' like that. The last time you said that was when we were at the lake and you saw that boat tied to the pier. We ended up taking a parked boat for a ride for the afternoon."

"There wasn't s sign that said we couldn't, now was there?" she snipped. "And anyway, it was a glorious afternoon, and we returned the boat at the end of the day, and nobody even noticed that it was gone. Hell, we probably could have stolen it and nobody would have noticed it."

"Gail, we did steal it."

"We brought it back, so technically, we didn't steal it. We just borrowed it."

"We stole it."

"Whatever."

Gail put the items back into the bag, everything except the money and the wig. After neatly folding them, she tucked the one-dollar bills in her pocket. She lifted her T-shirt and put the wig under her armpit, pulling her flannel shirt together and buttoning it as if she were hiding the blonde hair. While Henry was finishing his bologna sandwich, staring out the window in front of him as to try and not pay any attention to what Gail was doing, she reached under the front seat and discretely pulled out a metal object, and then tucked into the right side of her loosely fitted jeans.

"I'm going in and freshen up. You want anything?" she asked.

"Maybe a few lottery tickets. Winners only."

"I can do that. While I'm inside, why don't you pull out front and get on the edge of the onramp."

"Why?"

"Cause I said so, that's why."

"Cause I said so, that's why," he mimicked back. "That onramp is pretty far away."

"No need blocking the lane, and anyway, it'll save us some time. And I could use the walk."

"I'll say. You're starting to spread from sitting so much." Henry joked as he tried to pinch her left buttocks.

"And you need to be serving butter with those rolls you've got there," she played back with him, crunching his belly fat with her hand. "I'll be about five minutes."

Gail got out of the rig and as she headed for the building, Henry moved the truck forward, pulling onto the road and down to the onramp shoulder, completely out of sight of the truck stop. It was beginning to get dark, and he was a bit concerned about Gail walking by herself, but he also knew that she could handle any situation. He would always reassure himself about her well-being by saying, "Pity the poor guy that messes with Gail."

Five minutes turned into ten, and then fifteen. He was getting a bit nervous. Suddenly, he saw a figure in the rearview mirror running on the shoulder of the ramp, heading in his direction. Henry squinted as he tried to focus his eyes on the person approaching his rig. The passenger door opened.

"Get this mother moving and do it now!" Gail ordered. Without hesitating, Henry put the rig in gear and drove onto the interstate heading north.

Gail began to act mockingly flirtatious. "You like me with blonde hair?"

"What have you done and why are you wearing that wig?"

"You like rich girls? I hope so, cause this girl is rich!" She pulled out two handfuls of cash. "And here's your lottery tickets. Three rolls of lottery tickets!" She tossed the tickets at Henry and started counting the money as they headed up the road. "Close to five hundred dollars, I suspect," she said, gloating over her bounty.

"I wish you hadn't done that. You know, one day you're, I mean we're, gonna get caught."

"We're too smart for that. And I, I mean we, won't be needing this stuff anymore either." She took the blonde wig off, put it back into the bag, then rolled down the window and tossed the blue bag onto the interstate.

"Can't be convicted without evidence, and I don't see a blonde in this rig. Goodbye Rachel Wells, and thank you very much," she said, looking back into the darkness. She gave a gentle wave and then rolled up the window.

*

Ricky was hungry, but he wasn't sure for what. He was listening to his latest drag song CD collection, gesturing with one hand to the music while the other was on the wheel. *A White Castle cheeseburger*, he thought to himself, *at the next exit or the one after that*. He hadn't had a slider in about a month.

"What the hell?" Ricky screamed as he quickly and deliberately guided his Honda Accord to the shoulder of the road.

"Goddamn it, Ricky! What the fuck are you doing?" Don had just dozed off and was suddenly awakened by the loud crash and then the sound of a car pulling onto the shoulder.

It had been an uncomfortable three days for the twosome as they were on a get-away to work out the kinks in their new relationship. They had just moved in together after a whirlwind three-month courtship. Already, the partnership had become volatile, with disagreements over just about everything. Don was in his late twenties, and he was the jealous and insecure type, wanting to be in full control. Ricky was the younger of the two, slightly effeminate and cute, and also, for some reason, he wanted to do drag. He had friends who performed in a show in Louisville, and once he even entered an amateur contest. Though he didn't win, and he was somewhat convincing as a woman, his talent and on-stage presence was lacking professionalism. He was, without a doubt, a real "booger drag," the illusion raw and unpolished. Unfortunately, his friends showered him with praise and encouragement, and suddenly, performing in drag became his passion. The quick drive south to Atlanta and back was supposed to give the two the chance to come to some decisions about their future together; however, both were stubborn and not willing to concede to any demands set forth by the other. The only thing they could agree on was that the kitchen in their new house would be painted a bright yellow to accent Don's collection of Fiesta Ware left over from his last relationship. And the one issue that Don wouldn't budge on was that he was adamant that Ricky would not be a drag queen.

The car came to a halt, and Don was the first to get out. Ricky waited for the stream of cars to pass before opening his door to examine the damage. "I was just driving and then something hit the windshield. Fuck, look at it. It's cracked!"

"Look," Don said, pointing to the object on the hood. "It's a travel bag. How in the hell?"

"All I know is that a semi passed me and that's when it hit. I was right in the middle of 'I Will Survive' and then bam!" Ricky was starting to shake from the onslaught of adrenaline that had just filled his body. He wiped the sweat from his face with the sleeve of his flannel shirt. "At least no one is hurt. You're not hurt are you?"

"No, I'm fine. Probably queer haters. Why don't they just yell 'FAGGOTS' and then run like they use to?" Don quipped. He was still nervous about being openly gay outside the confines of his neighborhood. "Maybe it's a sign from above that we're on the wrong road, you know, you and me on the wrong road with this relationship."

"You and your signs from heaven theories. Don, you could be a little more optimistic. Maybe it's a sign that we're on the right road together, and that we have some bumps to overcome."

"Like that makes any sense. So it just came out of nowhere?"

"Yeah, just like that. Let's see what's in the bag. And if there's a baby in it, we're keeping it."

"If there's a baby in that bag, it's probably dead, and, in which case, we would definitely not be keeping it," Don bantered back.

Ricky opened the bag, and with the aid of the lights from the passing motorists, he could see the contents. "No baby," he said, cutely pouting his lips. "Let's get it in the car and see what's really in here."

"I'm calling AAA to see what we need to do, and we'll probably have to call the cops. Hell, we're almost home and now this. I swear it's a sign of some sort."

Ricky was in the car, with the interior lights on, rummaging through the bag like it was a newly opened Christmas present, while Don leaned against the auto attempting to use his phone to get some advice regarding roadside assistance.

"Damn, I can't seem to get any connection out here," Don hollered.

"Look, Don. It is a sign from God!" Don turned around to see that Ricky was wearing a blonde wig, fluffing it up with his fingers. "If this isn't a sign from above, then I don't know what is," Ricky exclaimed. "A sign from the drag gods!"

"What the fuck?"

"It's a bag full of drag stuff, stuff that belongs to Rachel Wells, whoever that is. There's a gown, CD's, makeup, shoes, jewelry, and this hot wig! There is a Goddess after all!" Seemed as though Don had been beaten by his own belief in fate. He felt everything in life was connected to a sign, an omen of sorts. How could he even dispute or explain the fact that a bag full of drag could fall on Ricky's car while he was traveling seventy miles an hour on the interstate, delivering the sign from God to a young man who desperately wanted to be a drag queen? Don was stunned.

"And how do you know it's drag stuff?"

"Cause I know what drag stuff smells like. You know, the bar smoke, the perfume, the hairspray, the sweat…"

"You've got to be kidding me."

A car was approaching on the shoulder. The two looked into the headlights. Perhaps some good Samaritan, though Don thought it could be someone out to bash queers. The car slowed then stopped. Suddenly, blue flashing lights appeared.

"It's about time," Don said, taking a sigh of relief. "Help is here, even without the assistance of the phone company."

A state trooper clutching a pistol got out of his car.

"Put your hands in the air! Now! And you in the car! Get out slowly with your hands in the air!" Ricky and Don obliged the officer. Within seconds, the couple found themselves face down on the edge of the highway. Don was still clutching his phone, and Ricky still had the blonde wig on his head. Soon, another police car arrived at the scene.

"Captain, it looks like we've got our armed robbers right here," Don heard an officer tell the one who had just arrived.

"Good job, Sergeant," the captain replied.

Ricky raised his head and began to speak. "There must be some mistake. We've done nothing wrong."

"Shut your mouth!" the sergeant said as he clicked the trigger on his gun.

"But we're not…"

"I said to shut your fucking mouth! Captain, this one fits the description to a tee. Blonde hair, flannel shirt, jeans, tall and thin."

Ricky put his head back down, the gravel seemed to pierce the side of his face. He looked over to see the look of fear in Don's eyes. It seemed like an eternity for the couple as one of the troopers opened the trunk to the Honda, pulling out and opening suitcases and shopping bags. There was cash on the console, and scratch-off lottery tickets piled on the front seat that they had purchased a few miles back. The captain pointed his flashlight on the blue bag. He pulled the gown out of the bag and started laughing. "By the looks of things, these guys were going out dancing later tonight."

Soon, he found the note and read it. "I'd say that they were going to toss this evidence out here on the highway and put the blame on this Miss Rachel Wells, whoever she is." He walked back to the two on the ground and leaned over to Ricky, putting the flashlight on his face. "Now that wouldn't be a nice thing to do to some innocent person, now would it?" For one fleeting moment, Ricky was craving a White Castle cheeseburger again. His mind worked that way: a thought here and then another unrelated one a few seconds later. Maybe a way to escape the situation.

Next, the captain turned and bent down in front of Don. "Young man, who is Rachel Wells?"

"I don't know who she is! We were driving and the bag came out of nowhere. It broke the windshield. Look at it if you don't believe me!"

"I saw the windshield. It's cracked, but not shattered. So where is she? Did you abduct her, or perhaps did you kill her?"

"I'm not saying another word without a lawyer!"

The sergeant walked around to the front of the suspects and said mockingly, "I'd say we got us a 'sweet' couple here. A 'sweet' couple of robbers."

"Yeah, let's book them. I'm sure we've got our truck stop robbers. And also a possible kidnapping and murder. We can't rule anything out. Let's collect the evidence and take these two in. Let's leave the wig on Miss Dolly. Makes him look real cute. We'll need to get a photo of him with the wig on when we get to the station."

"Captain, we'll also need to call in a 10-65. Purely procedural."

"Yeah. Can't be too sure that this Rachel Wells isn't a missing person. And hopefully, not a dead one. You put the older one in your car, and I'll take Miss Dolly in mine."

Petrified and without resistance, Ricky and Don were handcuffed and put into the backseats of separate squad cars. After backups arrived to collect the car and belongings as evidence, the two were whisked to the State Highway Patrol center in Elizabethtown. It was Don's nature to be nervous, always thinking the worst. He just knew that he would be thrown into a dungeon of undesirables, never to see Ricky or the light of day again.

On the other hand, Ricky was oblivious to what was really happening to the two of them. Being the optimist, he wasn't fearing any of the events of the past thirty minutes at all. In fact, on that night he had become a true believer in fate, and he had no doubt that all things would work out, and of course, for the best.

Fate is a strange and unexplainable thing, Ricky thought as he sat in the backseat. He leaned over a bit to the center of the seat to see his silhouette in the rearview mirror. He began envisioning himself performing in drag after all this misunderstanding was straightened out. He knew that he was here at this moment for a reason. That's what fate was all about. Perhaps he and the captain would have hot and torrid sex. The trooper would be his abductor and Ricky would give in to any and all of his lurid commands. "The captain called me Dolly. I will be Dolly from here on out." Not knowing all the words, he began to hum the title song from *Hello, Dolly!* while pretending to be riding in the back of a limousine.

"Keep it down back there!" the trooper shouted.

"Sorry," Ricky mumbled back, smiling. He stared at the back of the captain's neck. It was a thick and masculine neck. Then, for a quick moment, he thought of Don, and somehow he was happy not to be with him. Maybe Don was not the right one for him. Maybe this was what this whole episode was all about. Maybe he wasn't ready to settle down, at least not with Don.

The squad car made its way south to the first Elizabethtown exit. It was only about an hour or so earlier that Ricky and Don were in the same location heading north to Louisville, almost home before this incident of fate turned things around. Though it was barely dusk then, it was now dark, and eerily, it was like going back in time, though in a strange and myopic way. Ricky noticed the exit signs, and then the neon street lights on each side of the overpass. On the left was a White Castle. *Ah, that would be nice,* he thought. *A few sliders before the photo session and humiliation that waited ahead.* The squad car reached the traffic light at the end of the ramp, and then made a right turn without stopping. Ricky turned and looked back. Apparently, there would be no cheeseburger tonight.

*

Ricky and Don were released the next day after two bandits, a man and his female companion, were captured and identified as the real culprits when they attempted to rob another truck stop. At least Ricky and Don had been able to stay in the same cell overnight and, as luck would have it, they both caught up on their sleep.

The next morning, Ricky demanded an apology from the arresting police officers and asked that the blue bag with all its contents, including the blond wig, be returned to him. He received the apology, but the bag had disappeared from the evidence room where it had been tagged with an ID number and placed on a shelf.

"What do you mean it's not there?" Ricky asked. "Did it just get up itself and walk away?"

"Course not," the officer answered. "We all took an interest in the contents of that bag. It'll show up again in a few days or so. Why don't you check back with us?"

*

Months later, while driving north along Interstate 65, an elderly man from Florida noticed a blue traveling bag at a rest stop near the Kentucky border. The bag was on the ground beside a picnic table. The man went to the table and sat on the bench beside the bag. He waited a few minutes, eyeing the bag to see if anyone would show up to claim it. He fretted and worried that someone was watching him, then fretted and worried about someone deciding to take the bag before he made a move for it.

After a while, satisfied that no one had showed up to claim the bag, he decided to reach for it and look inside.

Silver Pumps and a Loose Nut

Daphne sat alone in the booth, stirring the half-empty glass of vodka and tonic in front of her with her fingertip, the fourth in the past hour. Her eyelids drooped from the weight of the oversized false eyelashes glued to her aqua blue-shadowed lids. She drifted in and out, thinking about being at the beach at sunrise to pay homage to Ursula Andress. As she listened to the honky-tonk country music in the background coming from the dusty jukebox, she gently shook her head and rolled her eyes in disgust with the selection of music. *Whoever heard of a honky-tonk angel*, she thought to herself. She hated country music, as it brought back memories of the time she lived with her evil stepmother in a trailer court south of Birmingham. Daphne knew well the perils of being a modern day redneck Cinderella trapped in a wide-load mobile home.

The soft amber lights cast a glow on Daphne's bright blond hair, teased high and hanging down past her shoulders. Her lips lacked color as her dark red lipstick had worn off. Too tired to reapply more gloss, and with the bar ready to close and no one there to even notice, she thought it would be a waste of time to even look halfway seductive at this hour of the night. Apparent that she missed the bar's prime time, she took off her four-inch silver heels and placed them next to her purse as if she were protecting them from some unknown foot-fetish thief. The pumps, two sizes too small for her size eleven feet and making her already six-foot tall willowy body even more towering, were her prized possessions. She had saved three months to get the silver pumps she had seen at Sears. The elaborate appliqués on the toes of the shoes sparkled with each step she took. More than anything else, walking in those glorious shoes gave her the swagger of self-confidence and womanhood that no pair of flats could. She stretched her legs under the table until her feet relaxed on the seat across from her. Her black dress barely covered the top of her thighs, and each time she flexed her legs and pointed her toes, her body shifted forward and the hem of her skirt would rise, exposing her bright red lacy panties.

Sitting alone wasn't the way Daphne pictured she'd be celebrating this night in Daytona. It was almost closing time and the only people in the place were the bartender, Daphne, and her ride for the night, Sam. Sam was a forty-something drag gofer from Birmingham who offered to take Daphne and her mentor, Stella, to Daytona for a contest at the Club Diva. The trip was really his excuse to visit with his old boyfriend, the bartender, who seemed to be trying his best to entertain Sam, though Daphne could tell that he really wasn't interested in his old flame. Daphne looked at the bartender, thinking he was around thirty or so, his muscles flexing through his t-shirt each time he picked up a glass or a bottle of Jack Daniels. *This stud*, Daphne thought, *could have any man he wanted if one was around*. Sam was foolishly in lust, and the bartender seemed content to be patronized by Sam's flirtatious jokes and come-ons.

Sam agreed to finance the entire trip. Stella was the big star back in Birmingham, and Sam did everything he was told to do by her, but a big star in the drag world didn't often come hand-in-hand with the big bucks needed to keep a girl in extra special gowns and designer hair-dos. Daphne didn't quite understand the relationship between Sam and Stella. She heard that years ago they were lovers but it didn't work out, and she also heard that Stella had blackmailed Sam for some unknown reason and he was working off his debt to her. What Daphne did know for sure was that she was near broke and at the bottom of the pecking order in this small ménage, having to be complacent with every decision, even waiting for the next meal to be provided during the trip. The only time the group would eat was when Stella was hungry. Fortunately, Stella was famished most of the time, as all of her two hundred twenty-five pounds craved carbs, bacon, cheeses, and most anything that didn't include lettuce.

Daphne yawned, admiring the small trophy sitting in front of her, her prize, along with fifty dollars, for finishing third in the drag talent contest. It was her first trophy for anything. Winning for Daphne was never in question, nor was it a quest, because she never won anything and never expected to. But with only four entries in the contest, Daphne was proud to have not finished in last place with no trophy at all. However, when the contest was over, she felt so sorry for the weeping last place loser that she almost gave the local queen from Daytona her trophy. That's just how Daphne was. But Stella interfered with the transaction telling Daphne to "hold on to that piece of cheap gold-plated shit, because when you get home, no one's gonna believe you were even here if you don't have evidence that says you were." Then she turned to the last place contestant, a crossed-eyed drunk who had too many shots of tequila during the night and thought she was Whitney Houston reincarnated, and told her if she took the trophy from Daphne she'd rip her a new asshole, and then she snapped her fingers and told the poor dear that it looked like somebody had already beat her to it, and then stuck it on her neck and called it a face.

Stella turned and added, "Girl, you are nothing but ugly! Is that a fart I smell coming out of your mouth? Come on Daphne, we need to get away from here before we suffocate from all that methane oozing out of her pores." Of course, Daphne followed Stella out of the dressing room, embarrassed, but still obedient to her mentor.

The fifty dollars Daphne won for placing third wasn't as much or as impressive as the five-hundred dollars Stella received for winning first place with her two talent numbers. Stella had a way of wowing the crowd at any show, and this contest was no different. She had the audience in her hands the first time she walked on stage during the parade of contestants wearing a yellow costume consisting of tights and a rhinestone vest loaded with strobe lights on the front and back, with compact speakers on the shoulders, and a huge yellow feather collar that reached higher than most headdresses. When she hit the center of the stage and turned on the battery pack, the lights came on and then sirens blared. And if that wasn't enough, the old rock song, "Wipe Out", filled the stage as she broke into a short shimmy routine. Some people have said she was a cross between Big Bird and the Roadrunner when she wore that outfit. Stella made all her outfits, and working during the week at Radio Shack with her employee discount gave her access to the electronic gimmicks that she used in her acts. Though Stella was an old school drag queen, usually confining her routines to old classic tunes and costumes, no other entertainer could compete with her.

But Stella's talent numbers for the evening were no less spectacular. The first was a rendition of "I Will Survive" as she brilliantly portrayed a kidney transplant patient in ICU, and of course, Stella always added flair to her acts. She would perform the operation on herself, pulling a donor kidney out of a cooler full of ice as she broke into the first lines of the song vowing that she could no longer live without the organ by her side. Stella had a way of taking a comedy concept that would normally be considered slightly entertaining or even offensive or in bad taste, and turn it around and deliver it in a dramatic fashion, totally serious, and get away with it. But it was her rendition of "God Bless America" that stole the show and secured the crown as she walked out on the stage with crutches portraying a battle-worn female soldier, her uniform torn by shrapnel, her right leg missing. And to top it off, she broke into "Boogie Woogie Bugle Boy of Company B," the whole time working the crowd into a frenzy with her energetic version of a combination of the Jitterbug and Quick Step, all on one leg.

Most people in attendance assumed Stella had her leg bent up behind her, her ankle taped up to her thigh, but Stella only had one leg. Stella, or Steve back then, was twelve when a group of middle-school bullies started to make fun of her during baton practice, calling her sissy and faggot. Not being one to back down, not even at an early age, she returned the taunts until the preteens began to chase her around the football field. Stella was fast, but in this case, too fast. Unable to stop her momentum as she left the confines of the school grounds, she darted into the street, and was hit by a car. A blue Chevy Camaro, one witness said. It was a hit and run. She lay motionless in the street, her body mangled, the baton slightly bent, but still clutched in her left hand. An ambulance arrived and whisked her away. She would survive after weeks of recovery, and she was able to go back to school, her right leg replaced with a prosthesis. Stella's middle school dream of becoming a high school baton twirler in the marching band had come to an end. It was on that day, as Stella would testify, she decided to become a drag queen, but not just any guy wearing a dress in the weekend shows. Stella would become the "drag avenger" out to conquer any evil or hostility that would threaten the peaceful world of the domestic gay man. In other words, Stella was out to beat up any bully that got in her way. But in essence, Stella had become a bully in her own right, though the connotation took on a different meaning when it pertained to a fat man wearing a dress.

Daphne, like most people, was intimidated by Stella, yet she revered the way her mentor performed and even admired her outlook on life. By contrast, during the contest, Daphne walked out in the parade of contestants wearing a White Castle uniform because she thought it looked original and Daphne just happened to like White Castle sliders. Of course, the audience didn't get it, and her applause was light. And for both her talents, she performed two different Britney Spears medleys, quite simply because Daphne thought of herself as a dancer. Unfortunately, Daphne's impersonation of Britney was nothing more than a bad six-foot-tall illusion of the pop star. Falling down at least three times during each act didn't help her score, but Daphne was of the mindset that regardless of her performance, with the help of her beautiful silver pumps and skimpy costume, she would receive style points to make up for her slips that landed her on the floor. Each time she ended up on her ass in front of the confused audience, she just rolled over and spread her legs, pretending to be sexy. But she reasoned she probably lost a point or two when her left nut popped out a few times, exposing a bit of her chicken skin to the front row. From her perspective, her talent acts were no different from the real Ms. Spear's performances, except Britney had no scrotum.

Daphne was a bit demure, never overwhelmed with excitement, and in many ways, Stella's opposite. Perhaps that was the reason they got along so well. Daphne was the passive one, and Stella was the protector, the assertive one. In so many ways, she wanted to be like Stella, but she knew it would never happen. Stella was a doer, and Daphne was a dreamer. In fact, one of the reasons Daphne wanted to come to Daytona was to spend some time at the beach, to take a dip in the water early at sunrise, to walk out of the ocean with the sun at her back and onto the beach like Ursula Andress in the James Bond movie, *Dr. No*. Daphne had a yen to replicate certain cinematic moments, even if they weren't accurate. Stella had been so kind to recreate the famous white bikini that Ursula wore in the 1962 classic, and give it as a present to Daphne. That gesture was rare and only the people close to Stella would have the chance to appreciate her generosity.

Yes, the Ursula Andress ocean experience was the real reason Daphne agreed to come to Daytona. The pageant was just an afterthought, and Daphne knew she had been purposely invited so she could carry Stella's costumes in and out of the club, or at least the unimportant items. Only Sam was allowed to carry Stella's glamorous costumes and wigs. Apparently, he had earned that honor, or perhaps Stella only trusted him to take on that chore, but Daphne was okay with the situation. Back home in Birmingham, following Stella around was a real privilege for her protégés. She had mentored many drags, and the first requirement to be a "Stella's girl" is to carry her things and do whatever she asks you to do.

The song on the jukebox changed. Some dejected woman was singing sadly about her divorce that became final that day. *Where do they come up with this stuff*, Daphne asked herself. Daphne heard the bar door open. She turned her head to see the bartender wave at a young man walking in the bar alone. She noticed by the way they greeted each other they must have known one another. Sam shook the man's hand and they engaged in conversation. Daphne took a sip of her drink, then leaned back, closing her eyes and resting her head on the wall behind her.

"Excuse me, can I join you?"

Daphne cautiously looked to her left, staring into the stranger's chest. He didn't look that low to the ground when he entered the bar, Daphne thought, but up close, he was really short. She paused, taking in the view by looking him up and down. Square jaw, black hair. He wasn't gorgeous, but he sure was cute. The cuddly kind of cute, she thought, and of course for Daphne, who was cursed with extreme height and an attraction to short men, she knew well the importance of judging a man for how tall he was laying down in bed as opposed to when he was standing up. For a moment, she got lost in the color of his eyes. They were a beautiful combination of Caribbean Ocean Blue and Bloody Mary Red.

"Hmmm?" she asked.

"Can I sit with you?"

"Sure," Daphne said, slowly coming out of her mental lapse. She moved closer to the inside of the booth allowing the young man to sit next to her. "Sorry," she said. "I was just thinking about some things."

"Like what?"

"Like, why do they play country music in places like this? It's such a downer."

"Yup, I agree."

"And like, why am I here when I should be out celebrating, partying where there are people, a lot of people?"

"Too bad, but I'm glad you're here."

"And like, what is your name?"

"Chuck. My real name is Charles, but people call me Chuck."

"You look like a Chuck. Let's see...Chuck, Chuck, bo buck, banana fana fo fuck. No offense, but that's the first thing that came to my mind."

"I guess you think that's the first time I've heard that one don't you?"

"Probably not. It just came out," she said as she took a sip from her glass.

"And what is your name?" he asked.

"Daphne," she replied in a soft voice.

"Daphne's a real nice name." He moved closer to her, the back of his hand touching the side of her smooth bare leg. Daphne normally didn't shave her legs, but Stella insisted if she were going to perform as Britney Spears and dance, she needed to do so without the restriction of dance tights.

She took another sip and said with a smile, "My real name is Buck." She put her hand on Chuck's thigh.

"Buck's not a very ladylike name," Chuck said, slurring his words.

"Who has to be ladylike?" Daphne asked in a playful way, realizing her lame attempt at humor wasn't being appreciated. "I'm kidding. My name's not Buck. Just call me Daphne." She glanced over to see Sam and the bartender watching the two nestled comfortably in the booth. The bartender gave a thumbs up. Daphne took that gesture to mean that Chuck was okay.

Chuck leaned over, facing Daphne and asked, "So, why don't we blow this hole and go hang out together?"

"Honey, that's sweet, but I'm from out of town, and Sam over there is my ride, and unfortunately, I have to go where he goes, and whenever he decides to go."

"I got a place to go, and a ride outside as well."

"It's getting late, and I have to be at the beach at sunrise," she responded. She took another sip of her vodka and tonic. "You been drinking tonight?"

"Yeah, earlier." He moved his hand to the inside of Daphne's leg. "Been smokin' pot for the past few hours."

"Thought so. I could smell it."

"You want some?"

"Sorry, I don't do drugs. Just drag and alcohol. Hey, you keep touching me like that and something's gonna fall out of place." Chuck just grinned. Daphne could feel a sudden shift in her loosely compacted crotch. She had not anticipated being sexually aroused and suddenly became worried that some part of her package might pop out.

"Come on, come with me," Chuck pleaded, his lips pouting.

"You're so fucking high. I hope you're not driving."

"No, I'm not driving. I got my best friend and his friend outside in the car. We got the backseat all to ourselves, and then we'll go down the road to my place. Ten minutes at the most."

"And you'll get me back to the motel later, before sunrise?"

"Sure. I promise."

"Well..." she paused not wanting to seem in a hurry. "Okay." Daphne was about to give in to the fact that she would be in Florida and not have a tryst. She believed that ever since Connie Francis sang "Where the Boys Are," no one goes to Florida without searching for that special beach boy encounter, unless of course, you're bringing your family to Disney World. And even then, the thought of dumping the kids with the husband after the second day and driving to the closest shore just to get a glimpse of tanned masculine flesh keeps resurfacing as you wait endlessly in line for the next ride.

Daphne nudged Chuck to get up from the booth. "Let me check in with Sam, then we can go," she said. She gathered her purse and put on her silver pumps and stood up, standing next to Chuck, but looking down at him with a crooked grin on her face. She grabbed her trophy and drink, and wobbled over to the bar, her legs stiff from too much dancing in one night. Chuck followed closely behind.

She handed her trophy to Sam for safe keeping, and took the fifty dollar bill out of her purse and tucked it into Sam's pocket. Daphne had been around long enough to know a hustler when she met one, and Chuck was definitely hustler material, which means anything of value should be put away. She assured Sam that Chuck would bring her back to the motel in a short time.

"I'll be there," Sam said. "And call me if you need me," he added reassuringly.

The bartender leaned over and whispered into Daphne's ear, "He's harmless. You'll be okay." He stepped back, then motioned for her to come near again. "He has a really big dick." Daphne arched her eyebrow, staring at the bartender.

"Is that all anyone thinks about?"

Sam jumped in and said, "Of course, we know that…" He paused, waiting for Daphne to put down her drink and set her pose, and together they completed the line from one of her favorite songs, "It ain't the meat, it's the motion," and then they both snapped their fingers in the air and laughed.

The bartender picked up his bar towel, grinned and sarcastically said, "Yeah, right."

"Come on Chuck, let's see what kind of chariot awaits us," Daphne commanded as she headed to the door. Chuck was right behind her, his hand holding the back of her dress as to not let her get away. Daphne stepped aside when she reached the door, and waited for Chuck to open it. He moved in front of her, his face even with her bosom, and looked straight up, his neck bent at a ninety-degree angle.

"Daphne?" he said.

"Yeah, what?"

"When we get in the car, don't let them know you're not a woman."

"What?" she questioned.

"I said, when we…"

"I got that part." Her eyes darted from his face to the door, and then back. She suddenly had reservations about leaving with him. It was obvious that she was a drag, especially standing next to Chuck. Most drags who want to pass as real learn early on where to stand and who to stand next to when they're in public. Daphne never pretended to be a real woman, and was satisfied being considered a drag queen as she aspired to one day being an entertainer like her mentor, Stella.

"Sure. Whatever," she said as she nodded for Chuck to open the door. The timing was not right to train him in the ways of proper etiquette. *He's cheap trade*, she thought as she sighed and opened the door herself. She followed Chuck to a black Lexus parked a few feet down the street. She was surprised when he opened the back door, but shook her head as he crawled in first. Daphne followed Chuck into the backseat, and as soon as she shut the door, the car began to move.

"This is Daphne, and she's coming over to my place," Chuck announced, his face beaming with nervous pride. Daphne wanted to start a conversation, but realized her baritone voice would definitely be a dead giveaway to her not being a woman. The driver waved and said, "Hello, Daphne," as he made eye contact through the rearview mirror. Daphne was only twenty-two, but she was well aware her gaydar was on target about the driver. She also sensed the handsome man in his early forties behind the wheel had her figured out as well. But even so, she stayed mute. The burr cut young man sat facing forward in the passenger seat, never uttering a word. Another hustler, Daphne thought to herself, but probably new to the game.

The ride seemed short, just a few miles down from the beach. The car stopped in front of a stucco duplex with small palms in the front lining the sidewalk. Daphne and Chuck got out, and the Lexus quickly sped off. The wind was blowing and Daphne could feel a few raindrops on her arms as they headed to the front door. She felt more and more apprehensive, not out of fear, but of not having control of the situation. Leaving the bar with a stranger was one thing, but walking into unchartered territory was another. As Chuck put his hand on the door to open it, he mumbled, "Don't forget, you're a woman."

"Now, how can I forget that?" Daphne playfully snapped back.

Chuck opened the door and led Daphne past the dimly lit living room, soft music playing, and then down a dark hall to the room on the left. As a precaution, Daphne scanned a bedroom lit only by the street lights shining through the window. No one was there. She walked in and sat on the bed as Chuck closed the door behind her.

"Why don't you get comfortable," he suggested.

"Here," she said as she turned aside, lifting her hair up over her shoulders. "Unzip my dress."

Chuck obliged her by pulling the zipper slowly down her back.

She grabbed her falsies with her hands, stuffing them into her purse as though she were hiding them. The top of her dress fell down to her waist. She kicked off her shoes. She was ready for that Florida fun that Connie Francis had been advocating for so many years.

"Hey, I gotta go to the bathroom. I'll be back in a second," Chuck said as he backed away and moved toward the door."

"Hurry up. I'll be here waiting," Daphne said, her eyes batting flirtatiously as she fell back on the bed, her hair framing her face. The door closed and Daphne waited in anticipation for Chuck's return.

Fifteen minutes passed and no Chuck. In the meantime, Daphne heard cars pulling up to the duplex in the driveway, their lights illuminating the room through the window with each arrival. The volume of the music rose, and an array of voices seemed to fill the hallway outside the bedroom. Being the patient person, Daphne continued to wait for what seemed to be another fifteen minutes or so, becoming more and more annoyed with each passing minute. She heard rain hitting the window panes, and more and more car lights were coming and going. Apparently, a party was going on, and there was Daphne, flat on her back on a bed in a dark room in a stranger's house, in some faraway town, and she liked the situation less and less. All she needed was an image of Dracula peeking through the window to create that old Hollywood version of a vampire movie. That thought certainly killed the mood for fun.

"That's it," she said out loud as she sat up. She grabbed her purse and rummaged through it for her phone. She wanted to check the time, and perhaps give Sam a call to come to her rescue. She had a rude awakening when she realized her phone was dead. "Shit," she mumbled as she threw it back into her purse. She pulled her dress up and was attempting to zip it up, when the door opened and Chuck walked in.

"It's about time," Daphne said, glaring at him in the dark.

"Sorry, I got sidetracked." Daphne could smell the stench of pot on him. He climbed onto the bed and pulled his pants down to his ankles, and then fell on his back. Daphne sat next to him, gazing down at his semi-erect cock. She thought of touching it, but before she could even lift her hand, Chuck reached over and grabbed her by the back of the neck and shoved her head onto his crotch. "Suck my dick, you bitch!" he yelled.

Daphne's immediate concern was that he was flattening her eyelashes as he pushed her face into his pubes, and her second thought was that he had a lot of nerve, and for a moment she had a notion to bite off his cock.

"You suck your own goddamn dick," she quipped back as she stood up. She wanted to beat his ass right then and there, but Daphne was the passive type and stood there stewing instead. "I need to leave and I need to go right now," she demanded. Chuck lay motionless. "Chuck, I need to leave now, and I need you to zip up my dress." Daphne looked worried. She nudged his side and then tried to shake him.

"My god, I hope you haven't OD'd on me," she said to herself. "What have I gotten myself into?" She stepped back, collecting her thoughts, and then pleaded, "Chuck, please don't be dead."

There was silence, dead silence except for the noise in the other parts of the house and the sound of the storm outside. Suddenly, Chuck began to snore.

At this point, Daphne was far from being amused. "You son of a bitch. You cock suckin' son of a bitch!" She sat on the edge of the bed, trying to figure out what to do next, how to get to the motel and the beach by sunrise. Chuck kept snoring and the sound annoyed Daphne so much that she contemplated putting a pillow over his face and holding it there. She sat for what seemed an eternity when suddenly the door opened and the lights came on. It was Chuck's friend with the burr cut. Daphne looked up at him, squinting, her eyes hurting from the bright lights. The guy was obviously disturbed, perhaps by a trick gone bad or the reality that his friend betrayed him.

"Chuck, get up," he ordered in a loud voice. He tried shaking Chuck, but to no avail. "Damn it, I said get the hell up!"

"He's passed out," Daphne said. The guy stood there, staring down at Daphne with rage in his face combined with a "what in the hell are you" look in his eyes. Daphne suddenly realized she should have used a less masculine voice, especially under the circumstances.

"Would it be too much to ask you for a ride to my motel?" Daphne asked politely in a more feminine manner.

"Fuck no!" he said emphatically.

"Then perhaps you could help me zip up my..." and before Daphne could finish her sentence, the young stranger turned off the light and left the room, slamming the door behind him. There again she sat, troubled by feeling helpless, but more so about not being at the beach by sunrise.

Then another thought occurred to her, that she might have to walk down through Daytona in broad daylight, looking like last night's stranded hooker. The scenario gave her the urgency she needed to contort her body, enabling her to reach around and zip her dress. She took her falsies out of her purse and put them in place, spread her legs and readjusted her testicles, then lifted her hair with her fingertips, and took a deep sigh and opened the door to the hallway. If she was going to have to walk back to the motel, she would do it now. "Face your fears, Miss Daphne," she told herself.

She walked down the hall, holding her silver pumps in her hand, and went past the living room where two men sat on the couch watching television. She made no eye contact, hoping they wouldn't notice her. She went to open the door when a gust of wind and torrent rain slapped her in her face. She pulled the door shut and turned around, and remembering to act like a woman, she said, "Excuse me, can you tell me how to get to the Red Roof Inn?" Until now, she hadn't even thought about which direction to go.

The two men stared at her, probably trying to analyze what they were looking at. Daphne figured they got it that she was a drag, but on the other hand, she sensed they might think she was a hooker picked up by Chuck, and now he was done with her. Regardless, she could tell they were both high. The dark headed man raised his hand and pointed to the door, saying it was about five miles down the road.

Daphne took a deep breath and turned around facing the door, when the other fellow spoke up. "Can I give you a ride?" Daphne sighed, relieved that she wouldn't have to walk five miles in the rain in drag. It would be a horror movie in the making.

"That would be nice. Thanks," she said, a quick smile of relief coming over her face.

They hurried to his car, and within minutes, they neared the Red Roof Inn.

"I like your voice," the driver said as he slowed the car down to a crawl. "It's low and sexy."

"Thanks," Daphne replied back softly, her face hugging the window. She sensed he was about to make a move on her, and of course, she was in no mood to be amorous, not to mention she was on a mission to make it back before sunrise. They entered the parking lot and he stopped the car.

"Why don't you ask me in?" he asked.

"I can't. There are other people in the room," Daphne replied. As she turned to quickly thank the man for the ride, he pulled her toward him, forcing his lips upon her mouth. Daphne grabbed the handle attempting to open the door. She pushed him away, again thanking him, and ran like hell in the rain to the oceanfront side of the motel, the surf a mere hundred feet away. She knocked on the door. No answer. The rain and wind pelted her, and she knocked harder. Apparently, Sam and Stella were inside, sound asleep, probably in a drunken stupor, and she was outside the door with no working phone and no key, and miserably wet. After about twenty minutes, the storm began to wane. Almost exhausted and defeated, she found a chair and pulled it next to the door, occasionally giving a knock in hopes that one of the two would hear her.

"Daphne, what the hell are you doing out here?" Stella was walking up to the door, still wearing her evening gown and tiara, the sound of her prosthesis slightly dragging on the concrete flooring.

"Please just let me in," Daphne pleaded. "And don't ask me any questions, just let me in." Stella was obviously drunk as she shuffled around in her black sequined purse to find her key. Once inside the room, Daphne looked at the clock and sighed with relief knowing she had about forty-five minutes before sunrise. Sam was not there, but he had the good sense to bring in the costumes and properly hang them up before going back out to spend the rest of the night with his boyfriend.

Daphne glanced at herself in the mirror. Her eye makeup was smudged and her eyelashes bent, her hair flat and wet from the rain. Simply put, she was a real mess. She pulled out a jar of Albolene from her makeup case on the counter, and began to remove the coat of last night's grease paint from her face.

Stella quietly helped Daphne by unzipping her dress. She limped across the room and stood at the open door and announced, "There's a hell of a party going on down on the other end. I just went by there and made an entrance. Straight guys, and they think I'm hot. I'm heading back down there."

"Stella, it's getting late, and well, you seem a little high right now, and…" Daphne looked up, her eyes barely open to keep the makeup remover out of her eyes. Stella was gone. "Crazy old woman," Daphne said out loud. A few moments later, she heard a commotion. She wiped her face with a towel and ran over to the door. Outside on the beach between the motel and the ocean, Stella was hollering at two men who seemed to be taunting her.

"You want some of this?" Stella screamed at the two. Daphne saw one of the men get physical with Stella, lightly hitting her with one hand as if he was trying to push her to the ground. Daphne had a flashback to a Nature Channel episode where two wolves singled out an old caribou cow, nipping at its hindquarters for hours until the poor dear was so weak it fell to the ground and the two carnivores began feasting on the carcass while it was still alive, no strength to fight back. Stella's voice was getting higher, and Daphne felt a sense of panic setting in with her mentor.

"Come on you cocksuckers, I'll show you who's more man than you are!" Stella yelled. One of the men lunged at her as she tried to kick him. He grabbed her leg, and she fell to the ground. The surprised bully found himself holding her prosthesis in his hands. Stella was helpless and the wolves approached. Daphne knew she had to do something, and quick.

"Give me my leg," Stella weakly demanded, sobbing in defeat. The old cow was down and the kill would come soon. She lifted her head and looked back at the motel to give one last call for help, when a blaring siren sound filled the air, and rays of strobe lights pierced through the early morning darkness. There stood Daphne wearing the Big Bird vest, her Ursula Andress white bikini, and she had a four-inch silver pump in each of her hands, her arms outstretched as she posed in the doorway. When "Wipe Out" began to play at full volume, Daphne's adrenaline and killer instinct kicked in like that of a mother bear protecting her cub, and she screamed like an attacking Apache as she ran to the beach, coming to Stella's rescue. Out of fear of the unknown, the two perpetrators ran like hell, one still holding onto Stella's fake leg. Daphne pursued the men down the beach until she overcame them, and after threatening the scared lugs with being beaten to death with her silver pumps, she retrieved the prosthesis and returned to find Stella alone sitting cowered on the beach.

"Stella, are you okay?" Daphne asked.

"You're wearing my costume," Stella responded, looking up like a wounded animal.

"Yeah, well the idea came to me, and…"

"You didn't ask my permission to wear my costume," she added, sounding a bit angry.

Daphne stared at the beaten down, but once almighty Stella. She took a sigh, and said, "Fuck you Stella," and she tossed the plastic leg right at Stella's lap. She undid the straps of the vest and dropped it to the ground, standing there in nothing but her white bikini, her wet blond wig, and a face with no makeup. The sun was about to peak over the horizon, the purple haze from the east casting muted hues on her flesh.

"Good bye, Stella. I have to go now," Daphne said as she gave Stella a brief forgiving smile and headed to the surf, first walking and then breaking into a quick run as if the ocean were calling her in. Stella watched in horror as Daphne made it further and further into sea. Within moments, Daphne was under water.

Stella was more than concerned for her friend, who she'd

always considered a bit delicate and suicidal. "Somebody help!" she screamed, still sitting in the sand. "Somebody's drowning out here!" she yelled over and over. No one came to the rescue, probably because of the crazy commotion a few minutes earlier, but a number of early morning joggers gathered around, curious about the creature in front of them who appeared to look like a beached whale in full Liz Taylor drag. As they circled Stella, phrases like "what the hell is that?" to "that poor dear thing" could be heard from the sparse group that did gather, when suddenly a woman said, "Look, over there!"

And just like in *Dr. No*, fifty years earlier, Daphne, reincarnated as a young movie sex goddess, rose out of the water, the sunlight at her back, in what seemed like slow motion. The small crowd clapped as the sultry silhouette moved forward, and Stella, just happy that Daphne was alive, reached into her bra and pulled out her phone to take pictures of her prized protégé coming out of the water.

"She's beautiful," one woman said in admiration.

"It's a man," another said. As Daphne approached Stella, the voyeurs dispersed, leaving the two of them alone. Daphne sat in front of Stella, the saltwater beading and running down her skin. They gazed at each other for a moment.

"Daphne, I'm so proud of you," Stella said, drunken tears of joy in her eyes.

"And why?" Daphne asked.

"I've never seen you more beautiful than now, but more importantly, I'm proud of you because, you see…" She paused, wiping her runny nose with her hand, leaving sand remnants on her upper lip. "Tonight, honey, you became a man. I know you don't want to hear that, but it's true. You stood up to those guys. You stood up to me. You saved my life and my leg. I will owe you forever. Here…" Stella took off her tiara and placed in on Daphne's head. "You deserve this more than I do."

Daphne blushed with pride, finally feeling the respect that she had always wanted from Stella. "Thank you, Stella," was all she could muster.

"Is that a nut I see hanging out there?" Stella said, pointing to Daphne's left testicle peaking out of the bikini bottom.

"Sorry," Daphne embarrassingly replied as she tucked it back. "I've had a problem with that all night long." The two laughed.

As Daphne helped Stella attach her leg, Sam appeared just as he always did, conveniently when all the drama was over. He helped walk Stella to their motel room and put her to bed.

The ride back to Birmingham that afternoon following a few hours of sleep was a quiet one, as no one really wanted to talk about what had happened the night before. Each of them would have a story to tell, to later embellish after a few drinks. But the dynamics between the three would be changed forever. Sam as usual, drove the sedan, while Stella, wearing a ball cap on her head, a red scarf around her neck and shades to conceal her swollen eyes, sat crunched up in the passenger side, shifting her weight around trying to find some semblance of comfort. Meanwhile, Daphne lay sprawled out in the back seat asleep, surrounded by feather boas and pillows, a tiara on her head, a trophy in one hand, and her silver pumps in the other.

The Scent of Honeysuckle

12:35 p.m.

"Maid service!"

Sammy's head was pounding as he rolled over, his body tangled in the sheets. He forced one eye open. The hotel room was dimly lit with the only light coming from the sun peering from the sides of the shades. He buried his head in the pillow.

"Maid service!"

"Crap," he mumbled as he rose up. He looked at the clock. It was already past noon, checkout time. "Just a minute!" he yelled. He stumbled to the door, unlatched the lock, and opened it to find a young Hispanic woman standing in the middle of the hall, her cart piled high with white towels and cleaning supplies.

"Can you give me thirty minutes?" Sammy asked, holding the sheet over his small frame. She nodded her head and proceeded to push her cart to the next door, then knocked and yelled, "Maid service!" Sammy closed the door.

Okay, he said to himself, *another hotel room*. He walked around trying to recollect anything from the night before. His clothes were neatly folded on a chair, his worn Nike tennis shoes beside them, and his dark blue hoody was draped over the lampshade on the bedside table. It was as if someone had taken the time to sort his clothing to make sure they didn't look unkempt when it was time to put them back on. He checked his cargo pants for his personal belongings. Tucked deep in his back pocket he found the three dollars that he had the day before. There were wadded up napkins with phone numbers from older men he had met the past few weeks. He frantically searched through his front right pocket, and with some relief he pulled out his Nana's old St. Christopher medal that she had given to him when he was six years old. Apparently, she lost interest in the oval shaped, iconic emblem of travel protection years before Sammy was born when it was announced that St. Christopher was not actually a saint. Like many other Catholics, she took it off and put it in her jewelry box with the other precious remnants of her past.

He remembered that day when she gave it to him. Sammy sat on the edge of Nana's bed while she posed in front of her vanity. He watched her brush her hair, and with each stroke he marveled at how her curly hair bounced back into place. She was enamored with him as much as he was with her. She opened her jewelry box, reached in and pulled out a modest pair of clip-on earrings, and fastened them to her lobes. Sammy thought they were the most beautiful earrings he had ever seen.

"Sammy, you want something special?" she asked, smiling at him through the reflection in the mirror.

"Can I have earrings like yours?"

"No, silly, but maybe when you get older." She foraged through the dainty white box and pulled out her St. Christopher medal. "How about this? It used to bring me good luck when I was your age. Maybe it will be good luck for you." She put it in his hand and said, "Keep it in your pocket, and it will keep you protected from all the evil spirits out there, especially when you travel." He put it in his pocket. Other kids his age had rabbits' feet for good luck. Sammy had Nana's medal.

As he glanced around the hotel room, Sammy sighed with relief knowing that his only possessions were still intact. He tried to recall anything that would trigger a memory from the night before. He faintly remembered a guy he met who bought him drinks at the bar. Everything between the first drink and this morning was a blur. Sammy couldn't even remember what the man looked like, what he was wearing, or even how old he was. And then there was the possibility that the one who bought the drinks may not be the one he spent the night with. Regardless, the stranger was already gone with no trace, not even a goodbye. For Sammy, it was another one night stand.

Sammy turned on the shower, standing naked under the spray attempting to awaken his consciousness. He lathered the soap in his hands, rubbing his face, his chest, his underarms, and then he ran the suds over his crotch and buttocks. His rectum hurt. *Probably got fucked*, he thought to himself. The warm water flowed over his head and down his torso, making its way to the drain. It was as if he were exorcising away the filth of the night before. After ten minutes under the water, he stepped out of the shower and began to dry himself off. He looked in the mirror, hardly recognizing who he had become. He was only sixteen, but the dark circles around his eyes made him look older. His arched eyebrows were growing back, and the stubble on his brow and upper lip made it uncomfortable for him to look at himself. He had lost so much weight that his ribs were showing. He looked anorexic.

He had always hated his body. He had no chest, and his hips were wide and out of proportion with the rest of his physique. And though he was small and underweight, he was still pear shaped. Looking through the mist on the mirror, he told himself he looked like a young lesbian, but a cute one. Not too butch, not too fem; just somewhere in the middle. He didn't mind looking like a girl, and at times he thought he should have been one. Of course, he had heard this before in ninth grade when he was tauntingly called a lesbian and a hermaphrodite in the shower after gym class. Sammy was the only boy in his class with no pubic hair, and his penis was also the smallest of those he'd seen. It was an embarrassing time for him with clothes or without, but to stand in front his peers with no means to cover up his nakedness and his physical deficiencies was more than he could handle. Soon, he started to miss school, and ultimately his grades began to suffer, and he struggled to make it to the tenth grade. That's when his father started to refer to him as a dumb ass, and he considered his son a waste of his money, what little he had. When Sammy decided to arch his eyebrows, he definitely crossed the line of tolerance with his dad, and suddenly the words "little faggot" replaced "dumb ass" as his father's words of choice when he addressed or referred to his son. Sammy had seen the public services ads that swore that "it gets better," but getting better was not an option at that point for him. His needed to get out.

Sammy rinsed out his T-shirt and used the blow dryer to take most of the dampness out. It was summertime, so with the heat of the afternoon on the other side of the door, it would dry in no time. He slipped on his pants, and then his T-shirt, and then he tussled with his cropped light brown hair with a handful of hotel soap. He had no gel and no brush, but he was told that lightly wet soap would act as the perfect solution to set his hair, at least until it rained or the humidity got high. He collected the extra toiletries from the bathroom, putting the small bars of soap and the complimentary bottles of lotion and cheap cologne in his pockets. He grabbed his hoody, put on his shoes, and walked out the door to face another day of survival.

2:43 p.m.

It was hard being homeless, and even more difficult for Sammy to keep up the appearance that he wasn't without a place to live. In the past few months he had learned from others on the streets where to look for food and shelter, as well as how to avoid trouble. For Sammy, constantly dealing with confrontations back home was what brought him to Louisville to start with. He was bullied as a child, and tortured as a teen, not only for being gay, but for just being different. Life in Corbin, Kentucky was tough for anyone who was odd, and especially for those who were introverted and unable to defend themselves against threats and abuse. But that was all behind him now. He vowed never to return to eastern Kentucky, no matter what. And it didn't matter that his parents had no idea where he was, nor did he even know if they were looking for him. He didn't care. He left everything in Corbin, including his ID, and even his cell phone. He avoided getting a job so that he wouldn't leave a trail for them to find him.

Though tired from the daily struggles of survival, and after losing quite a few pounds, he was able to walk with a swagger that he never had. Sure he was weak from not eating as he should have and not getting the right amount of sleep he needed, but on this day, and with a heavy hangover, he took pride in knowing that he survived another night against all odds. Right now he was hungry and he was trying his best not to spend the three dollars he had left over from the ten that a trick gave him two days ago for having a quickie under the Second Street Bridge. The rigors of sex were something that Sammy had learned in his short time in Louisville. In the past, he had often dreamed of the perfect man and developing a monogamous relationship, and then giving himself on that special night. He still had that dream of the ideal mate, but the purity of the relationship would never happen, for Sammy knew that he would have to do some things to survive, acts that his Nana would not approve, but here he was on the streets, living day to day, and Nana was in heaven. So often, he knew she was watching his every move, but when he was half naked in a back ally participating in survival sex, he disengaged her memory, only to feel guilty for his deeds when the act was completed.

The summer air was warm as he headed down Second Street to the Ohio River. Many office workers went to the riverfront to eat lunch while taking in the gentle river breeze and midday sun. It was also where quite a few of them would leave uneaten leftovers in the trash cans. Though initially humbled by the experience of foraging for food in garbage cans, Sammy soon realized that a freshly half-eaten chicken sandwich from a can swarming with flies was almost as delicious as one that Nana would make on a Saturday afternoon in her kitchen. But today, the pickings were slim. He found an orange and a few Cheetos. As with many of these ventures, some days would be better than others, and today, unfortunately, was worse than most.

Sammy headed to the bushes to relieve himself, only to wince in pain as the urine flowed from his penis. It was as if his whole dick was on fire. With cramps in his stomach, he broke into a sweat. It took a few minutes for the discomfort to subside, and lying on his back on the grass, he found shelter and comfort in the shade. He had never felt anything like that before, and he was alarmed. But what could he do? Where could he go to find help? Perhaps, in time, it would go away. He decided to relax and nap, just for a short time. He had nothing else to do.

He closed his eyes and took a deep breath. He could smell the scent of honeysuckle in the air. It reminded him of his summers in the country spent with Nana. She first showed him how to pull the blossoms off the honeysuckle plant and suck the nectar from the rear of the flower. It was a sweet taste that he remembered, and it took at least ten or more blossoms to really get a small amount on the tongue. "Some people say that the invasive honeysuckle plant is the revenge of the Japanese for losing that war, but I like to think the blossoms are a delicacy that those rich city gardeners just can't appreciate," Nana would say after a nectar session while running her tongue over her lips. "Ain't nothing like a good smell and sip of a honeysuckle blossom."

Nana always knew that Sammy was special. When he came to stay with her in the summers, it was like a vacation for the both of them. Sammy was her only grandchild, and she spoiled him rotten with whatever he wanted. She even shared her earrings with him. Once, when he was about ten, they put on aprons and earrings and went to the garden to pick squash and tomatoes for dinner. "But what if someone sees us?" Sammy asked, and Nana told him not to worry, that nobody ever came to visit, but if they did "...we'd just have 'em put on an apron and another pair of earrings and stay for dinner." And then she'd laugh. "Now you know not to tell your mom about this," she'd say in a very serious tone, and Sammy just smiled knowing that he was safe with Nana.

5:07 p.m.

The sound of rush hour traffic directly over Sammy's head woke him from a much needed rest. He thought it was odd that this oasis of riverfront splendor could be located right under the major intersection of interstate traffic. It was if the whole park was partially domed to provide shelter from the rain and sun for those seeking protection from the elements. For the homeless, sleeping during the day was much easier than finding a safe refuge at night. There was some comfort in the daylight hours knowing the surroundings, while the dangers of the night are rarely seen. Sure, it was easier to hide in the dark recesses of the alleys, but those few places were hideouts for others as well, and not too many street people want to share anything, let alone a safe place to rest.

Sammy stretched and stood up, staring at the Ohio River in front of him. There was something about the river that beckons young men, and Sammy was no different. He imagined how adventurous it would be to ride on one of the loaded barges and head south past Paducah and then maybe roll on down the Mississippi all the way to New Orleans. For a brief moment, he felt like Huckleberry Finn. But in a split second, he felt the whims of Becky Thatcher, knowing that if he were to ride down the river, it would have to be on the Belle of Louisville steamboat and not on a barge.

Walking with his head down and the hoody over his head to help protect his anonymity, Sammy headed south to Broadway. Often, he would attempt to make eye contact with drivers sitting at the few stop lights along the way. They would invariably look in another direction. He often wondered where they were going, what kind of family they had, or simply what kind of person they might be. No one ever smiled at him, inquired how he was doing, or even asked if he needed a ride. He passed the YMCA and decided to check out the area around McDonalds across from the community college. It was, after all, Friday and the night was soon approaching. Sammy was hoping to connect with one of the few "weekend" people that he had come to know. They were the characters that were always out on the weekends looking to hook up for sex or drugs, or even both. Sammy scanned up and down the street and saw no familiar faces. It was too early, he thought. He selected one of the benches that lined Second Street in front of the college to sit and wait. After a few minutes, he spotted a tall thin black man walking with a very distinct limp. It was Jess. Sammy met Jess when he first came to Louisville, and though Jess wasn't gay, they hit it off immediately. Jess became Sammy's street mentor, giving him all kinds of advice on how to survive. He was approaching and recognized Sammy.

"Hey, Sweet Baby!" Jess said, genuinely happy to see Sammy. "Been a week or two, hadn't it been?"

"Hey, Jess." Sammy stood up and greeted Jess with a knuckle bump. "Yeah, it's been a while."

"Sho' is good to see you still alive and well, but you look like you been losin' weight. You been eatin'?"

"Course, I've been eating. Remember, you taught me how to find the food..."

"The grub. Not the food, the grub."

"That's right, the grub."

"Grub is garbage, but good. Food is fine, but not necessarily good. Don't forget that, Sweet Baby." Jess patted Sammy on the back and looked cautiously around. It was his way of being aware of his environment and opportunity. He could easily comfort a friend with conversation, while looking for a buyer at the same time. Jess was a hustler who'd franchised his wares, and was now diversifying his trade by selling drugs. By his own standards, he had moved up the ladder of success and survival about a wrung or two. Though Sammy thought his friend might have been in his early twenties, to listen to him talk, Jess was old and wise and had done it all, and then some. It was his smile and his charm that pulled people in. He was almost like a con artist, but without the malicious attempt to do harm or be fraudulent. Sammy understood him, and he liked him. The two sat on the bench, their eyes taking in all that was happening around them.

"Sweet Baby, I thought you'd be outta here by now."

"I can't get out of here unless I know where I'm going, and right now, things aren't going so well."

"I didn't wanta say it, but you look like shit. I mean, you lost weight, you're clothes are dirty, and your hair looks like…what the hell you got in your hair?"

"Soap."

"Soap? I know us black folk do strange things with our hair, but why the fuck you put soap in your hair?"

"I didn't have any gel, and I heard that soap works like gel."

"Somebody clowning wit'chu. If it starts raining you gonna have soap suds on your head. Oh, Sweet Baby, you can't believe everything you hear out here on the streets. These streets are full of clowners and bullshitters, and you have to learn what's real and what ain't."

"I'm still learning," Sammy said, trying to defend himself.

"You still learning, alright, but you running out of time. You can't be out here forever. You don't have what it takes."

"I think I can. I've lasted this long."

"That's right, you've lasted. Not improved, not moved up or out. Just lasted. I told you along time ago, only the big dicks and the cuties get the sugar daddies out here. Pretty boys like you get used up and beat up. You either need to get outta here and get normal, or get a protector."

"A protector?"

"Yeah, a protector, someone who watches out for you, who takes care of you. But there's a trade off. You gotta do whatever the protector says, and if you don't, well, it ain't nice."

"You mean like a pimp or something?"

"Yeah, like a pimp or something."

"Jess, why don't you let me hang with you?"

"Oh, Sweet Baby, I work alone. You'd hamper my style, and anyway, I ain't a protector. I'm just me making my way, networking with who I can, and investing myself in the future with my wares."

"It was just a thought. I mean, you're like the only person I know here, the only one I can talk to."

"And you need to be getting back home where you'd be safe. I know they call you queer and faggot back home, but you still a queer and a faggot here. How many times you been beat since you been here?"

"Two."

"Two?"

"Well, three counting that old lady with the cane. That's when I met you, remember?"

"Yeah, I laughed my ass off, you trying to steal that old lady's purse and she beat the shit out of you with that cane. Your nose was bleeding. Remember what I told you afterwards?

"Yeah, never prey on the old women or the homeless, they're one of us."

"Yeah, one of us. And when you prey on them, you prey on yourself, and you never prey on yourself. That's just the law of the street."

"Jess, I hurt."

"You what?"

"I hurt, you know, down there."

"Ah, geez, Sweet Baby. I bet you've done got yourself the clap."

"The clap?"

"Yes, the clap. The drip. Gonorrhea. The STD. Oh, Sweet Baby, you been infected and it won't get better. You probably got the AIDS virus, too. You see how this ain't gettin' any better for you?"

Sammy began to weep, not because he felt that he was at the point of hitting rock bottom with his life, but because he was feeling shame in what he had become. His father had said he would become a disease carrying faggot, part of God's wrath, and perhaps he was right.

"Jess, I don't know what to do. I've never had anything like this before. Am I going to die?"

"Eventually, if you don't get it taken care of. Course, the pain will make you wanna die," he said as he mockingly grabbed his crotch and laughed. "I can't believe this shit. I thought you'd know better." Jess carefully looked around to see that no one was watching, and reached into one of his pockets, then lifted out a small plastic bag of pills. He started separating the large white tablets from the others.

"Here, there's four AB's…"

"AB's?"

"Antibiotics," Jess said, enunciating the word as if he were a doctor lecturing a patient with bad habits.

"And what do I do with them?"

"You take two now, and then two in a couple of hours or so, when it starts to get dark."

"Where'd you get antibiotics?"

"Sweet Baby, you ask too many questions, and anyway, it ain't none of your business where I got them. The fact is you're lucky I have them. Now take 'em like I told you, and know that they ain't gonna cure what you got. You gotta be down there at the clinic on Preston, you know, off Broadway, on Monday morning. It's four blocks that way," he said pointing east. "And don't you dare tell them I gave you anything for it."

"I won't."

"And promise me you'll be there on Monday morning."

"I will. I promise." Sammy put two of the pills in his pocket and he put the others in his mouth. They were so large and hard to swallow, especially with a dry mouth, but eventually, the tablets made their way down his throat.

"You eat today?" Jess asked.

"An orange. Some Cheetos."

Jess put his hand in his pocket and pulled out a small roll of bills. "Here, take this five and go eat at McD's."

"Jess, I can't take your money."

"Now, Sweet Baby, you take it or I'm gonna whip your ass all over this street, and I'll call you all kind of words, your favorite words like faggot and queer. You want me to do that right here in front of all these people?" He smiled as he pushed the five dollar bill inside Sammy's hoody and against his chest.

"You wouldn't dare," Sammy said, a smile coming over his face. He reached in his hoody and took the bill and folded it up, then carefully slid it into his pocket next to his St. Christopher medal. "Thanks, Jess. I promise I'll pay you back."

. "You can pay me back by gettin' the hell out of this town. Now, go eat."

Sammy crossed the street and headed to McDonalds. He turned to look back at his friend sitting on the bench. Jess waved his hand at Sammy as if he were telling him to go on, that he wasn't leaving until he was inside. Sammy ordered a double cheeseburger combo, and put the change in his pocket. He sat down at a table next to a window facing Second Street. He opened the bag, pulled out the burger and bit into it, savoring the first bite as if it were a slice of fillet mignon. It tasted incredible. He looked out the window. There was an empty bench. Jess had moved on.

7:12 p.m.

Sammy started to walk toward Old Louisville, the historic part of town just south of Broadway and north of the university. It was a quiet neighborhood with old Victorian homes. Sammy often walked to Central Park, just off of Magnolia and Fourth Street. He fell in love with the eclectic park with its visitors being old and young, black and white, gay and straight, and yes, even the homeless seemed welcome. But what he loved most were the squirrels. Yes, the park was home to hundreds of squirrels, and Sammy was fascinated with the audacity they had in approaching him when he sat on one of the park benches to observe their behavior. Back home in Corbin, people shot squirrels and sometimes they'd eat them. Perhaps that's why the furry tailed rodents were so elusive back home; they had the sense to know that they might be fodder for the dinner table. While watching them frolic around, teasing and eluding dogs, he acknowledged that there was no way that he could ever indulge in the act of dining on squirrel. Of course, he never thought he'd be eating out of garbage cans either.

The summer breeze felt so good on Sammy's skin. He felt as though the medication that Jess gave him was working, although the relaxation overtaking his body might have been from the meal he had just eaten a while earlier. He headed for the restroom. He stood in front of the urinal ready to scream, and as the urine began to flow, there was no pain, just some discomfort. Jess had saved the day, at least for the time being. After zipping up, he headed for the sink. He rinsed his face, avoiding putting any water in his hair for fear of what Jess said about soap suds forming on his head. Glancing at himself in the dirty mirror, he could see that Jess was right. He had let himself go. He looked thin and weak, and what bit of sparkle he once had was gone. He walked out and headed toward the spray fountain that the local children played in. It spewed about fifteen feet into the air, creating a mist and a relief from the summer heat. Sammy walked nearer and sat on the grass, watching the scantily clad kids running through the water playing make believe games of chase.

Sammy remembered the first time he went to the local swimming pool in Corbin. He was with Nana. He was five years old. She brought a picnic basket with bologna sandwiches, fresh fruit, and Ball jars with sweetened iced tea, and after laying a quilt on the ground in the corner of the pool to mark their territory, she led young Sammy to the edge of the pool. He remembered the excitement in the air, the kids jumping in the pool and splashing around. He also remembered how terrified he was about getting in the pool. Nana went in first, went under and the came up. "Now, it's your turn. Come on. Jump in. Come on Sammy, jump in. I'll catch you."

Sammy didn't really have a fear of the water or its depth. He was embarrassed to be standing there wearing only his swim trunks. Even at an early age, he was so self-conscious about showing his body, especially his chest. But, in all honesty, Sammy just didn't want to get wet.

Suddenly, a boy around ten swam from behind Nana and stood up. "Jump, you little sissy! Jump!"

Nana turned around, flailing her wet arm right into his face, knocking the boy under the water. When he surfaced with a stunned look on his face, she grabbed his wrist, looked him directly in the eyes and said, "If you ever say anything like that again to my grandson, especially when I'm around, I'll hold your little sissy head under the water until you see God coming to get you. Now get out of here, this is our corner of the pool. Scram!" The kid swam as fast as he could to the other side of the pool to get away, never looking back.

Nana had been Sammy's protector, he thought to himself, but she wasn't like a pimp. She was just always there when he needed her the most. Right now he could use her, but since her funeral, all he had left of her was her medal and memories. He watched the kids in the spray, their protectors sitting outside the range of the mist, watching over them. One day they would be on their own, with their own endearing memories of being wet in the park.

The sun was beginning to go down. Sammy decided to head back toward Broadway before the evening darkened. It was never safe in streets that were lined with trees and shrubs, no matter the class status of the neighborhood. That was just another piece of wisdom that Jess instilled in Sammy. "Be cautious of the night," he said more than once. As it was getting dark, the street lights began to slowly illuminate through the mighty oaks, casting filtered shadows onto the street. He remembered his doctor's orders and he swallowed his two remaining antibiotics.

10:23 p.m.

After making his way to the comfort of Broadway, Sammy followed the bright lights to Walgreens on the corner of Brooks Street. Inside, he marveled at the array of merchandise cramped into such a small space. He headed for the makeup counter, browsing through the hundreds of products and tools, anything and everything a woman would need to look glamorous, or at the least, presentable. He touched the magnifying mirror, turning it so that he could see his face. His pores seemed so deep, and he cringed thinking his brows needed tweezing and his facial stubble needed to be eliminated.

"Can I help you with something?" An older lady was behind the counter, attempting to look like a makeup consultant, but Sammy knew she was really there to make sure that no one stole anything.

"No, thanks. I'm just looking." Sammy moved down the counter gazing at the Cover Girl products. To his right, another middle-aged woman was testing different shades of lipstick. With her short hair and her sports shirt and polyester shorts, she didn't look like the lipstick type. And given her stocky build, she looked more like a high school gym teacher. Sammy found himself in front of the emery boards, eyelashes, scissors, and tweezers. He thought to himself how he sure could use the tweezers, but he didn't have the money for them. He stared at the assortment of eyeliners and eyebrow pencils. *If I only had a hundred dollars*, he thought. If he only had ten, he could make himself look decent again. He pulled the tweezers from the rack, and with deliberation, he selected a black pencil. Without hesitation, he put the two items in his hoody pocket. He continued to look at the other displayed items, gently running his fingers over them, caressing whatever he could. He loved the makeup counter.

"Excuse me," someone whispered.

"Yeah?" Sammy was startled to look up and see the customer who had been at the counter with him.

"I was just wondering what color might look good on me."

"What?" Sammy responded, looking perplexed at such a question.

"I'm just looking for the right color, and there seems to be so many. I was never any good with makeup, and before I waste my money on something that wouldn't look right…" She paused then said, "You look like you know something about makeup. Maybe you're an expert?"

"Well, I'm not an expert, but you definitely don't want to go with that darker color you have in your hand. Try that one. It should make your lips pop, but not too much." Sammy was flattered that she would take his opinion seriously. This was a rare occurrence for him. She put a dab of the color he had recommended on her lips and stood back.

"My gosh, you're good. This is the perfect color for me. Thanks for helping me out."

"Sure," he replied. "Thanks for asking for my advice."

"Listen, I don't want to see you get into trouble, but I think you should know that they've got all kinds of surveillance here in the store. The manager is probably watching you right now..."

"And?"

"I saw you put those two items in your pocket."

"And I'll pay for them when I leave the store."

"They'll put you in jail," she said. "You don't want to go to jail do you?"

"Of course not."

"And I bet you don't have the money to pay for them either, right?"

"Who are you and why are you asking me these questions?"

"I work at the shelter down on Market. I can spot a homeless person a mile away, and I'd say that you're not only homeless, you're a runaway as well." Sammy stared at her, confused about this special power that she seemed to possess. She couldn't pick out the right lipstick for herself, but she already had Sammy figured out.

"And what if I am?"

"I just want you to know that if you need help, if you need a place to stay, to sleep, or just to hang out, you can come anytime. The door is open. I don't care how tough you are, someone like you doesn't need to be out on the streets." He looked at her as she smiled back at him. He had seen that same kind of smile on Nana's face.

"My name is Tracy, and here's my card. It has my cell phone number and the address of the shelter."

"I know where it is. Four blocks up and then six, east."

"That's right. Now give me those things in your pocket, and I'll pay for them."

"I can't have you pay for them."

"They're obviously important to you or else you wouldn't be taking them out of here without paying for them. And anyway, I don't want to be seen as an accomplice to a potential crime. See that camera up there? Just give me the items, and wave to the good man behind the wall. Go ahead."

Sammy gave in to the wishes of the kind woman. He stood in

line with her as she paid for the items. They walked out of the store and she handed him the tweezers and eyebrow pencil. She also gave him the receipt.

"Thanks. That was very kind of you," he said, grateful for what Tracy had just done.

"It's not a problem. I'm on my way to work, so be careful out there and don't hesitate to come see me." She winked at him and turned away, heading up the street. Sammy watched her until she faded into the darkness. *She was a protector*, he thought.

12:20 a.m.

Sammy headed to Floyd Street, making his way to one of Louisville's largest and hottest nightclubs. A few weeks earlier, an acquaintance showed him how to get in the bar without an ID check and door charge. Seems the drag entertainers and other patrons used the side door to go into the alley to smoke pot and partake in other questionable activities. Even though the door was monitored, the entertainers would sometimes allow some guests to reenter with them. Sammy became one of Sheena's regular guests, waiting outside with other fans for the entertainer to take her "fresh air" break. Initially, Sheena and Sammy struck up a conversation, and she invited the under-aged boy into the dressing room, where he played with her makeup and jewelry, helped her get into her costumes, and then he found his way into the disco to dance and lose himself in the crowd. He would become intoxicated after drinking from half-filled plastic cups left on tables, and ultimately, he'd find someone to comfort and use him for what was left of the evening.

He was just over a block away when he heard the heavy bass of the disco. The closer he got to the club, he could feel the vibration, and the excitement began to build within him. He bypassed the front entrance and headed down the alley.

"Hey, Sammy. Come give Sheena some sugar." Sheena was wearing a sleek robe tied at the waist. With her blonde wig that was teased twelve inches high and her four-inch heels, she looked seven-feet tall. Sammy's nose barely reached her fake bosom. She had a joint positioned between her snap-on nails. She was holding court with about six others when Sammy approached her.

"Hello, Sheena. You look beautiful tonight."

"Thanks, sweetie. You want a hit?"

"Sure." Sheena handed him the joint. He took the smoke deep into his lungs, held it as long as he could, then let it out, rolling his eyes in painful joy.

"It's some good shit," Sheena said, smiling at her alley friend. "Take another." He did.

Without warning, a large man opened the door and informed the group that it was time for them to come back in the club. Sammy began to fall in line with the others when Sheena turned and stopped him. "Sorry, Sammy, but they're cracking down on us letting people come in the side door without a bar stamp. I can't let you in tonight. Sorry, honey. Maybe some other time." Sammy stood there as the door closed in front of him.

Eerily, it was quiet in the alley; the only noise was Lady Gaga singing "Born This Way," the bass reverberating inside against the walls. Sammy loved that song. He stood there for what seemed an eternity, trying to figure out what had really happened. Had he been rejected? Was Sheena really telling the truth? As he spoke out loud to himself, he could feel himself slurring his words. He began to feel dizzy and light headed. He was high, but he was coherent enough to know that it was not safe to be walking the streets in a vulnerable state. His heart was racing and he began to feel panicked. He reached in his pocket and pulled out Tracy's card. He would go to the shelter, just for the night. She would protect him.

He exited the alley and stumbled onto Market Street, heading for the shelter. It was a few blocks away. He was seeing double, and tried hard to stay focused by putting one hand over his left eye, then moving ahead. He saw the silhouettes of three young men heading in his direction. Out of fear, he wanted to turn and run, but it was too late. The men were right in front of him.

"Got a cigarette?" one of them asked.

"No, I don't." He proceeded to move forward. They blocked his path.

"Looks like a faggot, a faggot walking all alone. Give us your money." He could smell the stench of cheap liquor and sweat as they leaned over his frail body.

"I don't have any. Just let me go!" He tried to get by the trio, but two of the strangers held him as the other emptied his pockets.

"Goddamn shampoo and soap! Sweet smelling perfume or something! What the fuck? An eyebrow pencil? A couple of ones, three to be exact." The hoodlum stashed the money in his back pocket. "And what's this? A piece of jewelry? Hell, it ain't even gold."

Sammy felt a rage build in him that he had never felt before. "Give me my medal!" he screamed, and with one quick lunge, he kicked the robber in the groin. The man rolled on the ground in pain, and then stood up. With the others still restraining Sammy, the young man pulled a lug wrench from his pants and faced the frightened boy. He smashed the tool against Sammy's head. He hit him again, and then another time, with the final blow harder than the others. Without any more resistance, Sammy collapsed on the sidewalk.

"Faggot! And here's your fuckin' cheap jewelry!" The medal landed on the ground right next to Sammy's limp body. "Come on, let's go. Let the piece of shit die." The three perpetrators fled.

Sammy lay there, bleeding from the skull, gasping for breath, his St. Christopher medal just inches from his fingertips. He could see it, but he was too weak to grasp it. *Where was his protector when he needed one?* He tried to call for Jess, but his lips would not move. He tried to beckon Nana, but to no avail. The scent of honeysuckle blossoms filled his nostrils. It was the sweetest smell, the aroma of summer and content. His eyes were heavy and he felt tired. He started to drift off. All alone, he took one labored breath before slipping into darkness.

Spaghetti Kisses

Guided by the depths of her imagination, Danielle Campbell appeared to be a very precarious and happy child lost in innocent play most of the time. In the summer of 1955 she had a terrible crush on Joe Boy, another five-year-old who lived across the street in a tiny white house. All the homes in the rundown neighborhood in the quaint community in central Kentucky looked boringly alike to those who didn't reside there, but the families who lived in the remote cluster of homes near the end of town created their own means of identifying each building, like referring to the house on the left with the maple tree in front was where old man Davidson lived, or the one with the Christmas lights on the porch all year long was where the Simpsons lived, or the house with the big yellow dog chained to the stake in the front yard was where Sarah and John Mattingly lived. Danielle's house had two holly bushes growing perfectly on each side of the sidewalk entrance. Joe Boy's house was the plainest of all. Nothing in the yard, no shrubs around the base of the house nor toys on the sidewalk, not even a bike in the driveway. When darkness came, there were no lights on in the house.

When the sun came up in the warm summer mornings and the parents went off to work in the local distillery, the neighborhood children gathered each day after breakfast to play in the street. Joe Boy never spoke when he approached the small group of kids. He just smiled and that's what Danielle liked the most about him. His whole life seemed to be a mystery to her.

The children, including Joe Boy, usually paid no attention

to Danielle, almost shunning her when they played games of tag or when they sped up and down the street taking turns wearing used and broken roller skates. Danielle was never bothered by the reluctance of the others to engage her in conversation. At times they found ways to make fun of her size and her inability to keep up with them, often referring to her as "sissy" or "little girl." Most of the children were around seven or eight, and as an only child, she was fine with the omission of full inclusion in the group as long as she was allowed to tag along. This special playtime with others lasted each morning until noon as Danielle's mother, who kept a protective eye on her child from the front porch as if danger lurked on the streets, called her inside for lunch.

After eating a peanut butter sandwich and drinking a half-filled glass of milk, Danielle would routinely go to her bedroom. For most children, naptime was an unwelcomed inconvenience, but Danielle always found the quiet few hours alone the perfect getaway for her secret thoughts and conversations she had with her stuffed animals and dolls she kept neatly placed on her bed. She also looked forward to spending time in her special box. Her father had allowed her to keep the large cardboard box their refrigerator was delivered in back in the spring. Just stepping inside it was the gateway into her imagination. Alone, she'd take two Coca Cola bottle caps and placed them over her nipples under her t-shirt make believing she had grownup woman breasts. She'd wear one of her mother's old aprons, the strings wrapped around her twice at chest level to hold the bottle caps in place as the rickrack edged bottom barely touched the tops of her feet. She imagined the outfit to be a long flowing evening gown. She'd tie a scarf around her head covering her short brown hair, pretending the silk-feeling fabric was long golden tresses. With the muted sound in the background of the soap opera playing on the black and white TV in the living room, she took on the role of Cinderella in that cardboard box, and of course, Joe Boy was her Prince Charming. She simulated sweeping the floor and preparing dinner for the time when Joe Boy would come home from work at the distillery. She'd greet him at the door, the aroma of meatloaf in the air, and she would give him a kiss right on the mouth. They would live happily ever after. Soon, Danielle slid down to the floor of the box, pulled her apron under her chin, and drifted off into her nap.

On Saturday, Danielle and her mother went to see a movie matinee at the town's only theater. *The Lady and the Tramp* was the feature film, and as always, Danielle beamed with excitement. She loved the movies. The mother and daughter sat on the second row and Danielle watched intently as the big screen illuminated the room. She nodded off at one point, only to feel the pat of her mother's hand on her leg, gently waking her up just in time to see the Tramp and the Lady eat a strand of spaghetti and finally kiss. At that point, Danielle determined that she had just witnessed the greatest love story of all time.

As the movie ended and they exited the theater, Danielle held on to her mother's hand as they walked down Main Street, turning left after the drugstore and headed for home.

"Did you like the movie?" her mother asked.

"Yeah, especially when they kissed when they were eating that spaghetti," Danielle giggled.

"They call those spaghetti kisses."

"Spaghetti kisses? That's a funny name for a kiss. Mama?" Danielle asked with a puzzled look on her face.

"What is it?"

"When people fall in love, do they have a baby?"

Danielle's mother hesitated for a moment, trying to grasp the sensitivity of the situation. "Well, yes," she replied. "It can happen that way."

"I'm going to have a baby," Danielle exclaimed as she arched her back and pushed her stomach forward.

"Oh, Danielle. That doesn't mean you're going to have a baby," her mother said, laughing at the cuteness of the moment.

"Well, I love Joy Boy and I'm gonna have his baby," Danielle announced.

The protective mother abruptly stopped walking and pulled Danielle around, facing her. "Hush with that nonsense. You're only five years old. Don't ever bring this up again."

"But…"

"Don't 'but' me. I don't want to hear anymore talk like that. Now let's get home."

The two moved forward, Danielle with her head tilted down, not sure why she had been reprimanded. Her mother grimaced as they walked down the street to their home. But Danielle was resilient, and within a few minutes, she had completely forgotten about the conversation and she let go of her mother's hand and began skipping ahead. When she reached the front of her house, she turned around, waiting for her mother to catch up, and together they walked between the two holly bushes at the sidewalk entrance. Danielle couldn't wait to go to her room and play in the giant cardboard box.

Danielle's mother made a meager dinner that night. Pork and beans with mashed potatoes. It was her child's favorite meal, but she noticed the five-year-old wasn't very hungry. Her husband sat at the head of the table, eating his food and taking a sip of Miller out of a can after every bite. He was always quiet at dinnertime, and he expected everyone else to act the same. He hated small talk.

"Can I be excused?" Danielle asked her father.

"Not till you eat what's on your plate," her father ordered. Though barely thirty, his frowning facial features made him appear much older and intimidating.

"But Daddy, I'm not hungry," Danielle softly pleaded.

"Eat your food," he said, raising his voice.

Danielle's mother interrupted. "Perhaps we had too much popcorn at the movie today," she said as though she were trying to defuse an argument. "And anyway, we need to talk."

Danielle's father swallowed the forkful of potatoes in his mouth, then lifted his beer and took a drink. He sat the can down on the table, wiped his mouth with the back of his hand, and pondered for a few seconds. "You're excused. Go to your room."

Danielle quietly left the table and went to her room. A few minutes later, she could hear her parents arguing at the dining room table, their voices rising with every exchange. She stepped into her cardboard box to escape the uncomfortable emotions that frightened her. She had barely wrapped the scarf around her head when she heard the bedroom door open and her father's angry voice. Daphne peered from around the side of the box.

"I said, get out here, and take that damn scarf off your head." Danielle took a few timid steps, slowly approaching her father, as his imposing six-foot body towered over the frightened child. Danielle removed the scarf and let it drop to the floor. Her father squatted down to eye level. He was so close to her face she could smell the beer on his breath. She glanced up once to see her mother in the dark recess of the hallway, her face wet with tears.

"This girl stuff has to end and it ends right now. You are my son, not my daughter."

"But Daddy, I don't want to be a boy," Danielle said, her frail body becoming rigid with her brave attempt to stand her ground and make her case.

Her father stood up, and Danielle could see the rage building in his face. "God gave you a dick between your legs and that means you're a boy, and that's the way it is. Your name is Daniel, not Danielle. This nonsense is over, now say your name." Danielle paused, looking down to the floor. "Say, 'My name is Daniel Campbell' and say it now!" he screamed.

Danielle had always feared her father, but she had never felt as afraid of him as she did now. She took a deep breath and mumbled, "My name is Daniel Campbell."

"Louder!" her father yelled. "Say it louder!"

Danielle raised her head and with her lips trembling, she said, "My name is Daniel Campbell."

Within seconds, Danielle's father gathered all her dolls and stuffed animals, her scarf and apron, then he ripped apart her cardboard box and carried all that remained of Danielle's small world to the trash pile in the backyard. Danielle watched through her bedroom window as her father threw gasoline on the pile, igniting it into a blaze that seemed to reach the sky. Danielle was angry and confused, and though too young to fully understand the complexity of the situation, she was puzzled by her father's reaction. From that moment on, and out of fear, Danielle's soul retreated into secrecy, shielding itself from danger and shame, but never fully going away.

A few weeks later, Daniel sat on the porch step, watching Joe Boy's mother load up her car across the street with her sparse belongings. The rumor in the neighborhood was that she had separated from her husband, and now she and Joe Boy were moving to St. Louis to live with relatives. Daniel had a stick in his hand, pretending to be writing letters of the alphabet on the concrete below his feet. For a brief moment, he began etching tiny hearts and daydreaming about the love of his young life, and how he would never have spaghetti kisses with Joe Boy.

When the last load was packed into the car, Joe Boy came out of the house. Daniel waved to him, but Joe Boy barely made eye contact. In seconds, the black Ford was driving down the street. Joe Boy was gone without even a goodbye.

A Colony of Barbies

David had barely finished his breakfast and gotten in his car to head to work when he received a call on his cell phone from the rehab center, the nurse telling him that his mother, Janice, wasn't doing well. "Shit," he said out loud when he ended the call. Missing work was not an option for David, as he'd missed so many days already that his job was in jeopardy. Reluctantly, he called in, sensing his supervisor suspected that his excuse for not showing up was lame. "I'll get there as soon as I can," David promised his boss.

Janice resided in a new facility near the corner of Jackson and Jefferson in downtown Louisville. She'd been in rehab of some sort all of her adult life, but this time around, she was having major health issues due to long-term neglect in her diet, compounded with her smoking and drinking. Apparently, she'd had one too many Sterling beers in her life.

As much as he despised what his mother had done to him, he still felt the need to come to her rescue, or at least to put on a façade as though he cared for her. He was, after all, the only man in her life that didn't beat or abuse her. David hadn't seen his mother in six months, and the guilt of neglecting his only relative suddenly got the best of him, especially at this point when her health was failing her. So many moments in his life he just wished that she would drop dead without any warning, but now that her death was eminent, the thought of her passing left him uncomfortable. *Perhaps roses might cheer her up*, he thought, *or better yet, a six pack of Sterling beer*. But then again, she was in rehab, and no matter how bad off she was, bringing beer to a treatment center would definitely be the wrong thing to do. He pulled into the Shell station to fill up, and afterward, he walked in the store to get a soda.

"Will that be all?" the cashier asked.

David's eyes darted back and forth for a moment. "I'll take a pack of Winston's," he quietly replied. "I can't believe I'm buying cigarettes," he mumbled to himself as he jumped into his car and pulled away, heading down to Preston Street to buy flowers at a local floral shop.

A few minutes later, with a box of red roses in the front seat and a pack of Winston's in his pocket, he was on his way to see his mother. He always dreaded visiting her, but he thought that maybe this time would be different. His visits with her were laborious, to say the least, where he'd sit for what seemed an eternity, listening to her rant and rave about the past. She'd jump from one story to another about the dozen or so alcoholic men who came into her life, forced to act as surrogate fathers to her son in exchange for what always became a short-term relationship, each one pulling her down into the gutter of sin and shame. For as long as he could remember, David could sense his mother's vulnerability to booze and no-good men. David never knew his father, and whenever he asked about him, Janice repeatedly told him that Jesus was his real daddy and that was all he needed to know.

David and his mother hardly went to church unless the trip was connected to participating in Alcoholics Anonymous, but she was verbally zealous about her faith in Jesus, convinced that he forgave her for all of her sins. Only in her late forties, Janice had lived of full life of spiraled mania, each affair a torrid whirlwind of emotional and physical battering.

Yes, David had spent most of his adult life trying to understand how his mother could have gone down the path she did, and with each visit, sitting in a chair opposite his mother and listening to her vent only magnified the pains of his childhood. Even though their times together were actually no more than thirty minutes in length, he would become so emotionally disturbed he usually left without saying his goodbyes. David was hoping that his mother might not realize the long time since his last visit, but then he rationalized his absence by thinking that she never paid any attention to him to start with other than the awkward hello he received when he entered the room.

*

David did his best to keep the past from entering his world of the present, but no matter how well he honed his coping mechanisms over the years there would always be triggers that would set off the flurry of unwanted memories swirling around in his head. He didn't always want to blame his mother for how screwed up he was, but with every flashback that he had, he became more convinced that his mother was responsible for his miserable life. A gay man in his late twenties, David had never had a relationship with another man in fear of ending up like his mother. He chose a life of celibacy in order to avoid the pitfalls his mother had dealt with her entire life. On the outside, he would be a fine catch for any gay man. He didn't smoke and rarely drank. He was attractive at barely six-feet tall, with a thin swimmer's build, and thick blond hair. But the only element of his life that appeared organized was his immaculate wardrobe. He liked stylish cloths, and always matched his outfits down to the laces on his shoes. His therapist told him that his trendy façade shielded his fragile inner self just as the Armadillo has a shell to protect its weak underbelly. Even therapy wouldn't help him let go of the past. Many times there was no escaping those episodes of reruns running through his mind, each one becoming more twisted than the original.

Little did he know that on his way to the center to see his mother, David would be overcome with an array of emotions. He drove down 23rd Street, and right after he crossed the old L&N railroad tracks he passed a Goodwill store. He went by the same drop off for used clothing and goods everyday, to and from work, but as he drove by the building, he slowed down as he recalled when his mother stopped there one early morning, rummaged through the donation bin, opened the trunk of her car and threw three plastic garbage bags of early donations into the trunk, and then quickly sped off. David was around six or seven at the time and was in the back seat. He couldn't totally comprehend what he was witnessing, but he was aware of the expediency that his mother demonstrated when she left the scene.

"Mama, what's in those bags?" David remembered asking.

"Nothing, honey. Don't you worry about those bags. It ain't none of your concern. I need to stop in here and get some milk and bread."

Janice pulled into the Quick Mart parking lot, pulled her stringy, mousy blond hair into a ponytail and went into the store, leaving David inside the idling car. David always thought his mother was pretty. Even though she never wore makeup like the other waitresses who worked with her at the Waffle House, David often wondered what she would look like if she had lipstick on her lips, red lipstick to make her look like a movie star. When she wasn't working, she usually wore a T-shirt and shorts with flip-flops, even in the winter. Janice didn't worry about frilly clothes and fancy shoes. She was dirt poor, but never admitted to it; instead, she'd make up excuses that she didn't wear a winter coat because she loved the cold weather. She said she wore flip-flops because she didn't like her feet crammed into shoes. Of course, her favorite line she delivered to anyone, including David, who asked her why she didn't dress up once in awhile, was, "Who gives a shit?" David learned not to ask her about much, because she would invariably answer the same way, "Who gives a shit?"

She soon came back with a small carton of milk and a loaf of bread. They returned to their second story apartment on Second Street. David carried the loaf of bread. His mother lugged the carton of milk and the three bags of loot up the stairs. Once inside, she a filled a bowl halfway full of Cheerios for David, pouring milk on top.

"Eat it up and don't complain about it. It's all we have."

Even at an early age, David knew better than to sass his mother. He did whatever she told him to do. He was also aware he was an inconvenience to her. He sensed it in the way she looked at him, always with an air of disgust, like he was a mistake and she had to live with it. But being young, he worshipped his mother in many ways, wanting her approval, even if it was just minimal.

Janice started to open the bags, her small frame arched over as if she were waiting to pounce on the first thing that might jump out. David sat at the kitchen table, slowly eating his Cheerios like they were something special. "Bingo!" she yelled. "Baby, look at this." She held up a black sparkly dress. David remembered how it glittered when she moved it. Other than her waitress outfit, it was probably the prettiest thing David had seen. He hoped that she would put it on, to look glamorous, but instead, she pulled out another, and then three or four more. "Damn, these are party dresses. Mama's going out tonight." David kept eating his Cheerios, still enamored with the sequined dresses that now belonged to his mother.

Janice opened the second bag. She was not impressed as she pulled out men's shirts and pants. After emptying the bag, she returned those unwanted contents to the black plastic container, mumbling under her breath.

Next, she tugged at the drawstring on the third bag, and after a few moments of struggling, she just tore into the side of the bag. "Bingo!" she yelled again, but not with as much gusto as before. It was a bag of kid's clothing and toys, but not many.

"Baby, look. Little girlie clothes. They might fit you, especially the shorts. Hell, shorts is shorts," she said. David just kept eating his Cheerios, oblivious to the gender labels of the clothing. It wasn't until his mother pulled out a Barbie doll that David gave all his attention to what his mother was doing. "Hell," his mother griped. "A damn Barbie doll, and shit, there's more of them." One by one, she pulled them out of the bag. It was as if a colony of Barbies had been illegally smuggled across the border. And with each doll she pulled out, David was more and more enthralled. Though they were roughed up, a bit dirty, and their wiggy hair was matted, it didn't matter. To him they were the most beautiful things he'd ever seen.

"There's a ball and some puzzles. Baby, you want the ball?" his mother asked.

"I want the dolls." David remembered saying.

"I guess you can have a couple, but not all of them. And don't let Jerry see them. He'll be calling you names. Finish your breakfast, and then you can wash your face and play."

Jerry was Janice's newest boyfriend. Like the rest of the men she dated, he was a loser and an alcoholic. He was verbally abusive to David, who always tried to avoid being around him.

That evening after a dinner of beans and hotdogs, young David returned to the back side of his bed to play with the four dolls that his mother let him have. He was saddened that he couldn't have all the dolls, and he pretended that the ones he couldn't keep would all travel together in the taped up bag to another house down the street. He was sandwiched between the small space between his bed and the wall when he heard Jerry's voice.

"What the hell you playing with? Boy, you playing with dolls?" Jerry stood over David, towering so high that the ceiling seemed to touch his head. He reminded David of the giant in "Jack and the Beanstalk," except this giant never gave any warning when approaching. David was speechless.

"Janice! You got yourself a little faggot here. I told you so." David's mother was in the other room drinking her first of a nightly round of Sterling beer.

"Leave him alone and let him play. He ain't bothering anybody. Besides, they're keeping him quiet."

"Little fucking queer. Little faggot," Jerry said under his breath. "Yeah, you're a little faggot," he said a bit louder, but low enough that Janice couldn't hear him.

David didn't know what those words meant, but it was Jerry's tone and his intimidating expression on his face that frightened him. Jerry straightened up, shook his head in disapproval, and returned to the living room with Janice.

David took one of his newly found dolls and faced it off with another one. Pretending that the dolls were carrying on a conversation, the first doll said to the other, "You're a little faggot." He then positioned the second doll and said, "I like being a faggot." The first doll then asked, "You don't even know what a little faggot is, do you?" to which the second replied, "I don't care, I still like being one." Then he positioned all the dolls in front of him, their backs to the wall, and then assuming the role of instructor, he began his spelling lesson. Modeling his real teacher, Mrs. Valentine, he started to sound out the word "faggot" and then proceeded to write it on the white board, which in this case, was the light green bedroom wall just below eyelevel and unseen from behind the bed. With an orange crayon he scribbled his inventive spelling version of the word, starting with an "F" and then followed it with the letters "AGUT."

One by one, he asked his dolls to pronounce the word and then he pretended to have them practice it. "This will be one of our words for our spelling bee next week, so make sure you study it." David adored his teacher and he mimicked her classroom behavior as often as he could. She was, after all, the only positive role model that he had in his young life, and he seemed to understand and revere the importance of the impact she would have on him.

David was thrilled to have his dolls to play with, but it was only for a short time before they were gone. About a week after being introduced to his bevy of plastic pals, they all disappeared without any notice or warning. He was heartbroken on that morning when they were no longer camped beside his bed next to his wall, and when he inquired about the absence of the dolls, neither his mother nor Jerry gave an answer for their whereabouts. Though the specifics of his short time with his Barbie Doll family faded over time, he still remembered the joy they gave him, and the subdued outlet he had to express himself through play. Because he was young, he never really understood what "faggot" meant, but he remembered the word through all his years. At the time, the definition didn't matter. If Jerry didn't like faggots, then David was happy to be one.

Despite her apparent weaknesses, the one strength Janice possessed was that when she formed a relationship with a man, she fully obligated herself to being faithful, but the men she chose to be with were not as committed. Jerry and Janice were an item for about a year when she found out he'd been cheating on her with a sleazy divorcee who lived three doors down on the ground floor. According to Janice, the bleach-blonde floozy fucked anything and everything in the apartment complex. One summer night, and acting like she was high and mighty with the scruples of a nun, Janice condemned Jerry to a life in hell without her, and then in a fit of rage, she proceeded to take his clothes and his few belongings and piled them on the curb in front of the divorcee's apartment. Not to be outdone by a good dose of getting even, she dowsed them with lighter fluid and then squatted on the ground attempting to light Jerry's heap of old clothes. David watched from the second story window as his mother was demonstrating revenge on another man who betrayed her. He could see her hands trembling as she held her cigarette lighter with one hand and cupped it from the wind with the other, only to jump back every time it became too hot. After a few attempts, David saw his mother stand up and stare at the pile as the flames began to take off. Janice yelled unidentifiable words at the air, her fists tightly balled. Jerry was nowhere to be seen, probably at one of the local bars, totally oblivious to what was happening with his smoldering belongings. Even the divorcee wasn't in her apartment to witness the rage. In fact, the neighbors were the only ones watching through their blinds, all the while staying clear of the wrath of what many called the Second Street Bitch. Yes, Janice didn't get along with anyone, and those who challenged her for any reason found themselves in a shouting match that couldn't be won. Janice was notorious for just screaming at someone who had simply said "Hello" to her. "What the fuck?" she'd yell. "You don't know me and you want me to just stop what I'm doing to talk to you? Get the hell out of my face!" Yes, Janice didn't have any friends because no one could even get within two feet of her. Her schizophrenia made her behavior unpredictable. Of course, no one really knew she had been diagnosed with that condition. People just thought she was crazy and dangerous. Only when she was half-lit sitting at a bar could a man, and only a man with an extra Sterling in his hand, get even close to her, and then she was easy pickings for a quick tryst.

David often felt ashamed of his mother, but that moment he was proud that she made a stand and kicked Jerry out. He feared for their safety that night, wondering what would happen when Jerry came home to find out he was locked out of the apartment and all of his clothes were in a burnt pile on the curb. David slept lightly, rising up in his bed each time he heard a door open or close. He could hear his mother whimpering in agony in the living room, only to go into a rant a few minutes later, yelling, "You son-of-a-bitch! I loved you!" And then he heard the popping sound of a Sterling beer being opened, then the click of the cigarette lighter, and a couple of seconds later she'd say to herself, "Who gives a shit?" As she calmed down, David would pull his pillow to his face and slowly drift off until another round of noises or rants would wake him.

Jerry never came home that night. In fact, no one ever saw him again. Unfortunately, the blond divorcee continued to live in her apartment and didn't cower down to Janice's taunts and stares as she came and went. "Get a life, you crazy wench," David heard her say to his mother more than once. Though the scenario was a bit confusing for a small child to understand, there was something also very right about the neighbor. David was grateful to her. After all, if she hadn't been messing around with Jerry, he'd still be in David's life. He didn't know her name, other than the obscene connotations that his mother bestowed upon her, but he decided to call her Barbie. Yes, with her teased and matted hair, her skimpy and worn clothes, and her face full of makeup, she reminded him of one of the dolls that his mother had allowed him to play with. He never spoke to his new Barbie, but he smiled each time he saw her coming in and out of her apartment. She never knew the favor that she had blessed him with, but David felt a connection with her.

*

When David would have a flashback to the past about his mother, he usually allowed the full memories of an event to surface, and often times he would write about it. His therapist told him that writing down the memories was a way of suppressing them. Once the episode was recorded, especially if it were a traumatic event, he would do his best to never allow it to resurface again. At times, that would be difficult, but that was his way of trying to control the many diverse and confusing thoughts that constantly bombarded his consciousness. It was a strategy that kept his memories suppressed, a poor attempt to self-medicate his past away.

The light turned green. David was startled when he heard a horn blow. He didn't even remember stopping at the intersection. Embarrassed that he was holding up traffic, he shook his head and pushed his foot against the accelerator. He was sweating profusely, his heart pounding, his stomach nauseous. Often, these treks to the past brought on panic-like attacks. He pulled to the side of the road and opened the car windows allowing the cool morning breeze to fill the car. He closed his eyes, trying his best to relax, and as the nausea subsided, he fell into a light period of cautious rest as cars sped by, slightly shaking his car as each one passed.

David hated getting sick. Any time he became ill, his mother found a way to connect guilt, humiliation, and Jesus' wrath to the situation. His eyes still closed, he suddenly recalled when he was nine, and in the fourth grade, he had become ill at school, throwing up in the hallway and then being sent to the principal's office where he shivered with an extremely high fever. His mother was called in to pick him up and take him home.

Standing at the counter in the principal's office and glaring at the school secretary, Mrs. Pierce, his mother said, "What the hell is wrong with my kid?"

"The poor dear is so sick. He's in the next room. If you'll sign this release form, I'll get him for you."

David had just drifted off in a light sleep on the cot in the small sickroom designed as a holding tank for kids too ill to be in the classroom. His mother's voice woke him. "Come on, wake up. I've got things to do." He walked out to the school office to see his mother in one of her defensive stances, ready to take the school secretary down.

"No one is gonna tell me my son is sick or not. He's my responsibility." She saw David walk out into the office. "Let me take a look at you." David approached his mother, not sure of what she might do to him.

"But Mrs. Stoner..."

"It's Miss Stoner. I ain't married. Every time I come in here I have to make that clear. I'm Miss Stoner. Maybe you ought to write that down so you'd remember it."

"Miss, Stoner. I apologize. And I'm sorry David is ill, but the school policy states that if a child is too sick to be in class, then a parent or guardian will need to pick him up."

"Hell, he's a little warm," Janice said as she held her hand to his forehead. "It's just a little temperature. It'll go away soon."

"But Mama, I really don't feel very good. I threw up already and my head hurts, and..."

"You shut your mouth," Janice interrupted. Her voice level was beginning to escalate to where she was almost yelling. The school bell rang and suddenly, students were clamoring in the halls on their way to changing classes. The noise level was so high that Janice had no choice but to turn her voice up an octave or two, just to be heard.

"You called me to tell me my kid is sick and that I have to take him home," she screamed at the secretary, "and I have to leave my job at the Waffle House where I work to put food on the table to feed my kid, and now I'm gonna have to sit with him, on my ass, at home, until the little brat says he's feeling better and wants to come back to school."

It was when Janice said the word "ass" that the whole world stopped and stared. Though the word "ass" was not considered a real curse word to most adults, to elementary kids it was high on the list of things not to utter out loud. Cussing was not allowed in school, and of course, when an adult went into a fit of rage and used a curse word, it was time for students to take pause and listen. It was an embarrassing moment for David to have his classmates witness his mother berating him in the company of the beloved Mrs. Pierce.

"But Mama, I really am sick!" David yelled. His timing was unpredicted, but perfect. Without any notice, he threw up on his mother, covering her Waffle House apron with vomit. There was a quiet in the office.

Mrs. Pierce straightened her posture and stretched her neck into a position of authority. "Miss Stoner. Can you please sign this release form? Right there if you don't mind," she said pointing to the signature line.

Janice picked up the pen on the counter, putting the ballpoint tip on the form. "You little bastard," she said under her breath. "You did that on purpose."

She signed the release form and yelled at David, still wiping the upchuck off his chin, "Get your ass in the car and get it there now!"

She said "ass" a second time. The second cuss word in one trip to the office. *No one had probably ever done that before,* David thought. Ashamed that the whole incident had been seen by his peers, he burst into tears and ran out of the office. His tiny arms pushed the front entrance open with an enraged force and he headed to the car. He nervously waited for his mother to follow him. As he watched her march out of the school, heading toward him, he said to himself, "I'll never be able to come back here again." He was only in the fourth grade at the time, but he never went back to that school again. In fact, because of the public humiliation he endured over the years, David repeatedly refused to return to a school where his mother's tirades occurred, and Janice would end up transferring her son to another school, only to repeat the cycle of shame later in the school year.

*

David opened his eyes, the rumble of a loud semi waking him and bringing him to his senses. He took a drink of his soda, wiping his lips with the back of his cuff. Here he was again feeling the guilt that his mother, in partnership with Jesus, had bestowed on him from an early age. There was no escaping it. Maybe he should renounce his gayness and find a woman to marry and have his children. Of course, he knew that was a ludicrous thought. Perhaps he should start attending church, declaring the end to his atheistic views on religion and God. "Goddamn it!" he yelled. "Get the fuck out of my head!" And then David began to laugh remembering the first time he had gone to church with his mother. Finding humor in a situation was another method his therapist encouraged him to use. Sometimes it worked, sometimes it didn't. He turned on his turn signal and merged slowly into the traffic heading into downtown.

As he drove, he recollected the time when he was around eleven and in middle school when his mother decided she needed to find Jesus, again for the umpteenth time. Finding Jesus was an understood requirement when attending Alcoholics Anonymous, and for Janice, this was her fourth or fifth attempt to get sober. This time she intended to be more serious and dedicated than before, so serious, in fact, that she vowed to attend church every Sunday morning. David recalled the day they marched into the First Pentecostal Church in south Louisville. It was hot and crowded, and the church smelled of Old Spice and cheap perfume. Janice held David's hand as they walked down the aisle and stopped at the pew a few rows back from the front. It was already full.

"Excuse me ma'am, we want to sit here," she whispered in her church voice to the elderly lady who hugged the prize spot at the end of the pew.

The woman leaned over and looked down the row. "I'm sorry. I think we're already full," the woman replied.

"I think not. I see some spacing down there. If you'd all move your fat asses a little closer, there'd be room here for me and my son."

"But," the woman protested.

"Don't 'but' me," Janice said, raising her voice a bit. "Jesus has sent me here today and he's guided me to this pew." She looked up with outstretched her arms and yelled, "Hallelujah! Dear Lord I have come to you!"

David stood by his mother like a bystander, hoping no one would notice him. Janice continued to hold her hands face up in the air, now peering down at all of those sitting in the pew. Suddenly, just as when Moses parted the sea, the parishioners squeezed and pushed each other to the other end, and sure enough, there was room for Janice and David to have a seat next to the aisle.

"Praise Jesus," Janice said to the woman who had lost her position at the end of the pew. She put David in between the two of them, and the woman replied, under her breath, "Praise Jesus."

David remembered the long ceremony and the powerful, yet intimidating, sermon the preacher delivered. He also remembered the "old lady" smell that lingered around him, as well as the perspiration that penetrated his cotton shirt from the lady sitting next to him. He was sandwiched in so tight that he wasn't able to shift his body as his legs began to ache from not enough blood flow. David had never remembered going to church before, and the music and prayers seemed foreign to him. At times, he drifted off into a light sleep only to be wakened by an outburst of amen's from the congregation.

At one point, the minister asked if there were any new members who wanted to introduce themselves and admit to their sins. Without hesitation, Janice was the first to jump up, pulling David to his feet as well.

"My name is Janice Stoner and I am here to confess my sins!" As she hollered to the preacher, a chorus of "amen, sister" followed in unison. "I am here to confess that I love my Sterling beer, which makes me an alcoholic, and I sleep with men to whom I am not married, and sometimes I hit my child for no reason. The devil lives inside of me. I want to repent my sinful ways and rid my soul of the demon that controls my flesh!" David stood next to his mother, his head facing down, looking at his freshly polished black shoes that were at least two sizes too big. He wanted to run and hide, but there was no escaping. "And my son, David, a bastard child born out of sin, is here with me."

"Mama, stop," David said, his head about to burst as it reddened even more with embarrassment. He wasn't sure about the reference to being a bastard child, but he also knew that it wasn't a good thing. He was at the age where he realized that anything his mother said was hardly of any value.

"My son, who is ungrateful for his mother…" Her arms reached in the air, and the "amen sisters" kept coming. "My son, who lies to me…"

David was trying to use his undiscovered telekinetic powers by wishing the drapes on the old windows would burst into flames and send the whole congregation, along with his mother, out into the street, running for there lives. "My son, who is probably a homosexual…" The crowd hushed. The room was engulfed in silence. Not even the simple motion of a hand fan could be heard. David felt the life sucked out of him. He passed out. A bit later he came to, the kind women of the church leaning over his limp, wet body, wiping his face with cold washcloths. Soon after, he and his mother were on their way, briskly walking down the street to their apartment, the whole time Janice prayed out loud, holding David by the back of his collar.

"Jesus sent you a message today, young man, and you need to heed his wrath," she said, "or you're gonna burn in hell."

Hell couldn't be any worse than this, David thought to himself.

The next day when David came home from school, his mother sat at the kitchen table, four empty Sterling beer cans laid crushed to her right, another full one in her hand.

"What the hell you looking at?" Janice demanded as she glared at David. He said nothing. He expected her to say, "Who gives a shit?" but she didn't. He lowered his head and quietly went to his bedroom to be surrounded by the few things that made him feel secure. Janice's sobriety had only lasted a few days, and they never went to church again.

*

Still thinking about that church service, David smiled as he pulled into the parking lot next to the center. He grabbed the box of roses and walked through the glass doors facing the street. After signing in at the front desk, he headed to his mother's room. The facility looked more clinical in nature as opposed to the gloomy converted buildings she had been living in during the past few years. He rounded the last corner in the hallway and entered the first door on the left. Sitting alone in a winged back chair was a figure of a woman he hardly recognized.

"Mama? Mama, is that you?" David asked in a soft voice as to not startle the woman.

Janice looked up, her eyes sunken, the hateful spirit he so feared for so long was gone from her face. Her thin frame was smaller than before as if she had shrunk half her size, and her long stringy hair was pulled back in a bun. David never recalled her neck being so long.

"Of course, it's me. What the hell's the occasion? Somebody tell you I'm dying?"

Yes, the woman was definitely Janice. She had not lost her spunk, and David chuckled under his breath at the realization that this frail, beaten down frame of a woman was his really his mother.

"Nobody's dying, and certainly not you. You're probably too mean to die," he said as he walked over, knelt down in front of her and reached for her hand. "I just missed you, that's all, and I wanted to see you. What's wrong with that?"

"You still look like a faggot," she said as she scanned his eyes, thinking that perhaps he had changed.

"Yes, mama, I still am."

"I knew it the day you was born, but there was nothing I could do to change it. Lord, I tried to pray it away, but I knew I was being punished for my sins," she said with one hand pointing to the sky.

"Mama, it's okay. I just came to visit, to spend some time with you," David pleaded.

"Shit, you must be wanting something to be coming around, and you ought to know by now I don't have nothing to give you," she said, looking away from him.

"I don't want anything. I promise. I just came to visit for a bit. And look, I brought you these." He laid the white box on her lap. She looked surprised. "Open it up," he said to her.

Janice struggled taking the red ribbon off the box. "Pretty bow. I think I'll save it."

With David's help, she opened the box to find a dozen red roses. She lifted the bouquet up to her face and smelled them as she closed her eyes. David never remembered his mother receiving many gifts, let alone a dozen long-stemmed roses. She changed the pleasant expression on her face to a one of scorn, a look that he knew so well. "Somebody told you I was dying, and I ain't," she said, slightly raising her voice.

"Mama, nobody told me that. I just wanted to do something nice for you."

"Where's the chocolates? You could have brought me chocolates. Nadine down the hall gets chocolates from her son when he comes by."

"I can bring you chocolates next time. I didn't even know you liked chocolates."

"Who in hell don't like chocolates? We just never could afford them, especially the good kind."

"I brought you something else. And it's better than chocolate." David reached in his pocket, and making sure no one was watching, he pulled out the unopened pack of Winston's. "I know you're not supposed to have these, but I also know how sneaky you are. If anybody asks, I didn't give them to you."

"So, I ain't dead, but you give me something that's gonna kill me. Now that's taking care of your mama. It'll be our secret," she said as she took the pack of cigarettes and tucked it under the chair cushion.

"I would have brought a can of Sterling, but I know that's why you're in here. I remember how much you liked a good Sterling beer," David said as he sat in the chair next to his mother.

"Oh, I'm getting over that beer stuff. I only started drinking the shit when I was sad. Seems I was sad an awful lot, huh?" she said as a smile came over her face. It was one of the few times that David had actually seen his mother show an emotion other than hate and scorn. "I've been clean for about six months now. That's a long time David, you know, to be clean. Course, now I have other things to deal with. I take my pills for my mood swings, but now my liver ain't doing too well. Doctor says we have to wait and see, but I ain't going nowhere, at least not yet. Hell, I ain't even fifty yet. I'm too young to die." She laughed at herself, her eyes watering. "I've been a bad mother, haven't I? I know that's what you always told yourself. You never had to say it out loud. I could see it in your eyes."

"Mama, that's not true. I always thought you were mean and hateful..." David paused, a part of him wanted to open up, telling his mother how he really felt about her, but he was also quick to realize that this brief time with her was not the moment to disclose his hatred for all the misguided episodes from his past that he had to endure.

"Yeah, I was that alright," she giggled. "Mean and hateful," she repeated as she nodded her head in agreement with her son.

"But I never thought you were a bad mother. I've gotten older and I understand why you did the things you did. I think I know why you reacted to some of the bad things that happened to you."

Janice's eyes widened. "Like when I got mad at Jerry and burned his shit for fucking that blond floozy?" she asked.

"Yeah, just like with that blond floozy," David replied, chuckling in amazement that he would be finding some humor in what she had done to Jerry.

David spent over an hour sitting with his mother. As they sat there together, Janice nervously fiddled with the red roses, caressing each leaf, and every few minutes, she would lift them to her nostrils, taking in the sweet fragrance. The two took turns recollecting the events in the past that tore them apart, as well as the ones that pulled them together. David watched his mother, her body weak, her mind dulled by medication, and as she spoke, he suddenly had a different view of their relationship. It was an epiphany for him. For years he'd blamed her for so many of his own problems, and he spent so much time on working to not become her, when in reality he should have been learning from his mother about how to survive. That morning at the rehab center was probably the most cherished time he'd spent with his mother that he could remember, even better when she gave him the Barbie dolls that she stole from the Goodwill drop off.

By mid morning, Janice became obviously tired and needed to rest. Instead of just slowly walking out the door as he had done in the past, David hugged his mother goodbye and promised he'd visit her again, and soon.

"Hey," she said as David was about to walk out the door.

"Yeah?"

"Jesus ain't really your daddy."

"I know, Mama. I know."

"Don't forget the chocolates when you come back to see me," she said, her hand held up as she made a motion of goodbye with her fingers.

"I won't forget," David replied.

"Don't wait so long," she whispered from across the room trying to stay awake. With her head resting on the back of the chair and her arms clutching the roses, Janice fell asleep.

It was at that moment that David realized his mother was not a dreaded monster, but a mere mortal coming to terms with the demons that she'd spent her whole life trying to defeat. He felt remorse for her mistakes and misgivings, but he now understood that he'd been a witness to her battles throughout his young life, not the cause for her misery as he had always assumed. Janice was just a woman, like so many other women, who was trying her best to survive, as well as protect her child by any means that she could.

David smiled at his mother and quietly waved goodbye. As he walked down the hall, he felt elated that he had spent that morning with her, and he was happy she finally told him Jesus was not his daddy. It didn't matter at this point in his life who his father was, and David accepted the fact he would never know. He came to realize that after all the years of evading the question, his mother probably didn't know either.

*

Janice died peacefully in her sleep, David at her side. He had never seen his mother so calm as in that moment when the last bit of life left her body, her facial muscles relaxing allowing a faint smile to come across her mouth. David witnessed the demons rise from his mother's body, and even felt his own life-long pent up anxiety released. In those quick few seconds, David began a new life.

Six months later, he was strolling through the mall with his boyfriend, Ricky, the two meandering from store to store, making small talk like young teenagers on a first date. David now accepted his tormented past and he had made a firm and deliberate decision to move forward with finding a boyfriend. Lucky for him, his first sexual encounter and relationship were with Ricky, a well-groomed young man who had a need for the same kind of bond. Their shoulders brushed against each other just as they walked by a toy store.

"Hey," Ricky said. "Let's go in here."

"It's a toy store. It's for kids. You looking for anything special?" David asked.

"No, not really. I just happen to like toys."

Though uncomfortable with entering the store, David followed Ricky into the crowded abyss of endless stuffed creatures and children's playthings. Ricky seemed to bounce from one toy to another, totally enamored with the different gadgets and talking robots that were designed to keep children occupied. They turned the corner and walked down the second aisle.

"Oh my god!" Ricky exclaimed. "Have you ever seen so many Barbie Dolls in one place?"

David was awestruck, not because one complete side of the aisle was filled with a variety of Barbies and Kens, but because of the memory that suddenly crept into his mind.

"What's wrong?" Ricky asked, as he noticed the change of expression on David's face.

"Nothing's wrong," David replied. "It's a colony of Barbies. Look at all of them."

"So, I take it you like Barbie Dolls."

"No. It's not like that. When I was a kid, well, I… it's embarrassing to talk about it."

"You had a Barbie Doll, right?"

"How did you know?" David asked, a bit perplexed that Ricky would know that bit of information about him.

"Almost every gay guy I know either had one, played with one, or at least wanted one. And that look on your face is priceless. Let me buy you one."

"Oh, I couldn't. I mean, I'm a grown man and you want to buy me a doll? I would be totally embarrassed to take it to the counter. What would people think if they saw us walking out of here with a doll?"

"Who gives a shit?" Ricky retorted.

"What did you say?"

Ricky slightly contorted his expression. "Who gives a shit?" he repeated a bit more deliberate with his enunciation.

"I can't believe you said that," David said softly.

"I didn't mean to offend you by cursing," Rick said apologetically.

David chuckled. "I'm not offended. My mother used to say those words all the time. I just never heard anyone else say them."

"And I hope you listened to your mother," Ricky said playfully. "Come on, pick out a doll. I prefer the blond ones."

David smiled, and after a slight pause, he said, "I do, too. Let's get that one. She reminds me of an old neighbor I had when I was a kid."

Duplicity

As she sat quietly huddled next to Chris, the security guard, Mary Kay tried to take her mind off matters by picking minute pieces of lint off her red Christmas sweater loaded with Santa appliqués and sequined snowflakes. The perky secretary in her early forties was quite notorious for wearing holiday sweaters everyday to work. Most were traditional, but some were considered offensive, but she paid her critics no mind. Though she routinely wore bunny sweaters during Lent, she always made sure that she donned her Good Friday sweater each year, the one with the words "Jesus Will Rise Again!" written in rhinestones just below the brown felt cross glued to back. Or with the vast assortment of her autumn and Thanksgiving knitted wardrobe she made sure at least once during turkey season to put on her most offensive sweater, the one that had a cute Native American princess sarcastically saying, "Thanks, white man, for the STD's." Yes, Mary was outspoken in an odd sort of way. Her sweaters allowed her to express herself without opening her mouth. The daily operations at the adult education center revolved around Mary Kay, and despite her minor outbursts of isolated, yet scheduled expressions, oddly enough she was the most normal of all the employees.

Mary Kay had never been a hostage before, and now she found herself helpless and frightened, and despite having an armed guard on the premises, she and her coworkers were being held in the center against their will, at gunpoint by a deranged student. It was just a few hours earlier, the day before the Christmas break when Rudy arrived at the center on First and Chestnut to check and see if he had passed his GED. He even brought cupcakes he baked himself the night before so he could celebrate with his teachers when the good news was to be announced. Unfortunately, when Rudy learned that morning that his scores were not high enough, he whipped out a pistol from his pocket and went ballistic, vowing in a fit of rage that no one would leave alive unless he was awarded his diploma. There was some fleeting comfort for the hostages in that they were confined to the community room where Mary Kay's makeshift office was carved out in one corner, a kitchenette in another, and off to the side was a restroom. The only difference from any other day in the facility was that the only door to the outside world was boarded up with a makeshift barricade of tables, file cabinets, and bookcases. Yes, there was running water and a toilet available, but still, waiting out the day not knowing what the outcome might be was a bit disturbing, at least for Mary Kay. The others were not so bothered by the change in their routine. She watched the others pass the time, improvising a game of Go Fish using math flash cards. It seemed to be a coping mechanism to keep their minds off the situation.

Anna eyed her cards, running her sixty-year-old fingers over each one. Though she had years of experience teaching, her peers considered her a nitwit. And actually, she inadvertently lived up to that reputation. Being almost totally deaf along with her stuttering speech only reinforced her image, but it was her genuine absence of a short-term memory that made communicating with her almost impossible at times. "Shirl, do you have anything divisible by three?" she asked after a long pause while studying her cards.

"You must be looking at my cards again," Shirl replied.

"You need to breast your cards," Anna snapped back.

"Breast my cards? What exactly does that mean?" Shirl inquired, truly unaware of the meaning of the phrase.

"Yeah, hold them close to your breasts so no one can see them. The cards, I mean. You know how you talk with your hands all the time, and when you do, I can see your cards."

"Please, Shirl, just give Anna the cards she asked for and keep this game moving," said Gary in his usual disrespectful tone of voice.

Gary hated his job, his students, and more than anything else, he had no patience for his coworkers, especially Anna.

"But I just never expected any of you to remember what you saw," Shirl pleaded. Shirl was a whimsical instructor whose New York accent and early Barbara Streisand hairdo puzzled many of the southerners she encountered. If there was a half cracked Oreo in the bag of cookies, it would be Shirl, whose background was in special education before she began teaching adults. "Okay, okay, I'll keep it moving," she said laughing aloud. "With my neck brace on, I have to hold my cards out here just to see them," she said as she stretched her arms out in front of her halfway across the table. "It's almost impossible for me to breast my cards and see them all at the same time. So in all fairness Anna, you shouldn't be trying to look at my cards. Apparently, I'm not going to get any sympathy, or the simple accommodations that I need while we play this game," she said as though she were talking to herself. "Here. Three times three is nine…that's divisible by three, so take that one. And this one has a sum of twenty-seven, and that's divisible by three. I think that's all I have."

Anna reached for the cards and placed them with the others she held tightly in her hand. "What about the three times one card?" she asked wryly.

"Three times one?" Shirl held her cards out, searching for the card that Anna had asked about. "Oh, that one. See you did look at my cards," she exclaimed.

"No, I didn't," Anna argued back.

"Then how else would you know I had that card?"

"Because, I gave it to you… to you the last time you asked me for it," Anna stuttered.

"I still can't believe that you could even remember that. Here. Take it. I hope you're happy."

Anna took the card, and then asked, "And what about the three times four card? Give it up, Shirl," she demanded.

"Anna, you're taking the fun out of this game. What the hell? Here, take that one, too."

"This is exciting, isn't it?" Anna said, holding her cards in front of her like they were prized possessions.

Gary leaned back, his aging stout body too large for the chair. At sixty four, he was ready to retire and start his own business as an interior decorator. Though never one to put up with nonsense, he'd been somewhat resigned to the situation that morning, avoiding any conflict with Rudy and the others, but now his patience was running thin with the whole ordeal. "There's no fun in playing Go Fish with flash cards. We're just here biding our time until that homegrown, illiterate terrorist decides to knock us off one at a time."

"We could call this game Go Flash! Get it? Go Flash?" Anna announced, oblivious to Gary's comment.

"Anna, that's the stupidest thing you've said all day, and the list of stupid things you've said is getting longer by the minute," Gary said, raising his voice. "For one, I'm not exposing myself to anyone here while playing a card game, as the name implies. And there's no way in hell that I would want to see the likes of you and Shirl without your clothes on either."

Shirl gave no regard to Gary's short rant and added, "And to make it more authentic, we should all be wearing trench coats, don't you think?"

Anna giggled. "I suppose it is a bit chilly in here... a bit chilly to be flashing. You know what they say about men and the cold."

Gary sighed in disgust and said, "If you're referring to shrinkage, Anna, then you need to look no further than in the mirror and glance at what's left of what used to be your breasts."

While the game of Go Fish continued, Mary Kay looked over at Rudy, studying the complexity of a hostage taker. She was determined to get through the dilemma, even thinking about a new sweater to mark the occasion, one that might say "I was a hostage and I survived," or "No one can keep me down." The variety of verbiages kept running through her mind as she squinted her eyes from the glare of the sun coming through the high built-in window designed to allow light in the room without the ability for someone to look in or out. "Look at Rudy sitting there, all perched below the window, being stubborn and mean," she said to Chris. "I never knew that side of him. He's always been so sweet and kind. I just can't believe that he held a gun to my head. I mean, he put it right here," she said pointing to her temple. "I could have been shot dead, or worse, wounded and never able to walk again."

Chris turned to Mary Kay, tapped his fingers on his security guard badge and said, "I would never let him hurt you." Chris was an overly macho man with the Barney Fife syndrome, who also believed that he was God's gift to women. All women.

"That's very nice of you, Chris, but he's got a gun and we don't."

Chris leaned in. "Mary Kay, I've been trained to deal with nutcases like him. The time will come when he won't be totally alert and then I'll take him down."

"But that sounds dangerous, and someone could get hurt. We just need to wait. Miss Mims will handle this. I know she will."

Chris sighed and said, "It's been four hours since you left that message and she still hasn't called. She might be so busy with that auditor that she hasn't checked her voicemail yet. We don't even know if she's aware that we're in trouble here."

"Chris, Miss Mims is the ultimate program director who does everything right, well except for collecting all of our cell phones during this morning's meeting just because someone forgot to turn theirs off. But anyway, she checks her voicemail constantly. And when Rudy told me to put the main phone on voice mail, I actually forwarded all the calls to Miss Mims' number instead. She would be getting all the calls coming into the center, so her phone light would be on at all times. If anything, she'd be pissed off about the calls being forwarded to her line, but under the circumstances... well, I'm sure she's working on getting Rudy a GED. Somehow."

Chris nodded his head in agreement then added, "If she heard the message, then she has to follow security procedures. That means that right now we're completely surrounded by police. In other words, the building is in a lock down... no one in and no one out. Probably a SWAT team outside. That door could come down at any minute and when it does, just hit the floor to miss the deadly bullets that will fill the air, no doubt aiming at Rudy, but ricocheting into the many hostages in the room. It might be ugly, Mary Kay, but just hit the floor and cover your eyes."

"It sounds like something out of a movie," Mary Kay said as she folder her arms.

"Movies are based on real stories, you know," Chris added as though he were trying to make the situation more dramatic.

"Hey," Shirl yelled. "Can you two get over here and play with us?"

"It would be my pleasure to play with you," Chris said as he headed for the table.

"Oh silly, not like that," Shirl said, flattered by Chris's insinuation. "We need some fresh blood in this game."

Anna looked up, her eyes a bit limp. "Yeah, we've created a new game called... called... Go Flash! Get it? We're playing Go Fish with flash cards. Thus, Go Flash! Get it?" Anna repeated.

As Mary Kay approached the table, Gary interjected, "Yeah, they get it," then he turned to Mary Kay and said, "Trust me Mary Kay, this game is probably not as exciting as you might imagine."

"Well, I'm ready to play," Mary Kay replied as she sat in the chair at the end of the table. "I need to do something to take my mind off this horrible day."

Standing up, Shirl announced, "Well, if you don't mind, I need to use the little girl's room." She leaned slightly over, cupping her mouth with her hands as though she were telling a secret. "It's a shame there isn't a window in there. One of us could crawl out and go for help."

As Shirl turned to walk away, Anna hollered, "Yeah, if there was a window in there we could go in one at a time and crawl out... and crawl out, and before you know it, no one would be in the room but Rudy."

"That's brilliant Anna," Gary said sarcastically, "except for the fact that he's stationed himself by the bathroom door, and even though he didn't pass the GED exam, I'd say the boy can count to... let's see... one, two, three, at least five, don't you think? Not to mention that he heard every word you said and now he thinks you're plotting to escape."

Mary Kay looked at Anna. "Are those hives on your neck?"

Anna tried to twist her neck to see the hives rising on the skin just below her chin. "They're on my arms, too! And they itch a little," she said as she started to gently scratch her thin frail arms.

Mary Kay became alarmed. "You must be having an allergic reaction to the nuts in the cupcakes. I can't believe you ate them."

"And I'm having a reaction to the nuts in this room," Gary mumbled.

"Well, Rudy insisted that we all have a cupcake and I didn't think it would be in our best interest not to do what he asked us, right? Especially, when he's got a gun," she added emphatically. "He's got... he's got a gun," she stuttered. "But honestly, the hives don't itch too much. In fact, I really feel lightheaded, kind of like when I take too many Benadryl tablets. I feel a bit ditzy."

Gary grinned. "You are the queen of ditzy."

Anna smiled and said, "It sort of reminds me of the late sixties, with pot..."

"And acid... psychedelics..." Chris added.

"I never did any of those ludicrous things," Gary declared. "But I have to admit that I'm feeling a bit of a buzz right now, sort of like the one I get when I've had one scotch on the rocks too many and I insist on driving."

The bathroom door swung open and Shirl made an attempt at what she would deem to be a grand stage entrance. With her arms in the air she began to sing the words from "Aquarius" while scooting to the table. Mary Kay thought Shirl's behavior to be odd, but then again, Shirl was odd. "Come on, sing with me!" Shirl yelled. Then, while trying to find some semblance to the original medley, she belted out, "And something about peace will guide the planets... how does it go?"

"And I will steal the stars!" Chris sang out.

Mary Kay watched as everyone but Rudy joined in, singing a pathetic version of "Aquarius." Even Gary attempted to harmonize with the group, but no two people sang the same lyrics or melody. After about three minutes of group adulation, they finally reached the pinnacle as each held a note at the end, trying to find some means of creating a finale. They broke into laughter when Anna held the last note longer than the rest.

"Hey, we're better than the Fifth Dimension!" Chris announced.

Even Gary seemed to enjoy the short moment of inclusion. "Sounds more like a bad imitation of the Lennon Sisters," he said as he patted Chris on the back.

"Funny, Gary!" Chris responded. "If you'll excuse me, it's my turn to visit the little girl's room!"

"It's the one on your right, or it could be on your left," Shirl directed, her speech a bit slurred. "I guess it depends on how you're looking at it! You do look at it, don't you Chris?"

Chris turned back around. "You wanna look at it?" he asked suggestively.

Gary reverted back to his curmudgeon persona. "This is getting vulgar. And anyway, there's only one little girl's room in here."

"Oh, Gary, we're just kidding," Shirl said to Gary. "We have to make light of everything. What else can we do?"

Just as Chris closed the bathroom door behind him, Anna screamed, "And don't pee on the seat!" She then clasped her hands together and confessed, "I hate it when... when... when men pee on the toilet seat."

Mary Kay sensed that something wasn't right with her co-hostages. Though each one of them had a strange personality, they appeared to be high. "You guys are acting a bit weird to me," she said.

"Probably a little cabin fever," Shirl surmised. "You know we've been locked up for about four hours now. I'm starting to feel a little like Patty Hearst. Remember her? Soon we'll be looking at Rudy and falling in love with him. He is a sweet dear, don't you think?"

"And he'll be able to have his way with us all," Anna added. "Oh my, that could be wonderful. Let me, let me, let me be first," she stuttered with a lustful gleam in her eyes.

Mary Kay stood up. "Well, he's not having his way with me, not if I can help it. Rudy, may I come over and speak to you?"

Still perched on the floor below the window, Rudy looked at Mary Kay. There was worry in his light blue eyes. "You think because I'm over here I haven't been able to hear anything you've said? I've heard everything. I'm not an illiterate terrorist. I don't want to hurt anybody and I don't want to have my way with everyone, especially Miss Anna. Sorry, Miss Anna, no disrespect, but you are old enough to be my grandmother. So what do you want to speak to me about?"

Anna grabbed the deck of flash cards as though the subject might change. "Should we deal you in, Mary Kay?"

"Yes, deal me in. I'll be right back."

Anna laughed out loud. "Put on your trench coat, honey!"

With apprehension, Mary Kay walked slowly toward Rudy. She sat in the chair next to him. "Rudy, these people are acting a bit goofy, not that they aren't already capable of that, but it is a little strange that they're singing and laughing so much. They never do that. By any chance, would those cupcakes be laced with anything?"

"Laced?"

"Yeah, laced. Did you put anything in them to make people high?"

"No, of course not," he said, obviously concerned. "You're not high are you?"

"No, and I'm the only one who didn't have one of your cupcakes."

Rudy glanced down at his shoes as he attempted to recollect the night before. "I made two batches of cupcakes, one for my teachers here at the community center, and one for my friends for later this evening." His eyes suddenly widened. "Oh, my god. I brought the wrong ones here today, didn't I? How stupid of me. I can't believe this! I've gotten my teachers high on pot. And you ask me why I can't pass my GED? I'm stupid, that's why. Now I'm really in trouble. Kidnapping, and now distributing drugs."

"Rudy, this hole you're digging keeps getting deeper. You've got to realize that at some point, the police will get here and probably arrest you."

"I know. I know. But I want to get my GED, and I won't let anyone leave here until I get it."

"Well, I'm pretty sure that Miss Mims will come through for us all and get a diploma for you, so let's be patient and promise not to hurt anyone."

"Mary Kay, I can't promise that. No one takes hostages and says that they won't hurt anyone."

Mary Kay paused, not wanting to push Rudy too far. "You're right. But don't let them know they're high on pot, especially Anna. It would freak her out, especially at her age."

"I can promise you that," Rudy said as he looked into Mary Kay's eyes. "Mary Kay, I'm sorry I put the gun to your head."

Mary Kay sensed a feeling of remorse from Rudy. "Look at them," she said with a quick smile appearing on her face. "They do look like they're having a good time, don't they?" she said as she tried change the subject. She was afraid of falling into the allure of his gaze.

"Mary Kay, did you hear me? I'm sorry," he said again.

"I heard you, Rudy," Mary Kay said softly, still looking away.

Rudy was about to say something else when Chris opened the bathroom door as the sound of the toilet flushing echoed through the room. Chris tightened his belt and said, "Before anyone says a word, just remember that a man's…"

Shirl gasped for air. "Oh my god, we're being gassed! It's Auschwitz all over again!"

"Who… who… who…" Anna stammered.

"Anna, it's not "who," but "what" just died?" Gary stated as he covered his nose and mouth with his hands.

"As I was saying," Chris said, raising his voice above the others, "a man's stink is a sign of his manhood."

Gary retorted, "Somehow, you left the measure of your ego out of the equation. Good god, what on earth did you have for dinner last night, a carton of deviled eggs?"

"Let's light matches!" Anna chimed in, clapping her hands.

"Can't do that on school property," Mary Kay said to Anna. "Against the law. I have some spray in my desk. Rudy, if I may?"

"Yeah, please do," Rudy said, his face grimacing from the retched odor.

"Come on now, it ain't that bad," Chris said, his arms outstretched as though he wanted acknowledgement for the level of rankness that he'd just released in the small confined space.

Shirl rolled her eyes in disapproval. "Chris, that's just horrible."

Anna spoke out in Chris's defense. "What's he supposed to do? There is no window... no window or ventilation in the bathroom, and he had to go." She then turned to Chris and said in a scolding manner, "I hope you didn't pee on the seat."

Of course, Gary had to add his two cents. "I hope we won't smell like this when the police come to rescue us. They'll open the door and with one whiff, they'll turn around and leave us here, thinking we're dead and rotting away. You know this stink will get in our clothes, don't you? It's like cigarette smoke. It will linger for days."

Mary Kay popped the top off the aerosol can and began to spray the floral scented mist around the room. "This spray should help. It's Springtime Lavender," she said proudly as if she were in a commercial.

"Ah, that does smell better," Shirl said as though she was inspired to go out and buy a can that very minute.

Gary frowned and stated in a snarky manner, "Oh good, now it smells like a cow shit in the flower garden."

"Smells fine in here now," Anna said as she finished dealing the cards. "I say let's play Go Flash!"

Shirl glanced over to Chris and whispered, "Chris, I hope you washed your hands."

"You did wash your hands, didn't you?" Mary Kay asked. She was a person who insisted on cleanliness.

Chris only responded to the inquiries by staying silent as he held his cards in his hands, sorting them in place. Gary took the unanswered questions to mean that Chris did not wash his hands.

He pushed himself away from the table and firmly announced, "Oh my god, I'm not touching those cards!"

Mary Kay ordered Chris to put down his cards and go wash his hands.

Chris stood up and headed for the bathroom when he stopped and turned, facing his coworkers. "Geez, being kidnapped is like going camping, and how many of you wash your hands when you go camping?" he asked.

"Let's just say we have some non-campers here, so Chris, just go wash your hands," Mary Kay ordered as though she were talking to a child. "And leave the door open so we know that you did."

"Oh, alright. I'll go wash my little pinkies," Chris said as he held his little fingers in the air. The group sat in silence as they watched Chris wash his hands through the open door.

Gary took the opportunity to address Rudy. "When is Ethel going to take care of this problem that we seem to be having? I mean it's been four hours. Surely, Rudy, you're not going to keep us here overnight, are you?"

"Soon as I get my GED we can all leave."

"Rudy, why is it so important that you get your GED today?" Mary Kay asked.

"I want it and I want it now. People have called me stupid and retarded my whole life just because I couldn't do well in school. I just can't seem to make the right decisions at the right time. I'm always being laughed at, and I never seem to know why. My whole life has been nothing but one big failure."

Anna looked up from her cards. "Can we sing 'Aquarius' again?"

Mary Kay put her hand on Anna's shoulder. "Anna, Rudy is trying to tell us something very important. We can sing later."

"I thought that if I were to get my GED, people would not look at me the way they always have. They wouldn't laugh anymore."

Chris returned to the table. "Okay, my hands are clean now."

"Chris, please," Shirl said, quietly scolding Chris. "You're interrupting Rudy. He's explaining why he wants his GED."

"Sorry. I just wanted everyone to know that I even used soap this time."

Rudy waited for Chris to sit down. "I'm tired of failing, and more importantly, I'm tired of working so hard to only fall short. We've been doing this for three years now, you know, working on my GED."

"Maybe three years is not enough," Mary Kay said, trying to comfort Rudy. "Maybe you need more time. You've been so close."

"But you don't realize that I'm ready to move on with my life. There are things in my past that I have to leave behind, and I want to do it now. I want to move on."

"Rudy, we all have things in our past that haunt us," Shirl stated, "things we try not to think about, but they creep up on us at unexpected moments. Well, not exactly unexpected moments, but times, let's say, that are not perfectly scheduled for reflecting."

Anna curled up her wrinkled face. "That's confusing. What did she... she... say?"

"We're talking about the past, Anna," Gary interjected, "something you can't seem to recollect."

"You all are sitting here high and mighty, with good jobs and making great money," Rudy continued. "You'll try your best to convince me that the past isn't important, and we have to put those things that bother us behind us."

"Let's play a new game," Anna stated, clearly trying to change the subject again.

Rudy raised his voice in anger. "Yes, Miss Anna, let's do. Let's tell secrets. Our own little dirty secrets," he said as he walked over to the table.

"I don't think I like where this might be going," Shirl whispered to Gary under her breath.

"What's to be afraid of Shirl? Ghosts in your closet?" Gary asked.

Mary Kay rose from her chair. "Rudy, we work together. I don't think that we should share our deep dark secrets, if there are any, with each other. It might make some people feel uncomfortable."

"More uncomfortable than we already are?" Rudy shot back.

Anna set her cards down on the table. "Who wants to have their way with me first?"

"Anna, no one's gonna have their way with you," Mary Kay replied.

"I think Miss Anna should go first," Rudy demanded.

"See, he does want me first," Anna said, smiling at the group.

"No, Miss Anna, I don't want you first. I want you to go first."

"To...to...to do what?" she asked.

"Tell us a deep dark secret. Something about your past."

"I don't have any secrets."

"Sure you do," Rudy said persuasively. "Go first and tell us something about yourself that nobody here knows."

"I said I don't have any!" Anna yelled.

"Tell it!" Rudy screamed back as he clutched the pistol in his hand.

Mary Kay quickly analyzed the confused look on the elder instructor's face. "Anna, I think it would be a good idea to just tell us something that we don't know about you. I'm sure there's something interesting that you could share."

"Yes, do tell us about the different dinosaurs you used to fight with every day before the great extinction," Gary snidely said, elated that Anna would be the first to tell her secret.

With tears beginning to swell in her eyes, Anna looked up and said, "I don't know how to start."

Rudy lowered his voice. "Just say, 'There's something about me you don't know,' and then tell it."

"There's something about me you don't know..." Anna paused, wiping her eyes, thinking about what she wanted to reveal about herself. "Well, let's see. There are so many things." Suddenly a smile came over her face. "Oh, this is one you don't know! One thing I've never shared with you all is that I... I... I...won a beauty contest when I was eighteen."

"Anna, I didn't know that," Mary Kay said as she tried to comfort Anna. "That's very exciting."

"Yeah, real exciting alright. Miss Oldham County 19... 19... oh I can't remember the year. I remember that my cousin said I should enter because there was a cash prize of one hundred dollars, and I thought about all the clothes I could buy with that kind of money. A hundred dollars was really a lot of money in those days. My... my... my mother gave me her blessing and even made my dress for the runway walk. It was pink and full, and came right to just above my ankles. My father hated the idea of me parading around in front of strangers. I could tell. But he said nothing. When I won and came home with the money, my father just walked away with this disgusted look on his face. I guess it was his religious beliefs or, well, I really don't know, but he always said... he said... he said women belonged in the home. I didn't want to play that role. Don't get me wrong, I loved my father and my family. I just... I just... I wanted to see the world, to see things that I could never see if I stayed in Kentucky. I took the money and bought some clothes, and then I bought a bus ticket out of there."

Shirl seemed to beam with pride. "Miss Anna the beauty queen," she said, stretching her arms out as though she were reading those words on a marquee. "Anna, I think that's a marvelous story."

"So, where did you go?" Rudy asked, totally enthralled with the story and wanting to know more.

"I went to New York. New York City. It was a glorious place. I had a friend in high school who moved there and we used to write letters to each other. When she found out I won the contest, she invited me to come to the big city and stay with her. She... she... she said work was plentiful. Well, she was wrong. I had a hard time finding work, and well, let's just say that my welcome didn't last long. I was soon out on the street and I was ready to go back home. Can I have some coffee? My mouth is so dry."

"You know coffee might make you pee," Mary Kay whispered in Anna's ear. Anna had a weak bladder and was known to lose control every now and then after drinking too much coffee.

"Well, the bathroom is right over there," Anna responded out loud. "We have any cupcakes left? I'm feeling very hungry, too. Yeah, hungry, too."

"Anna," said Mary Kay, "we're all out of cupcakes, but I think it's okay to have some coffee."

"Do we still have to pay for it?" Anna asked referring to the fifty-cent fee for coffee.

"Well, under the circumstances, I don't think Miss Mims would mind if we had a cup or two at no cost," Mary Kay said assuredly. "Just remember that the bathroom is right over there. Let me get your coffee."

"Yeah! Free coffee! I'll take two cups," the old woman hollered as Mary Kay went over to the kitchenette to prepare the java.

Shirl was intrigued with Anna's story. "How did you get back, back to Kentucky?"

"Well, I didn't come back, at least not right away. I was out on the street..."

"Scaring people, I'm sure," Gary interrupted.

"I... I... I was looking for work when I saw a sign in this window that said they needed a dancer. I went inside and they hired me right there on the spot."

Shirl put her hands to her face, excited to find out that her coworker had been a dancer. "Anna, I had no idea you could dance. So what kind of dancing did you do, the mamba, samba, polka?"

"Well, it was quite sometime ago, and yes, I had... well... a little rhythm and I had good looking legs. At least that's what folks told me. But no, none of those."

"So what kind of dancing did you do, Miss Anna?" Rudy asked. "Don't tell me you were a stripper or something like that."

"Well... something like... like... like that," Anna said, the tone in her voice dropping in embarrassment.

Gary slapped the table with his right hand. "I can't believe what I'm hearing. You, Anna, a stripper? Now I think I've heard everything."

Mary Kay was returning to the table, carefully holding Anna's cup of coffee. "Gary, is it that hard to believe that Anna could have been young and adventurous when she was young? I bet she was gorgeous and sexy, and all that. Here's your coffee, Anna."

"Well, I did turn a few heads," Anna commented as she cradled the coffee cup with her hands, warming her fingers from the heat.

With shock and disgust on his face at the same time, Gary said, "I just can't imagine her with all of her clothes off luring men into some nasty frenzy. It just seems inconceivable to me."

"Gary, I wasn't a nude dancer. I danced burlesque."

"Burlesque? What's that?" Rudy asked.

"Well, I'd dance with feathers, lots of feathers. Feather boas, feather fans, feather headdresses. No one ever saw my body. Just… just… well, just my legs and my face. That's all they'd see. It was called a strip tease. I'd just give the men a glimpse… a glimpse here and there. My featured dance was in a champagne glass. Not a real champagne glass. It was huge and full of bubbles. I'd lay back and lift my legs up in the air…"

"Please Anna," Gary pleaded, "we don't need the extra visuals."

Shirl was totally enjoying the story. "Anna, this all sounds so exciting, so exotic, so…"

"So vampy," Chris added, the look of lust in his eyes.

"I was getting some… some… some notoriety. Anna Folanna, they called me. People would come from all over to see me. And the money was good, too. I got my own apartment, more new clothes. But it all ended one night after work when… when… when I had just gotten out of my cab and was walking across the street and… and… and I was hit by a car. The car never stopped… just kept going. I remember hurting and then I blacked out. I woke up in the hospital with two broken legs and a concussion. I was told that I might not ever walk again, let alone dance. I was also told that I might have some mild short-term memory loss. I was devastated. My new world was coming to an end. The only thing I could do was to go home, home to Kentucky. My family was glad to see me, even my father. Yes, he was especially happy to see me come home. I never told him or actually anyone else the kind of work I did when I was in New York. He always thought I worked in a candy factory. Funny, huh? Me working in a candy factory. Well, I did learn to walk again and I went to school to become a teacher, something my father approved of. But I still think about my dancing days. The... the... the freedom, the thrill." Anna took a sip of her coffee, a happy grin on her face. "And anyway, they said burlesque wouldn't last forever, and they were right, it didn't."

"So without the accident and the decline in burlesque, you would have started doing lap dances to pay the bills," Gary dryly said.

"Oh, I would never," Anna said as she looked around the table. "But please, I... I... I don't want anyone to know about this. No one, I mean no one knows this part of my life and I want it to stay that way."

"But Anna, it's a great story to be shared," said Mary Kay.

"I understand her request," said Shirl. "Let's agree to swear, never to share what is being said today. Okay?"

Mary Kay concurred, and one by one, the hostages agreed to swear not to share the secrets, despite Gary's mention that the agreement would have to be nullified if they were asked to testify in a court of law about the events of the day. With a little nudging, he reluctantly said, "Okay, okay, I swear not to share any of this silly crap that I hear today."

"And Rudy, what about you?" Anna asked. "Will you swear not to share my story?"

"Yes, Miss Anna, I swear," he reassuringly replied. "Now, who wants to go next? Come on, who's next? Who wants to share their deep dark secret or something from the past?"

"I feel like I have cotton in my mouth," Anna stated as she tried to moisten her lips with her dried tongue. She took another sip of her coffee.

"That's odd... I do too," Shirl added.

"Maybe we're all dehydrating and we'll soon shrivel up and disappear," Gary said.

Chris laughed and added, "Like a vanishing act."

Gary turned to Rudy. "You can't really be serious to think that we'll all have to tell something about ourselves, something that's nobody's business?"

"I'll go," Chris announced.

Gary stared at Chris in disbelief. "You can't be serious. We can't give into his demands."

"I don't mind, and anyway, I've got something I need to get off my chest. It's something that's killing me inside and this might be the time and place to talk about it."

"Then go ahead," Rudy directed, glaring at Gary as though the captive had defied his captor.

"Well… let me just get it out," Chris started. "There's something about me you don't know." Chris took a deep breath and then blurted out, "I've been having an affair with Ethel, Miss Mims. There, I said it."

Mary Kay smiled. "Chris, I hate to tell you this, but we all knew that you were having an affair with Miss Mims."

"Really?"

"Yes, really."

Anna sat her cup of coffee down on the table next to her stack of cards. "I know I've already shared, but this would be a good time…a good time to tell you, Chris, that most of us in this room have probably had an affair with Ethel."

"What?"

"Yeah," Shirl confessed, shrugging her shoulders. "I'd say that most of us have at one time or another found solace in the arms of Ethel."

"Perhaps everyone but me," Gary objected. "I'd rather die than get that close to the old dragon."

"Now Gary, we're talking about our boss so be nice," Mary Kay intervened. "But I want to add that I view Miss Mims as strictly in a supervisory role and have never been sexually involved with her, nor will I ever allow myself to do so. It just isn't right. It's not professional."

Anna leaned over and with her finger pointed in the air she said, "Never say never, my… my… my dear."

"Anna, you too?" Mary Kay said in shock.

"Yep, can't remember exactly when, but it did happen. Probably more than once."

There was a moment of silence when Chris said in a broken voice, "Wow, I knew she loved sex, but not that much. But it doesn't matter. You see, I think I love her."

Gary stood up, not believing what he was hearing. "Oh dear god!" he exclaimed.

"I know what you're thinking," Chris said, "that she's just infatuated with the uniform. But, I think she might love me, too. You see, when you look past this badge that says "security," you'll see a man full of personality and love."

Shirl folded her arms and sighed. "Oh, Chris, that's so beautiful. But aren't you already married?" she asked.

"Yes, I'm married. I'm eight times married."

"Eight times? How did that happen?" asked Anna.

"I got married then divorced, married then divorced, married then divorced, married then..."

Mary Kay interrupted. "We get it, Chris, but what Anna really meant was, what led to the string of marriages? I guess it's okay to ask that, isn't it?" she said, looking to Rudy to make sure she wasn't breaking any hostage rules.

"Sure, Mary Kay. It's fine," Chris reassured Mary Kay. "You see, I used to be a dental student at the University of Louisville. I didn't have a full scholarship, so I took a part-time job as a security guard at the mall. I loved, and still love women. But, wow, I had no idea that women loved the uniform so much. I married my first wife before I could finish school, and then she left me when she found out I was screwing around with the woman who would be my next wife. Now don't get me wrong. I knew that I needed to finish school, set up my own dental practice, and make lots of money with a grand home in the suburbs and a couple of really expensive cars. But the uniform. The uniform. The uniform would get me everything I wanted. Lots and lots of pussy, free pussy, whenever I wanted it. That's all I wanted. I realized that I didn't need to get the home, the car, the practice. And anyway, I'd eventually lose it all one day to an ex-wife and to alimony payments. Living the life of a security guard would allow me to play and not pay. You know what I mean?"

"But eight times?" Anna asked in awe.

"Yeah, eight and still counting. I hope. The problem now is that I'm married to a woman who doesn't care that I screw around. Now that ain't right, is it? She's supposed to want me all to herself. I'm afraid that I might not get out of this one. I may be stuck for the rest of my life with this woman that I no longer love."

Mary Kay had a puzzled look on her face. "You don't love her because she has committed to you for the rest of her life and she loves you no matter what?"

"Yeah, I think the thrill is gone. And you see, it's Ethel that makes my heart beat loud now. I love her. I really do."

Shirl, strangely moved by the story, pulled a tissue from her pocket and wiped her eyes. "Oh Chris, that is so lovely."

Gary was not impressed with Chris nor his tale of lust and love. "Shirl, you think everything is lovely and beautiful. He's a man whore, a confused man whore in a security guard uniform. I personally can't see what these women have seen in him."

Rudy calmly responded to Gary's comment by asking, "What do people see in you?"

"What do you mean?" Gary asked, suddenly put on the spot with no clever reply.

"Just like I said, what do people see in you? You seem so full of hate and spite. Are you really that full of anger?" It was obvious with Rudy's tone that he had a dislike for Gary and his evil tongue.

"That's none of your business," Gary arrogantly responded.

Rudy approached Gary from behind, pointing the pistol to Gary's left temple. "Let's make it my business." He then cocked the trigger. "Why don't you tell us what makes you so hateful?"

"Nothing!" Gary screamed with fright. "There's nothing that I need to tell!"

"Oh, I think you can think of something," Rudy said as he ran the barrel of the gun back and forth on the side of Gary's head.

"I was a battered child!"

"I don't buy that," Rudy responded.

"I lost my mother at twelve!"

"Not good enough."

"I always wanted to be a singer." There was a pause. Rudy shook his head. "I posed as a nun while substituting in a parochial school," Gary added. "One time I went to church drunk."

"Not good enough! Let's tell us what everyone wants to hear."

"And that would be?"

"Come on, say it. Tell them all that you're one great big faggot. Tell them!" Rudy demanded.

"How dare you!" Gary yelled defiantly.

"Say it! Say it or else."

"Or else you'll shoot me?"

Mary Kay, her eyes nervous with fear, waved her hands in the air trying to get Gary's attention. "Gary, just say it. You just have to say it."

"Okay, damn it, if I must, I'll say it. I'm gay! Damn it, I'm gay! Is that what you wanted me to say?"

Rudy backed away. "Now was that so hard?"

Anna put her head down on the table. "Hell, we... we... we already knew that he was a homo," she mumbled.

"Yeah, it was obvious you didn't share the love for women like I do," Chris admitted. "Not once did I ever hear you talk about, you know... *pussy*."

Anna raised her head. "I love pussy cats, too. You can talk about my little pussy anytime you want. You want to see a picture of my little pussy?" She reached down, searching for her bag. "I have one here in my purse."

"You're on the wrong page, Anna," Mary Kay said, embarrassed for Anna. "We're not talking about cats."

Anna paused, then simply said, "Oh."

"I knew you all knew," Gary said as he wiped the sweat from his upper lip with his hand. "But what you don't understand is that I could never bring myself to say it. So what you really don't know about me is that I never could say it."

Shirl surrendered her used tissue to Gary, which he reluctantly used to wipe the sweat from his brow. "But Gary, you always talked about you and Raymond and the vacations you'd take together. He's so sweet, isn't he, that Raymond. We just assumed…"

"And how you loved Cher and the Miss America Pageant…" Mary Kay interjected.

"And don't forget about the baby grand piano in your living room," Anna said as she rolled her eyes. "God knows how many… many… uh, many times we had to hear about that damn piano."

"Okay, I said it. So there, I'm gay. I said it and now it's out in the open. I'm gay! I'm gay, gay, gay, *gay*! And yes, I love Cher and the Miss America Pageant, and I love my baby grand piano, and I love Raymond. What else do you want me to say? Huh? Is that enough? I'm gay, goddamn it, I'm just one gay old fag who doesn't like having a gun put to my head!"

Anna looked at Gary and calmly said, "Gary, it's okay that you're gay. It was only a secret to you. We've all known. It's fine." She then stood up and like a maestro leading the orchestra, she began chanting, "Let's all say it together… Gary's gay! Come on, Gary's gay!" Everyone but Gary followed suit in unison.

With a half smile of relief on his face, Gary interrupted. "I get it, I get it. I'm gay, but I'm still spiteful and hateful, and full of anger and that will never change, no matter how gay I get."

"That's so lovely, Gary," Shirl said in admiration.

"Somehow I knew you'd say that," he replied, handing the used tissue back to Shirl.

Rudy cleared his throat, and smiled at Shirl. "So Shirl, what's in your big closet?"

"Clothes, Rudy. Lots and lots of clothes," she replied with laughter. No one else found her response amusing.

"I don't think Rudy was referring to your clothes," Mary Kay said to her.

"I know. I was just trying to make a light joke. I guess it was too light, huh? Well, my story will sound silly, almost perverted, but for some reason I feel compelled to talk about it. And we are sharing with each other. So please don't judge me…"

"We swear not to share," Anna said as she crossed her heart.

"What you don't know about me is that... well... what you don't know about me is that I've not been completely honest."

"About what?" Rudy asked.

"Let me explain. You all know that I'm with my second husband. My first marriage didn't work out. Too young and idealistic, I guess. After my divorce, I tried all kinds of dating, but nothing seemed to click for me, if you know what I mean. One of my friends suggested that I go on the Internet, you know, to meet someone. I tried it and I met this wonderful man... Ben. His bio listed his likes and his dislikes, he loved the race horses and his favorite singer was Barbra Streisand, and he just sounded so romantic and mature. We exchanged emails and I really liked him. One evening he wanted to talk on the phone. I was so nervous about it, and I was feeling so insecure. I didn't want to sound like a country bumpkin so I changed my whole persona before I called him."

"You changed your persona?" Mary Kay asked, seeking clarity in Shirl's confession.

"Yes. You see... I know you all think I'm from New York, but I'm not. I was born and raised in Mississippi. Jackson, Mississippi."

Mary Kay hesitated but said, "Your accent isn't southern. I always thought you were from New York."

"Yes, I know, but I'm not. Never even been there, and actually, I never said I was from there. But, I figured that since he loved Barbra, and she is one of my favorite entertainers, well... I decided to talk like her. He loved my new northern accent and our conversation went so well. Then he wanted to exchange pictures. I had no choice but to change my hair and make up. Overnight, I became Barbra Streisand, except I could never sing like her, of course. I even pretended to be Jewish, not a Southern Baptist. One thing led to another, we started dating, and then we married. To this day, he still thinks I've always talked like this and that I'm from New York, not Jackson Mississippi."

"So your whole marriage has been a lie, a scam?" Gary asked with some sincerity.

"Gary, I don't look at it that way," Shirl stated. "My intentions were never to hurt anyone. I mean, those of us here don't always tell everything we know about each other. That's obvious just from this little experience we're having here. Someday I might reveal my roots..."

"Speaking of roots, you could use a bit of a touch up," Anna interjected.

Of course, Gary could not ignore the opportunity to cajole and commented, "Anna, I do believe you're thinking like a gay man."

"You're both on the wrong page again," said Mary Kay.

Shirl giggled and said, "I might tell him one day. But the timing is not right, not right now. You see, there's more. When we first got married, we had sex all the time. But soon it started to wane. I didn't know if it was too much Barbra Streisand, or if I needed to change my personality again. Ben is a good catch, and he's so sweet, and I'm determined to do anything I can to make it work. No offense, Chris, but I don't want to be married eight times."

"None taken," Chris responded, enamored with Shirl's tale of deception.

Shirl continued, "Two years ago, when I sprained my ankle... you all remember that don't you? Well, when I came home from the doctor with my foot in a bandage, he pampered me and was the perfect nurse, waiting on me hand and foot. It wasn't long after that he proceeded to make love to me like never before. Shortly after that, we were in church one Sunday when I leaned over and told him that my back was killing me. We had to wait until the pews were empty and everyone had left the church because he couldn't stand up."

"He couldn't stand up?" Anna asked.

"Anna, he had an erection, and it was quite noticeable. When we got home, he massaged my aching back, and boy did he ever massage my aching back, if you know what I mean. Later, I started thinking about it and then I realized that Ben gets turned on when I'm in pain, or at least if it appears that I'm hurting. I don't know if there's a medical or psychological term for it, but I figured what the heck. So when you see me wearing bandages and casts, and this neck brace, then that's why. I love him so much, and apparently it's important to him that he can take care of me."

Trying to analyze the Shirl's behavior, Mary Kay asked, "Isn't that a lot of work, and isn't it uncomfortable to go through the surgeries and the rehab just to have a good sex life?"

"Mary Kay, it's like the accent. Once you get used to it, it just becomes natural. It just becomes the way. Well, that's my story. And as I said earlier, please don't judge me. Not too weird is it?"

"Does Ben know any of this?" Mary Kay asked.

"Oh my, no. It would break his heart if he ever knew the truth."

Chris sighed and said, "Well, it sounds a bit kinky to me, but I gotta tell you, I'm feeling a little aroused right now just listening to you.

"Okay, ladies," Gary warned. "Don't be wearing any bandages to work unless you want to get attacked by the raging hormonal security guard."

Anna raised her leg out from under the table. "Anyone wanna see the bandage on my thigh?"

"It's not a bandage," Gary said with the authority of a physician. "Probably just old loose skin that's wrapped around your bony leg."

"Gary!" Mary Kay scolded.

"Hell, Mary Kay, he might be right," Anna said jokingly. "Hey, I wanna go again!"

"Oh please," Gary objected. "You've already bored us enough with your trivial 'I could have been a star' story. Let's not give her another turn, or better yet, Rudy, why don't you not waste a bullet on this old fag and use it on that old bag?" he said pointing to Anna.

Rudy pondered a moment, and then agreed with Anna. "We've got time for more, so go ahead, Miss Anna. Go ahead and take another turn."

"Thank you, Rudy. You're so kind to me," she said to her captor. "Another thing…another thing you don't know about me is… Hell, I can't remember the other thing."

"That's okay, Anna," Mary Kay said comforting Anna, "and we are killing time, but..."

"But be nice to Miss Anna," Rudy interrupted. "She is after all, one of my favorite teachers..."

"Who helped you to NOT get your GED," Gary added.

"Be nice Gary," Mary Kay said as though she were disciplining a school bully.

"That's okay, Mary Kay, he doesn't scare me," Anna said. "So, let's see. Another thing you don't know about me. How should I say this... another thing is. Well, this is odd, I suppose, but maybe not as odd as Shirl... as Shirl wearing all those bandages and casts, but... but it does involve wearing things."

"We gotta guess what you're wearing?" Chris cried out with a twinkle in his eyes.

Mary Kay expressed her disgust with Chris and his luring looks at Anna by reminding him of the age difference between the two and that he should respect his elders. "Damn, I wanted to play that game," he said in disappointment.

"God, you straight men will settle for anything," Gary said as he mockingly gagged with disapproval.

Anna told everyone to calm down, that she was ready to share. "Okay, let me start over. I'm ready. Another thing that you don't know... that you don't know about me is... well, I like to wear men's underwear." There was silence in the room.

"You what?" Chris sheepishly asked.

"I like to wear men's underwear. I think they feel... they feel better than women's underwear, especially the Fruit... the Fruit of the Loom briefs. Of course, I do like my Calvin's."

"Now I think I can die," Gary added, bending over as if he were throwing up.

"They're just clothes," Anna pleaded, "and they feel better than the lacy and frilly...the lacy and frilly kind that most women wear. Sometimes, sometimes I wear boxers, depending on if I'm wearing a skirt or pants. After all these years, it... it... it feels so good to let it out."

"So you're a cross dresser?" Gary amusingly asked.

"Oh my, no. I just like the feel of men's underwear."

Shirl crossed her legs, tilting her weight to one side. "Anna, I know a cross dresser, and he says the same thing about women's underwear. I don't know, it sounds to me like you might be a cross dresser."

"Or one of those transsexual people," Chris said seriously. "You know that's how they all started out. You know, wearing their mother's clothes. You ever wear your old man's clothes?"

"Yeah, but I'm not a transsexual, I don't think."

"You ever think about having sex with a woman?" Shirl asked.

"Yeah, I don't have a problem... you know... a problem with that, but I love men. I really love men and sex with men. That's my preference, even at my age... my preference for sure."

"Sounds gay to me, you know, preferring sex with men. I hear that all the time," Gary said proudly.

Shirl uncrossed her legs, repositioning herself in her chair. "Anna, this could be really complicated. I mean you could really be screwed up in the head, you poor dear. I think there's more to it than you think."

Chris leaned closer across the table. "Like you could be a closeted transsexual who's into men, which means if you had a sex change, you would be a man into sex with men. Sorry, Anna, but you're gay. I'll be damned, I never would have thought it. You had me fooled. Now Gary here, I had him all figured out from day one, but you? No way would I have ever thought you were... you know... gay."

Anna looked stunned. "Now I'm really confused. I never tried to analyze why I like to wear men's underwear. I thought it just felt more comfortable."

Chris winked at Anna and gave her one of his notorious come-on smiles, and then said, "You ever thought about wearing a thong?"

"I... I... I have, once. I mean I actually wore one, but I didn't think about it... think about it."

Gary snidely commented to Shirl, "I didn't see that one coming, nor would I want to see it again."

"It was very uncomfortable," Anna continued. "I suppose that I could get used to it, but…"

"I wear them," Chris confessed.

Shirl, a bit startled with the revelation, perked up and said, "Oh, really?"

Chris had taken control of the conversation. "Yeah, as a matter of fact, I have a colorful assortment that I use for special occasions. You know the ladies love the male stripper movements. Wanna see a few?" he asked, raising up from his chair.

Mary Kay was fast to put an end to the thong topic. "Sorry, Chris, but you're giving us too much information, and anyway, you've already shared."

"Sorry, Mary Kay," Chris said as he shrugged his shoulders and cowered back down in his chair.

Being analytical, Shirl shifted the attention back to Anna's issue. "So, Anna, let's get back to your problem, or rather, your preference for men's clothing."

"What's the big deal?" Anna snapped back. "There was a time… a time… a time when only men wore pants, and look at you all now. At some time or another, you've all worn pants, so does that make you all cross dressers?"

Shirl nodded her head in agreement. "I know what you're saying, Anna, but Fruit of the Loom?"

"Nobody sees them but me, and anyway, it's not my turn to defend myself. I'm… I'm… I'm supposed to be sharing and that's what I've done. So there, and I'm through."

"You're a cross dresser. A nitwit cross dresser," Gary interjected with a bit of condemnation.

"That's enough, Gary," said Rudy, and then he turned to Mary Kay. "So, Mary Kay. What is it about you that we don't know? You can't be little Miss Perfect all the time, so share that big dark secret with all of us."

Mary Kay sat up straight in her chair. She knew that eventually she'd have to share something, but Mary Kay had always been open about her life. "Well, I hate to disappoint you all, but I've had a wonderful life that's had little ups or downs, and I've had very few problems. I have a great husband, wonderful kids, a beautiful home, and a job that I dearly love. I mean, sure, there are things about me that you don't know, but I don't have anything to tell you that would be of any significance. Maybe I should have gone first."

"Come on, Mary Kay, nobody has a perfect life," said Gary, challenging the secretary. "You're either being evasive or you're telling a lie."

Shirl came to Mary Kay's defense. "Gary, that's not nice. Of all people to call a liar. I can't imagine Mary Kay telling a lie."

Gary persisted. "So, what is it, evading the truth or are you lying about your perfect life?"

Mary Kay paused, gently biting her bottom lip in angst. "Well, Gary, maybe it's a little of both. You, see, I have been lying and I've been avoiding talking about it, about facing the truth. You're right. What you don't know about me is that I have been lying to you all."

"About what?" Anna asked, a bit stunned that Mary Kay would admit to lying.

"About Missy," Mary Kay replied. "You know how you all ask me how she's doing and what's going on with her since she left working here for her new job? And you know how I always say that she's doing fine and we're going to have lunch one day? Well, the truth is that I haven't spoken to her since she left. Oh, I do leave messages on her answering machine almost everyday, but she has yet to call me back. Not once. I thought we were good friends and that when she got her new position that we would still stay in touch and be the best of friends. I still feel that way. Guess I need to get over it, but part of me says that she'll come around one day and call me. This is humiliating, but there, I said it, and I feel better already. I'm sorry for not telling you all the truth, but honestly, my intentions were good, and I did expect her to call one day, but after six, seven, eight months, I suppose it's not going to happen."

Shirl reached over to hug Mary Kay. "You poor dear."

"And that's it?" Gary demanded. "You've been pretending to be in touch with a friend and former coworker who won't give you the time of the day, and that's the worst thing about yourself that you can come up with? You're right, Shirl. You poor dear."

"Well, I think it's sad," Anna said sympathetically, "kind of, you know, hoping for... hoping for your friend to call. I had that happen to me once, well, maybe more than once..."

"And they found out you were a cross dresser, huh?" Gary said, laughing out loud.

Mary Kay turned to Rudy and said, "I told you my life was not exciting, but it has been good. And I've liked it that way. I told you I should have gone first. It's been hard to compete with the likes of stories of strippers, gays, sex fiends, and cross dressers, no offence Anna."

"None taken," Anna responded as she brushed her white hair behind her ear.

"I've come clean, and I'm sorry for not being honest from the start, so please forgive me. Can we move on?"

Shirl was the only one to answer. "Of course you're forgiven. I mean, you were only lying to yourself, kind of like we all have been."

Anna peered around the table. "Looks like everyone's taken a turn but you, Rudy."

"Yeah, everyone but me... I've said that phrase so many times," Rudy said.

Anna clapped her hands. "Bravo, Rudy. You know what a phrase is! You remembered!"

Rudy acknowledged Anna's compliment. He had been working on his English grammar with her since he'd been coming to the center. "Thanks, Miss Anna. I have been working on that one, thanks to you."

"So are you going to share with us, some horrific part of your past?" Gary inquired.

"I can."

"Rudy, you're so young," Shirl said to him. "What could you possibly tell about yourself that would be so horrible?"

Rudy hesitated, a frown on his face. After a few moments, he spoke up. "What you don't know about me is that when I was four years old, my brother and I were playing in the front yard. Nathan wouldn't let me play with his Legos. I guess he was like any six-year old who didn't want to share his toys with his kid brother. I remember how he was building this castle with his Legos on the driveway. I was occupied playing war with our assortment of GI Joe's. Seems like we had at least seven or eight of them. I could hear my mother and my father arguing. They argued all the time. They were loud. On that day, my father ran out of the house in a fit of rage and jumped into the car, started it, put it in reverse, and backed it up. He backed it up over Nathan. I will never forget how my father looked through the passenger window at me with this incredible look in his eyes. I just stood there staring back at him, sort of frozen in time. He jumped out of the car and ran back to see about my brother. Nathan was just laying there. My father just kept screaming, and my mother came out and she became hysterical. The next thing I remember was the ambulance and the police arriving. They took my brother away. He was dead. Died on impact, they said. He suffered no pain. It seemed like the whole thing was surreal, like I was on the outside looking in. I was numb to the pain and grief that everyone was feeling. Later that night, my father turned and looked at me and said, 'Why didn't you tell me?' He blamed me for Nathan's death, not outright, but he blamed me. When he asked me why I didn't let him know that Nathan was behind the car, I knew that he felt it was my fault that my brother was dead."

Mary Kay was totally moved by Rudy's story. "Oh, Rudy. That's so horrible."

Even Gary was touched by the tragic tale. "I'm sorry Rudy," he said. "I mean I should have never been so condescending with you. It was unkind."

"My father never let me forget my brother died in front of me, or the fact that he felt it was my fault for his death. He always referred to Nathan as the smart one, the one who had a future, the one who was good. One time at a parent-teacher conference when I was in fourth grade, my father told my teacher that it was a shame that she didn't get to know Nathan. He talked about what a good reader he was and how he liked to write really funny stories, even at six. He wasn't slow like me. Me, the family idiot." Rudy began to weep. "He hated me. Nothing I did would be good enough, and even though my brother was dead, he could still do it better than me. My father finally left my mother when I was around eleven, but my mother wasn't much better. Even though she never blamed me for Nathan's death, she was so eaten up with grief that she started to drink, couldn't hold a job, and didn't really care what I did. And as you know, I dropped out of school and just hung out, and eventually, I came here to start over."

Mary Kay rose up out of her chair, and without asking for approval, she approached Rudy with her arms outstretched. "Rudy, I think you need a hug," she said as she embraced him in her arms.

"I've needed lots of hugs, but no one was there," Rudy said as he cried on Mary Kay's shoulder.

"We're here, for you Rudy," Mary Kay assured the young man. "I want everyone to hug Rudy. Come on, everyone show him we care," she demanded of the others. One by one, first Shirl, then Gary, and finally, Anna, stood up and followed Mary Kay's example, hugging Rudy, then offering him apologies.

"Rudy can I be your grandma?" Anna asked. "I'd be a good granny."

"Sure, Miss Anna. That would be nice."

Mary Kay noticed Chris hadn't given Rudy a hug like the others had. She understood the feminine nature of comforting was foreign to the macho instincts that Chris had honed over the years. "Come on, Chris, let's give him a big old bear hug," she encouraged.

"Oh, alright," he said. "Come here kid." Just as Rudy put his arms up to be hugged, Chris came close to him, attempting to grab his gun. The two fell to the floor, each wrestling to gain control of the other.

"Chris, what are you doing?" Mary Kay screamed. "Stop before someone gets hurt!" Within seconds, the gun went off. Silence engulfed the room. Anna collapsed, hitting her head on a chair before she landed on the cold tiled floor. Rudy stood up, the gun in his hand.

"Oh my god! Anna's been shot," Mary Kay shouted, the fear in her voice replaced by rage.

Rudy stood there stunned. "I didn't mean... is she? Is she alright?"

"No, she's not alright," Mary Kay answered as she knelt over Anna's limp body. "I think she's... she's dead. Rudy, she's dead. You shot her," she said, releasing her pent up emotions.

"Anna! Oh my god!" Shirl yelled at the top of her voice. "You've killed Anna!"

Mary Kay, without hesitation, stood up and faced Rudy. With authority she said, "Rudy, this has gone far enough. Give me the gun," she demanded, staring the scared young man in the eyes. She got even closer to him. Sternly, she said, "Damn it, Rudy, just give me the gun and give it to me now before someone else gets hurt. Come on, give it to me." Reluctantly, he handed her the gun.

Rudy dropped his head, and looking down on Anna's body said, "I didn't want anyone to get hurt. I just wanted my GED. That's all I really wanted. I just wanted my GED."

Mary Kay ordered Chris to take Rudy outside. "You've got it," he said, his security guard attitude coming back. He looked at Mary Kay, Shirl, and Gary, as he reached for Rudy's arm and pulled it behind him. "You guys pull that barricade away from the door. Come on kid, let's go. It's all over now." Within seconds, the barricade was dismantled, and with the door opened, Chris led Rudy outside to the police who were waiting for them.

The three remaining hostages stood over Anna's lifeless body, their eyes filling with grief and remorse for their fallen comrade.

Gary was the first to say his words of remembrance. "She was so wonderful. So giving." He paused. "Is that pee on the floor?" he asked.

Shirl ignored Gary's comment, saying, "She was my best friend. I just can't believe it. And now she's gone, gone forever."

"Who will I make fun of now that she's no longer with us?" Gary added, sincerely feeling the loss. "I guess I'm the old one now, soon to be the victim of ridicule by my younger peers."

Anna opened her eyes and raised her head from the floor. "Has he had his way with me yet? Did he just do it and leave?"

"You're alive!" Shirl hollered with joy.

"Oh my god, like the creature from the *Black Lagoon*... it just won't go away," Gary said with dread and disappointment in his voice.

"Oh, Anna's fine," Mary Kay reassured her coworkers. "When the gun went off, it set Anna off into one of her seizures, you know, the kind that make her faint when she's startled by loud noises."

"You mean, she wasn't shot?" Shirl asked. "She just had one of her seizures and you knew she wasn't shot?"

"Yeah, the old seizure and fainting spells paid off this time. When I realized that she wasn't hit, I thought it would be the perfect time to get the gun from Rudy and end this whole mess," Mary Kay stated with affirmed relief. She pointed to the ceiling. "Look at the bullet hole up there. Probably went right through the attic and through the roof."

As Mary Kay and Shirl squatted down to assist Anna, Gary just stood over them, shaking his head in disbelief. "Can you believe it? With a little bit of divine intervention, the old goat probably saved our lives."

Mary Kay looked up at Gary and said, "She sure did. She sure did."

*

Months later, as Saint Patrick's Day was approaching, obvious by the bright green sweaters Mary Kay had been wearing for the past week, the center was busy as students took a renewed pledge to commit to earning their GED's. Even the instructors were invigorated by the onset of spring just around the corner. Mary Kay was going through the morning's mail when she spotted a letter to Anna. Gary, Shirl, and Anna were taking their mid-morning break, sitting at the same table where they spent those grueling few hours as hostages just before Christmas. Chris stood next to the table, monitoring the center as he always did.

"Look what I have here," Mary Kay announced as she approached the table. "It's a letter to Anna."

"A letter for me?" Anna asked, surprisingly.

"It's a letter from Rudy," Mary Kay said as she handed over the letter. Anna opened the envelope, pulling the one page letter out, peering over it.

"Come on, Anna," said Shirl. "Read it out loud."

Anna looked around, proudly toying with the idea of sharing the letter that Rudy had written to her, to her and no one else.

"Well, alright," she said. She began to read her letter aloud. *"Dear Miss Anna, Thanks so much for writing to me in jail."*

"She writes him once a week," Mary Kay interjected.

"Hush up, Mary Kay," Anna said like a giggling teenager. "That's... that's nobody's business but mine."

Shirl agreed. "That's right, Anna. You have that right. Please read on."

"I... I..." Anna stuttered. *"I enjoy reading your letters to me and letting me know what's going on at the community center. Things have been going fine since I made the plea bargain. I have new friends and everyone treats me... treats me real well. The only thing I'm scared of here is Big Larry. He looks mean, acts mean, but most of all, he... he... he is mean. I've seen him in the shower and he's really big, too, if you know what I mean. Ha, ha. Don't tell Gary. Ha, ha."*

Gary sarcastically rolled his eyes, but he was also beaming with pride that he had been mentioned in Rudy's letter.

"I... I... I've started working on my GED. My new teacher says that I should be able to pass without any problems. I've heard that before. Ha, ha. Once I get my GED, I'll take college classes. Since I'll be here for the next ten years, I should have plenty of time... plenty of time to get that done, and it won't cost me a dime. Isn't that something? I think I want to be a lawyer, a doctor, or maybe a security guard."*

"Isn't that sweet?" Shirl commented.

"Imagine that," Chris said. "A security guard like me, no doubt. I'm proud of that boy aspiring to be someone honorable like myself."

"*Please keep writing, and tell everyone hello for me. I wrote down that recipe for the nutty cupcakes that you asked for on the back of this letter. I hope they come out alright.*"

"I thought you were allergic to nuts," Mary Kay said.

"I am, but… but this is a special recipe that I don't have a reaction to," Anna replied, a big smile coming across her face. "*Good bye, and please visit. Love, Rudy.*"

Mary Kay shook her head with approval as Anna passed the letter around, each one scanning over the handwritten note from prison. "Isn't it funny," she said with no apprehension. "Here we are at work everyday, earning an honest dollar and trying to make ends meet, while the kidnapper gets all the benefits that the law allows. Free meals, free boarding, a free education. This a great country," she said.

"Thinking about a sweater for the occasion?" Anna asked.

"Already got one started," Mary Kay replied. "An American flag with guns and dollar signs floating around it."

"That sounds so derogatory," Gary interjected.

"It's free speech, Gary. Free speech," Mary Kay repeated with authority. "And free speech doesn't have to make any sense."

Mary Kay returned to her desk, quietly acknowledging the changes that had taken place with the staff at the center since the hostage taking. She listened intently and smiled as the trio at the table traded barbs with each other.

"Oh, Gary, you know better than to ask me about my new bandage," Shirl laughed.

"Wearing your Calvin's today, Miss Anna Folanna?" Gary whispered.

"Shut up, you old homo," Anna quipped back. Chris stayed close to the table, never saying a word, his only intent was to hear more about Shirl's arousal strategies and the kind of underwear Anna might be wearing.

It was a good day at the center. No one ever shared the secrets that were revealed that afternoon in December, but the bonds between the five hostages grew stronger after the big event. Oddly enough, and indirectly, even Rudy was now part of the menagerie on First and Chestnut.

Learning to Sashay
Like RuPaul

Ermina stared into the makeup mirror, methodically moving her head from left to right, making sure each stroke of eyeliner matched the other. Ermina believed that having perfect symmetry meant having the perfect face. Periodically, she stood up, her hands cradling her face, posing in front of the dressing mirror to the beat of the DJ's muffled music as if she were a Vogue model, each new stance a framed photo of the glamorous star that dwelled in her mind. Wearing a light blue silk robe and a rose colored scarf around her head to cover her thinning hair, she ignored what she considered her few masculine flaws, instead focusing on the facial canvas she was covering with layers of makeup, powder, and heavy blue eye shadow. She'd always told herself that wearing makeup did not create the star; it was the timely process of the application that allowed the character to emerge from within. She'd painted her face a thousand times over the years, but each time she applied the makeup, there seemed to be more foundation needed to cover the blemishes of time. Yes, Ermina was an aging drag queen, but her beauty was still esteemed by other entertainers and her adoring fans. She was the queen of queens, and though her glamour needed constant reinforcing, she still maintained the air of unmatched royalty. She also possessed a wicked sense of humor that kept others on their toes.

The dressing room door opened allowing the deafening dance music to engulf the room. Dante, Ermina's overweight costar at

Club 82, paraded in clutching a black plastic bag in her hands. Her brightly painted pink nails stood out against the dark bag, each one meticulously manicured. "Hey, girl!" she yelled. Always loud, Dante projected her voice as if the person she was talking to was on the other side of a football field.

"Hello, Dante. What's going on with your bad, black-ass self?" Ermina asked, not looking away from the mirror.

"Wait till you see the new hair I got today."

Ermina looked up, arching her left eyebrow. "It better not be like any of mine. You know I hate copycat competition, especially with hair."

"No, honey," Dante said, snapping her fingers in the air. "They're nothing like anything you've got. As a matter of fact, you'll be trying to copycat me after you see them."

"If the day ever comes that I imitate you, it'll be the day that I quit drag," Ermina responded. "And I don't intend to be retiring anytime soon," she said as she playfully snapped her fingers in Dante's face.

"You better not make any promises you can't keep."

"Well, settle down and pull the damn fur balls out of the bag," Ermina demanded as she set her powder puff down and turned to Dante, giving her fellow entertainer her full attention, or at least pretending to.

Dante sat in the chair next to Ermina, then reached into the mystery bag, feeling the contents, slowly deciding which to pull out. "First," she announced, "the Venus wig. Voila!" She held the blond wig in the air as if she were a hunter pulling a prized pelt out of a sack.

"That's very nice, Dante. But it is so very common," Ermina calmly stated as to appear not too impressed. "You can understand its blandness is why I never bought one."

Dante looked down, slightly deflated by Ermina's words. She was hoping for some shared joy regarding her purchase, not a condescending comment. She suddenly made excuses for why she bought the wig in the first place. "Well, I knew you didn't have one, and I do like the style, and it was on sale."

"You don't plan to wear it on stage do you?" Ermina asked, professing to care about Dante's established stage image.

"Yes, ma'm I am, and tonight, too," Dante said proudly.

Ermina turned away, looking into her mirror and started to apply red lipstick on her upper lip. Casually, she said, "I'm not sure you should, Dante. Wearing new hair on a big show night can confuse your fans. They might not like it, and they might not tip you like they normally would. And you know how much you rely on your tips."

Dante rolled her eyes. "My fans will always give me the ducats because they love me. It doesn't matter what kind of hair I have on my head, they would still love me."

Still acting nonchalant, Ermina looked up as she placed her hand on her chest and said, "I refuse to argue with you, my darling Dante." She turned back to the mirror and softening the tone in her voice she asked, "What does the other one look like?"

"You won't like it," Dante replied, trying to dismiss Ermina's comments about the other wig.

"Shut up, Miss Thing, and show me," Ermina demanded.

Dante stood up. "I love it when you force me into things." Energetically, she turned her back to Ermina, leaned over, and then spun back around holding a black curly wig in her hand. "Voila," she announced. "The Diana Ross Sixties wig!"

"Ew, I mean ooohhh! That is sooohh gorgeous!" Ermina said with pained excitement.

"You think so?" Dante asked. "I didn't think you'd like this one. You don't think it's too old fashioned, do you?"

"Old fashioned? Of course not." Ermina continued to apply lipstick. "You should wear the Ross wig tonight," she said under her breath, but just enough for Dante to hear her comment.

"But you said wearing new hair on a big show night might confuse my fans. That's what you said."

Ermina paused. "I did say that, but this hair is simply gorgeous." Of course, she was being pretentious, and Dante was one to be easily misled. Ermina leaned over, pulling her friend back down into her chair. "You wouldn't want to deprive your fans of an evening of glamour and bliss, now would you? And a night wearing a Ross wig would only excite your fans into a frenzy," she said as she massaged the back of Dante's hand. "And anyway, I think it was you who said that your fans would love you no matter what you had on your head."

"Will you help me get it ready for tonight?"

"Of course, I will, Dante," Ermina said convincingly. "Go ahead and put it on your head and I'll start working on it right now."

Dante pulled off her dark green T-shirt, exposing her overweight upper body. Ermina hated it when Dante wouldn't wear a robe while preparing for the shows. Ermina felt it was improper to be half naked in front of others. But after she and Dante argued about the issue so many times in the past, Ermina finally just accepted the fact that she would have to look at Dante's bulging gut and sagging man boobs while the two shared the dressing room. Picking the right battles was important for Ermina, as, according to her, staying on top was the result of well-planned and orchestrated schemes. Creating friction over partial nudity, even though Dante's flesh was repulsive, would only hinder the status between the two, and with Ermina already having the edge on the pecking order, she decided to save her energy for the more serious conflicts in the future. Dante faced the mirror and leaned over the dressing table, pulling the wig snug on her head. She raised her head, the unkempt curls dangling in all directions.

"Oh, my!" exclaimed Ermina. "Look at how that makes your jaw line so much smaller."

"I think you're right," Dante concurred as she jerked her chin in.

"And when I tease the bangs up and comb them back to one side, it will be an incredible look. Trust me, everyone will talk about your new look tonight."

"I love it already," Dante said as she admired herself in the mirror.

"Yes, it's the T! The real deal!" Ermina said as she continued to tease the hair, acting like the hair stylist that she never was. She picked up a can of extra hold Aqua Net. "Close your eyes and let me spray here in the front."

"Careful not to get the spray in my eyes" Dante warned. "You remember how they swelled last time. I had to do oriental drag the whole night because my eyes were closed shut."

Ermina paused, and being coy, she smiled and said, "I do remember. I also remember how you were introduced that evening as Dante's cousin from China because you were so embarrassed to go out as yourself. You certainly fooled the audience that night."

"It was your idea to do that, remember?" Dante added. "You said it would devastate my fans for them to think that I might be deformed or injured. You were right, as always. I didn't make many ducats that night, though."

"Yes, yes, how well I remember. Your cousin from China didn't make many tips that night, and I think it was because she was a little awkward on stage."

"Awkward?" Dante said, raising her voice even louder. "She was dancing blind on that stage because she couldn't see with her eyes shut tight."

"Perhaps you should have put on shades and pretended to be Stevie Wonder in drag."

"Thanks, I'll remember that next time."

Ermina finished spraying a heavy layer of Aqua Net on the wig. The swirled hair and stiff plastic sheen reminded her of a giant black tulip. Of course, she knew better to refer to Dante as a tulip head. She stood back and proudly said, "Okay, my dear Dante, open up. You like it so far?"

Dante's eyes opened wide with excitement as she beamed with pride looking at her new image in the mirror. "Oh, yes, baby. It looks fine, sooohh fine. It's the bomb!"

"Well, it's a shame you spent all that money on two wigs," Ermina said as she pampered Dante's ego. "After wearing this one, you'll probably never wear the other one. I mean, the Venus wig will look so very plain and common after wearing this one."

"You think?"

"Well, look at the two side by side." Ermina grabbed the uncombed Venus wig and held it up next to the Ross wig. "Here, look."

"Not much to look at is it?" Dante said as she compared the two through the mirror.

"No, unfortunately, it isn't," Ermina said, nodding her head. "Hey," she said, "I have an idea. Out of the kindness of my heart, why don't you let me buy the Venus wig from you? At least you won't be starting the night out in the hole. How much did you pay for it?"

"I got it on sale."

"Well, I'll help you out. I'll give you twenty for it."

"But it's new, and I paid forty for it," Dante stated firmly.

"My dear, you can either be forty in the hole or twenty in the hole. It doesn't take a brain surgeon to figure this one out. As you know, I hate math, but I can see the deal on this one."

Dante thought for a few moments, looking at herself in the mirror. "You're probably right."

"And I'll even throw in finishing the back of your hair for tonight… for *free*."

"Okay, it's a deal. Twenty ducats and finishing the back of my hair."

"Deal," Ermina agreed. She took the teasing comb and gave the back of the wig a few strokes and a spray of Aqua Net. "And look," she said as she threw her arms in the air, "I've just completed the agreement. It's done."

"But that didn't take two minutes," Dante complained.

"It would take someone else thirty minutes, but me, only two. Why waste time?"

"But…" Dante tried to continue.

"But honey, it's gorgeous, Miss Dante DeBusse!" Ermina exclaimed.

Before Dante could even object any further to the scam job that Ermina had just pulled on her, Angel entered the dressing room, a bar tray in his hand. "Anyone need drinks?" he asked. Angel was Billy the bartender's newly and unofficially adopted child. Billy and his partner, Mike, took the twenty-two year old in after his grandmother threw him out of her house when he confessed to her he was gay. Of course, Angel was totally new to the gay world, and he was still enamored with the bar scene, and even more so with the drag shows. He worked part-time at Mike's deli in the daytime, and now was enjoying his first week waiting tables at Club 82.

"Well, hello my little Angel," Ermina said as she leaned over giving Angel a no-touch European kiss on each cheek.

"Hey girl, Miss Salami Mommy," Dante yelled. "You like my new hair?"

"It looks uh... uh..." Angel was not sure how to respond. He was confused at being referred to as 'Miss Salami Mommy,' a reference, he thought, to working at the deli. He wasn't sure if the comment was a compliment or just another bully taunt like the ones he had endured over his short life. He didn't want to be disrespectful, and he still had a fear of the unknown, especially in this situation, with men who wore dresses.

"Don't frighten the boy, you big cow. Come over here, dear," Ermina said to Angel, guiding him away from Dante. "Be nice with your words, Angel," she said softly in his ear. "Miss Dante is still getting accustomed to how it feels to have really short hair on her head for a change. Don't you think it makes her jaw line look smaller?"

Angel paused, not sure what to say. Dante had a very large, well, some considered it huge, jaw line, but perhaps the new hairdo did make it appear smaller. "Well..." he began to say.

Ermina interrupted. "And look at her neck. It doesn't look near as thick as when she wears those long tresses that she likes to wear, trying to cover up her neck most of the time. She does have a beautiful neck, don't you think so, Angel?"

Angel reluctantly agreed. "Why yes, yes she does. Either of you want a drink?" Angel was feeling a bit more than just awkward as he tried to change the subject.

"Not right now, baby," Dante answered. "Maybe in a little bit. You know I have to wait for my first drink after my makeup is on," she added. "Hey, wait a minute. Are you inferring that I have a thick neck?" Dante was usually slow to react to Ermina's comments. Sometimes, it could take thirty seconds or more.

"Dante, my dear. We've been over this so many times. Your neck is lovely. It's just that it's not as long and elegant as mine, and you are a big girl, so a little more girth would be expected."

"Ermina, would you care for a drink?" Angel asked.

"Later for me, too, sweetie," Ermina added as she sat down in her chair. "Angel, I have a present for you."

"For me? A present?"

"You're still entering the amateur night show in two weeks, right?" Ermina asked.

"Yes. Yes, I am."

"Do you have a wig yet?" Ermina questioned.

"A wig?"

"Yes, a wig... hair, you know, the crowning glory."

"No. I don't have one yet. I think Billy and I are going to go get one."

Ermina bent over, reaching under the dressing table, and pulled out a wig box. She sat it on her lap and slowly opened it, lifting a perfectly quaffed up-do of auburn hair. "Here," she said. "My ballad hair. I want you to have it."

Angel was taken aback. He had seen Ermina perform during the weeknight shows, and she was famous for her ballad hair. "But I can't..." he said in awe.

"I won't take no for an answer. And anyway, I just bought new hair for tonight, and I have been looking for a different look. Let's try it on."

"Now? Try it on now? I can't. I have to work."

"Hell, it won't be busy out there for at least another hour or two. Come on. Sit right here," Ermina coaxed as she guided Angel to sit in her chair.

"I can't believe this. I hope Billy won't mind. I mean he still doesn't want me to enter the amateur night. He says I shouldn't do drag."

"Funny that he would say that, you know, with him helping you with your costume and then taking you out to go wigging shopping. But never you mind. You let me worry about Billy. We go way back. I know how to handle him. You ever have a wig on before?"

"No," Angel replied as he tried to get comfortable in Ermina's chair. He felt honored that she would allow him to sit in her space.

"It will feel different at first, maybe kind of heavy, but after awhile, you won't even know it's on your head. Am I right Dante?"

Dante looked up from his mirror, patting his face with foundation makeup. "Yes, baby, you're always right, girlfriend."

"Now hold it by these curls while I pin it on." Ermina meticulously placed numerous bobby pins, locking the wig in place and securing the ballad hair atop Angel's head. "Almost there. One more... and there!" she exclaimed as she let her hands do a magical dance into the air.

"It looks funny. Like a helmet," Angel said out loud as he gazed at himself in the mirror.

"No he didn't call your wig helmet hair," Dante said, bursting into laughter.

"I'm not paying any attention to you while you foolishly try to create some resemblance to a woman," Ermina snapped back at Dante.

"I didn't mean to make fun of the wig," Angel said apologetically.

"No offense taken. It looks glamorous, my dear Angel. And dark hair was made for you, too."

"You think?" Angel questioned as he patted the sides of the wig with his fingertips.

"Why, of course."

"I like it." Angel said, a tepid smile coming across his face. "Did I tell you that my mama had dark hair?"

"No, you didn't. And I bet she was very pretty, too," Ermina said as she placed a few strands of loose curls into the right positions.

"Yeah, and it was long and wavy, and she was pretty, so very pretty," Angel added.

Ermina picked up the container of red blush, twirling the makeup brush around to gather a good amount on the tips of the bristles. "Let's put a little blush on those cheeks," Ermina politely demanded.

"I don't know about the blush. Billy might not like me wearing that while I work."

Ermina stepped back, placing her hand on her hip. "It's a drag bar, sweetie," she said, her tone of voice becoming more serious. "Even some of the other waiters wear blush and eye liner. It only enhances the features of the face, especially when the lights are so low. And I'll bet you'll make more tips, too. Pretty people always make more tips. Isn't that right, Dante?"

"Yes, baby, they do," Dante answered without looking away from the mirror as she outlined her nose with dark contouring to make her nostrils appear smaller. "The girls with the most makeup always take more ducats home."

"And you might even get a boyfriend or two," Ermina added, contorting her face in mock pleasure.

"Really?" Angel innocently asked.

"Yes, really. Guaranteed," Ermina said in a reassuring manner. "Just tilt your head back a bit and close your eyes. Yes, that's perfect. Normally, we'd put on a makeup base before we decorate the cheeks, but we're just playing tonight. When you get ready for amateur night, you'll want to do it right with all the makeup."

Angel sat patiently in the chair, his head tilted just enough to let Ermina apply the blush on his face. "Can I look now?" he asked like a kid wanting to see his Christmas present.

"Not yet. Just keep your eyes closed while I fan your face. Gets all the dust off so it won't get in your eyes."

"And you don't want to get anything in your eyes... everrrr," Dante said in an affirming voice as she watched Ermina dust Angel's face with the red powder.

Ermina glared at his dressing room partner while he continued to make Angel's cheeks redder than a Washington cherry. "Hush, Dante. You don't want to frighten our little Angel."

"Oh, I'm not scared," Angel interjected, his eyes still shut.

Ermina smiled at her new protégé. "Of course you're not," she said as she stood back, thinking about the next step in transforming Angel into a creature of the night. "Mmmmm… let's work on those eyes," she said out loud. She fluttered her fingers over an array of makeup tools, finally reaching for the eyeliner applicator. "A little eyeliner is what we need. Be still," she ordered. "I'm not going to take your eyes out. Just relax. Think pretty. You know, beauty does not come easy for most people. Only a few have been graced with natural beauty, and the rest of you, unfortunately," she said looking at Dante, "must suffer through endless hours of beating your face with the makeup sponge and powder pad. It's the price you have to pay to be pretty." She stepped back again, feeling that she had made the perfect additions to Angel's face. "There now, take a look."

Angel slowly opened his eyes, not knowing what to expect. He looked in awe at the person in the mirror. "Oh my… Oh my God. Is that me?"

Dante stopped primping and looked at Angel as if this was a special moment to remember. "This is bringing back memories of my first time in makeup."

"They didn't manufacture makeup for prehistoric cave bitches like you," Ermina quipped.

"Score one for you, Miss Quickness," Dante said, as she turned her attention back to the mirror. "But that's because you cock roaches were hoarding all the ingredients needed to invent makeup."

"Score one for you, too, Miss Dante. We're tied, but who's counting? You know how I hate to keep score," Ermina said, pretending to recoil her nails in midair. There were times she was outwitted by Dante, though not often, and she was easy to retreat, convinced that her dry wit was a trait that Dante was emulating. As a mentor, Ermina was flattered that Dante admired and looked up to her. The two played like two small puppies, but Dante knew in the back of her mind that Ermina had the skills to go mad and rip her throat out if necessary. Understanding and respecting the pecking order at Club 82 kept peace among the employees, and every member of the staff knew that Ermina was at the top of the pyramid. She was Cleopatra, the Queen of England, and Jackie Kennedy all rolled into one, along with a bit of Hitler to totally scare the crap out of any newcomers who dared to challenge her.

"I can't wait to show Billy. Do you think he'll like it?" Angel asked.

"Of course he will. And even if he doesn't, who really cares? You have to be your own person. The real question is, do you like it?"

"Yes. Very much," Angel answered, admiring his new eyes.

"What about the lipstick?" Dante asked. "You gonna put the lipstick on?"

Ermina pondered for a moment, trying to toy with Angel. "I don't know," she said as though she were attempting to make a major life changing decision. "You know the lipstick is the ultimate touch when you're putting your makeup on. It's the final commitment to being a real drag, a new woman, a real woman." She paused then looked right into Angel's eyeliner framed eyes. "Are you ready for it, Angel?"

"I don't want to be a real woman. I just want to be pretty."

"A reluctant and humble participant," Ermina said under her breath.

"I never wore lipstick before," Angel confessed. "Well, one time I remember sneaking my mama's. It was red. And it was just a little."

Ermina patted Angel's arm in a reassuring manner. "Oh yes, we've all snuck into mama's lipstick haven't we? I have some red right here. Ready?" she asked, gently holding the tube of lipstick as if it were a piece of Godiva chocolate.

"I guess so," Angel answered, still a bit apprehensive.

"Now I want you to pull your lips over your teeth like this." Ermina demonstrated the proper way, according to her, on how to apply lipstick. "Now, you do it, okay? That looks good, but hold it steady. We'll do the top first...and then the bottom." She began by gliding the red lipstick over the top lip, and then gently over the bottom. Angel tried his best to follow Ermina's directions, but his lip began to quiver. "Hold still. We're almost done. There, very good. Now rub them together," she said rubbing her lips together, modeling the procedure for Angel. "Yes, very nicely done." She backed away and stepped behind Angel, her hands in the air, an artist's work complete. "I present to you, the fabulous beauty called Angel!"

"Girl, you look wild!" Dante said, slapping her right hand on the dressing table in approval.

"But I don't want to look wild." Angel's words were meek. He appeared confused and disappointed by Dante's description of him.

Jumping to the rescue, Ermina tried to restate Dante's comment. "Dante means that you're absolutely gorgeous... beautiful..."

"Pretty?" Angel asked.

"Yes, baby, pretty," Dante stated. "But wait a minute, you're missing something." Dante stood up, giving Angel the once over. "You don't have any tits."

"I need them?" asked Angel. He had that look of a dental patient sitting in the chair who just had three teeth pulled when the dentist turns around and says, "Let's just pull one more."

"Relax, baby," Dante said trying to comfort the apprehensive young man in front of him. "It's like this. You can't go out there with a woman's head and a man's body. You'd be looking like a freak or something."

"Don't get carried away Miss Dante DeFreak," Ermina said as she began to pull her jewelry out to polish it before the show. "You carry the patent on freakishness."

"And I inherited it from you, Miss Thing."

"That you did," Ermina responded proudly.

"Here, baby. Take your shirt off," Dante said as he encouraged Angel to the next level of transformation.

"I don't know..."

"Come on, unbutton it and take it off." Dante was intimidating, and Angel opted to follow her orders. He stood up and took his shirt off, feeling naked as he stood there in front of these two creatures that he barely knew. Dante opened a duffle bag, and pulled out a strange contraption. "I'm gonna give you your first bra," she said.

"But that's so big," Angel protested.

"That's because Dante has very large man boobs," Ermina jabbed.

"It doesn't matter what you think, Ermina," Dante said in her own defense. "The men just love the extra flesh that I possess. They'd rather chew the fat than gnaw on the bone."

"That's interesting, because my boyfriends love the bone," Ermina quickly retorted as she held a pair of rhinestone earrings up to her ears.

Angel was still staring at the extra large bra. "Well, I don't know… I think it's so…"

Dante held the brazier up and handed it to Angel. "Come on, put it on," she said.

Angel began to laugh nervously as he tried to figure out how to maneuver his arms into the strange getup. "I guess these go in the front?" he asked as he pulled the bra up to his torso, the wide cups protruding from his body.

Dante was quick to aid the young man in assisting him to make the bra fit right. "You're learning fast, Miss Angel. It's not a training bra, so let me pull these straps to make them fit. There, and let's pin the back to make it snug, 'cause you don't want the breasts to sag down to your waist at the wrong moment." She fastened the snaps and pinned the straps together in the back, making the undergarment feel secure. Dante reassuringly eyed the fit as she turned Angel around so that they were facing each other. "Now, let me see. Wow," she commented. "They do stand out, don't they?"

Ermina tugged at the tissue box to her left, grabbing two handfuls of Kleenex. "Here, stuff them with tissue so they won't go flat when your boyfriends decide to cop a feel," she said as she laughed at her own words.

Angel obliged his mentor's request, staring into the mirror as he stuffed each bra cup, making adjustments so one resembled the other. "This is a lot of work. Do I need to wear a dress? I mean, can I put my shirt on now?"

"No, sweetie, you don't need a dress, Ermina said emphatically. "You've got time for that later."

"Yeah, that's right," Dante agreed. "You don't need a dress. Let's put your shirt on."

Angel followed Dante's directions and put his white button-down collar shirt back on. Standing there looking helpless, he said, "So now what?"

"Now let me show you a trick to glamorizing this look," Dante said, again happy to take the lead in showing Angel how to dress up his attire. "Leave the buttons unbuttoned. Pull the two bottom ends together and tie a knot right under the bra just like this. Good, it looks good. Then let's unbutton the collar and pull it up with the points sticking out. Oh, yes, baby." Dante did a final primp then snapped her fingers in approval. "Now look in the mirror. The new you!"

"I don't even recognize myself," Angel declared as he stood in front of the mirror admiring the shapely figure in front of him. Standing there wearing Ermina's auburn ballad hair, with his eyes outlined in heavy black eyeliner, his cheeks heavily blushed, and his lips a vibrant red, he felt like Tina Louise from *Gilligan's Island*. "Do you think Billy will recognize me? What about Mike?"

"Of course they will," Ermina said reassuringly. "No matter what you're wearing, you'll always be Angel. Here, I want you to keep the lipstick," she said as she put the top on the tube of lipstick and handed it to Angel.

"And I can keep the wig, too?" Angel asked.

"Yes, sweetie," Ermina replied. "I told you it was a gift. Now go and make some money."

"But wait," Dante interrupted. "We need to work on your walk and the attitude. Come here."

"Oh, God," Ermina moaned. "Not the walk."

"What's wrong with my walk?" Angel asked.

"You need to twist your hips when you walk, like this." Dante went to the other side of the dressing room, posed with her hands on her hips, and then proceeded to prance back to where she had been standing. "You have to sashay, like Miss RuPaul," she announced.

"RuPaul?" Angel asked.

"Yes, baby, Miss RuPaul," Dante leaned in ready to give Angel a lesson in drag history. "Drag extraordinaire from the eighties, a goddess, the creator of that drag race show. She sings to me when she does her 'Super Model' song."

Ermina gently slapped her temples in disgust. "Dante, if you go into that routine, I'm gonna..."

"I wouldn't give you the thrill of watching, so just pretend you're not here," Dante retorted as he turned away from Ermina. "So Angel, baby, like this..." and Dante demonstrated the sashay model walk that RuPaul was so famous for. "Sashay, sashay...and with the right walk, you've got the right attitude. It all works together."

"Honey," Ermina said as she stood up trying to protect Angel. "Don't listen to everything she tells you. Real girls don't sashay."

Dante took a deep breath, cocked her neck sideways, and snapped her fingers in defense. "Miss Angel is not a real girl, either," she said to Ermina. She turned and faced Angel and stated, "Now you can either go out there walking bowlegged and not make any ducats for the night or you can sashay your pretty ass and go home with cash in your pockets. And anyway, the men love to watch the ass sashay." She paused, once again taking control of the situation. "Now, watch me... sashay, sashay, sashay," she said in cadence as she moved across the room. "Now you do it."

"Do I have to say, 'Sashay' when I do it?" Angel asked, batting his eyes. There was some discomfort wearing eyeliner that made him feel like some creepy critters were making their homes on his eyelids.

"No, baby, just do it," Dante ordered. "You can sashay in your head. Now let me see it."

Angel walked across the room, attempting to imitate the movements that Dante had just shown him. "How was that?"

Ermina tried not to pay any attention at this point. She provided the make up and application tips, but as far as she was concerned, the walk and the attitude was a job for Dante. It was obvious that Dante was becoming a bit irritated with his new student, who was apparently not a quick study. She shook her head and said, "Girl, that's not very good. In fact that was just plain pitiful. Did you sashay in your head?

"Yes... I did."

"You might need to say it out loud until you get it together. So say it out loud this time and walk at the same time. Ready? Go," she ordered.

Eager, but reluctantly, Angel began to walk. "Sashay, sashay, sashay," he said out loud over and over. He stopped after making two laps around the room. "That's hard to do," he said as he rolled his eyes in disappointment that he couldn't do a task so simple as this one. It was as if Angel had two left feet and each of them a loosely attached prosthesis.

Not one to give up, and suddenly acting like a drill sergeant, Dante lowered his already baritone manly voice and said, "Keep going. Do it again."

"Sashay, sashay, sashay..." Angel obeyed Dante and continued to walk around the dressing room, chanting in a monotone voice.

"That's much better," Dante announced. "Here's your tray. Now go up to Ermina and pretend you're waiting on her."

"You mean, ask her if she wants a drink?"

"Yes," Dante answered.

"Okay. I'll try my best." Angel cleared his throat, and holding the tray in front of him he began to walk toward Ermina. "Sashay, sashay, sashay..." he recited, and then he stopped around six inches away from Ermna's face. "You want a drink?"

"I want you to move back about two feet before I cut you in half with that goddamn tray that's too close to my face," the diva ordered. Angel was stunned by the Ermina's reaction and stood dumbfounded, unable to move. Dante quickly broke the silence.

"Oh, sweetie," Dante said as she nudged Angel away from Ermina, who was still glaring at the baffled waiter. "The first rule of survival in Club 82 is to not get in Miss Ermina's face. She doesn't allow her personal space to be intruded upon." Angel backed away, still in shock with the response to his getting too close to Ermina, who now responded with a silent nod and a polite smile on her face. The tension, for now, was over.

"Angel," Dante continued, "you are not going to impress the

customers by walking that way. Here. Give me your tray. Let Dante DeBusse demonstrate the proper way to greet the customer." Walking across the room while jerking her hips from side to side, placing one foot before the other with each step, tossing her head as if she were wearing three jacked up wigs at the same time, and exuding enough attitude to melt a dress of plastic sequins, Dante stopped and posed with her tray perched on her shoulder. She blew an exaggerated make believe kiss toward Ermina, who was trying her best to ignore the whole scenario as she began to glue a set of thick black eyelashes to her lids. "Hello, baby," Dante whispered in a somewhat weird but erotic voice. "Your lips must be parched and your eyes in shock with what you see. Can I get you a delicious cocktail to quench your thirst while you adjust your eyes to the great beauty that stands before you?"

Ermina slowly looked up and sighed. "Have you lost your mind? The only thing that's shocking right now is being at eye level with your sagging man boobs. And if I'm at all thirsty it's because I'm getting flashbacks to when my mother nursed me as an infant."

"Angel, don't pay any attention to her," Dante said defiantly. "She's just a bitchy customer who realizes that she might have to buy her own drink...again."

Ermina then turned around and said, "Angel, just be yourself, but have fun, too. Just sashay your ass out there and make some money. Don't think about it too much. Just do it."

"I'm a little nervous," Angel confessed. "Do you think people will make fun of me?"

"They might not even notice how different you look," Ermina said. "And anyway, some of the customers have never seen you before, so they won't know how different you look. Now go sashay... we have a show to get ready for."

Angel took his tray, and took one last glance in the mirror when the door opened. Billy walked in. "Have you all seen Aaaannn...gel?" Standing about four feet away, his eyes wide open with what he saw before him, he questioned, "Angel? Is that you?"

Proudly, yet with a hint of tentativeness, Angel replied, "Yes, it's me. You like it?"

"Why, you look just..." Billy was at a loss for words. The short frail young man he unofficially adopted and brought to work was now decked out in harsh stage makeup, a bouffant wig, and sporting breasts that were at least a forty-four D cup.

"She looks fabulous, Billy," Ermina demanded. "Say it... fabulous!"

Following orders, he said, "You look fab... u... lous. Just fabulous."

Angel could sense that Billy had been coerced into saying how good he looked. With self-doubt he asked, "You think I look funny, don't you? You think I look ugly?"

Billy was quick to realize his mistake and tried his best to erase the expression from his face. In all his twenty-something years in the bar business, he'd thought he'd seen it all, but he was truly startled with Angel's appearance. But he wanted to be protective of the sensitive young man. "No, Angel. I'm just surprised. I mean, I just saw you as Angel a while ago, and now I walk in here and you're somebody else. I'm just surprised, that's all. You look very good."

"You think I look pretty... just a little?" Angel asked, pleading for some semblance of approval from his good friend and mentor.

Billy acknowledged Angel's request and brandished his large toothy grin of approval. "You look very pretty. Now, what I came in here to tell you is that you have a few customers at your table. I think they need to be waited on... like now, if you know what I mean."

"Oh. I forgot about my tables. I better get out there," Angel said as he headed toward the door.

"Don't forget to sashay, Miss Angel," Dante hollered.

Angel looked back and smiled, and doing her best imitation of Dante, he said, "Okay. Sashay, sashay, sashay," and then left the dressing room.

Immediately, Billy's facial expression went from pleasurable surprise to scorn while Ermina and Dante, knowing their activities would soon be questioned, kept their faces in the mirror. Billy tried to take a moment to decide upon the right words to use, but before he had any time to think, he said with frustration, "What in the hell are you two tired bitches doing with Angel?" Dante was used to being talked down to, but she gasped that anyone would say such a thing to Ermina.

Slowly, Ermina turned to face Billy, and closing her eyes she took a slow deep breath. "Come on, Billy. We're just giving Angel a little encouragement… adding a bit of spice to his life."

"Encouragement? Spice? He looks like a fuckin' clown at a rodeo," he said raising his voice in anger. "And what's with the sashay stuff?"

"Calm down, Billy," Ermina demanded. She stood up, retying the belt to her robe. "It's a goddamn gay bar… excuse me, a goddamn gay *DRAG* bar. Where else can you get away with looking a little freakish?" she asked as she snapped her head around, pointing at Dante.

"Why do you look at me every time you use that word?" Dante asked sheepishly, hoping that Ermina would face Billy without her help.

Ermina walked over to Billy and calmly said, "I know you worry about him, but he's in safe hands here. And anyway, if he's gonna be in the amateur night show he might as well get used to wearing a wig before the night he's suppose to perform, don't you think?"

"I just don't think…"

"Oh, and how's his dress coming along?" Ermina asked sarcastically. "And aren't you the one who's helping him 'sew' the damn thing? Billy, you know we love you dearly, but don't come in here condemning our behavior when you're doing the same goddamn thing." She paused knowing that she would win this battle. She reached out and gently rubbed the side of Billy's bicep, a sign that the argument was over, that she had once again prevailed. "I see you've been working out a bit. That's good." Getting closer, she said, "Now, sweetie, is there any special song you want me to perform tonight? Slow or fast?"

"I just worry. You know how he is, you know, slow. He's so easily swayed."

"I know, sweetie, but he's okay. He just wants to be pretty like they all do. Everyone of those young patrons out there would love to have the nerve to do what we do. And the ones that are the ugliest and sometimes the most pathetic are the ones who are almost always lured into this world of drag glamour. They just want to be pretty, not realizing that it takes more than makeup to turn someone into a beauty."

"But right now he looks like a clown, a bad looking clown," Billy said, making his last plea.

"To you, maybe, but right now he thinks he's prettier than ever. And granted, I might have gone a little too heavy on the blush, but Billy, we've known each other for so very long. You know that I wouldn't do anything to hurt you nor him. Now go. I bet you've got customers, too. Go on…things will be fine."

Billy headed to the door, then turned around as he took his hand and turned the knob. "Any song will do. You're great with anything you do. You know that. Maybe wear the flame red dress?"

Ermina smiled at her old friend. "Of course, Billy. Just for you. You are my number one fan, right?" Billy gently shook his head in agreement and then left the room. Ermina sat down and resumed her primping. The show would start within the hour.

"Well," Dante said after a brief moment of silence. "He's not happy."

Without looking away from the mirror, the queen of queens replied, "Who is, Miss Dante? Who is?"

Within minutes, and in silence, the two completed their makeup routine, their faces heavily painted for the patrons in back row, and their drag personas emerging from within. Sitting side by side and ready to don the final touches of hair and costumes, Ermina was the first to speak. "Look at us oozing with so much glamour. Have two creatures ever looked more beautiful?"

And as they did every night before the show they posed in front of the mirror and chanted, in unison, "Welcome to the fantasy called Club 82, where the girls are girls and the boys are, too. Where he's become she's, and you become me, come live vicariously at Club 82."

Batting her eyes in self-adulation, Ermina said, "Now let's go put on a wonderful show for all those little butterflies out there who want to be pretty. Who will be their inspiration, Miss Dante?"

Without hesitation, and understanding the pecking order in the club, Dante replied, "You will, Miss Ermina Furr. You will."

Starting Rumors

"May I take your plates?" the waiter asked once he'd scampered his way around the slightly crowded café to the table where Cindy, Victor, and Emily were just finishing their lunches.

"Well, the plates are obviously empty, so unless you think we're going to sit here and lick them clean, then yes, you can take them," Cindy said sarcastically, her brassy voice as large as her body.

"But you didn't finish your garnish," the waiter quipped back. "You know you're supposed to eat your parsley sprigs. They're full of nutrients."

"You know I don't like parsley, and I bet you put that piece of green shit on my plate just to annoy me, didn't you?" Cindy said as she raised her eyebrow, challenging the youthful, but experienced waiter. Not only was the young server an expert at his craft, he was just as adept at back talking with his customers, especially Cindy.

"I did," he replied as he stacked the dishes on top of one another. He put Cindy's plate on the top, displaying the small sprig of parsley. "I'll just save it for the next time you come in. No need to waste good vegetation," he said jokingly as he smiled, then turned away heading to the kitchen.

"I love that little fucker," Cindy uttered under her breath as she followed the waiter with her eyes squinted. Cindy was first hired as a history teacher at the community college over twenty-five years earlier, working her way up the academic ladder earning numerous degrees and tenure along the way, but she was still content in staying in the same department, delivering the same lecture year after year. She was also a frequent patron of the slightly off-campus café for as many years and was considered a common fixture in the establishment, rewarded with the right to have her own favorite table and waiter ready whenever she dropped in for lunch, which was almost daily. She felt compelled to joke with the staff, encouraging them to sass her in return, and they obliged her request, but also understanding that they could never win a bout of good humored cajoling.

"We come here a lot," Victor explained in his high-pitched effeminate voice as he looked at Emily who appeared to be amused, but temporarily taken aback by the bantering.

Cindy gently wiped her lips with the white-cloth napkin. "Everyday," she clarified. "Yes, we come here almost every day, you know, to eat." She quickly ogled the young woman sitting across from her. "Emily, I thought a little thing like you would be a vegetarian, but you put that burger away like a hungry lumberjack."

"I hope I didn't appear to be too hungry," Emily said, slightly blushing. "I probably don't eat as healthy as I should. The past year has been an incredible whirlwind for me, you know, getting married, and of course, earning my degree, and now this new job. I usually eat and run." Newly hired as an instructor at the community college, Emily was assigned to be mentored by Cindy and Victor. Though in her early twenties, with her red hair quaffed in a tight bun and her dark grey business suit with low heeled pumps, Emily had "conservative" written all over her. She was obviously well mannered and schooled in proper etiquette.

Victor shifted his torso, half crossing his legs near his ankles, his elbows on the table. At forty, he still had a youthful appearance about him, primarily due to the quarterly Botox injections he received to diminish his frown lines around his mouth and the crows' feet near his eyes. He taught biology on the campus, taking the job many years earlier out of the need to work. Like Cindy, Victor hated change, and so after many years of working in the same classroom and laboratory, he didn't aspire to seek anything else. Unlike Cindy, who was content with her static career, Victor actually hated biology, or at least the lab portion of the course. He refused to touch dead specimens even while wearing latex gloves and the smell of formaldehyde made him deathly ill. After every class, he stood in the hallway, spraying Lysol disinfectant over his entire body, fumigating himself from head to toe and ridding himself of the stench of preserved animal flesh. Because he used surgical masks during class to filter out the smell of death that permeated his nostrils and mouth, students often had difficulty understanding his lectures. Despite the obstacles they might have during the semester dealing with Victor's quirks, his pop tests and exams were notoriously easy to pass, so students rarely complained about his odd behavior.

Victor delicately picked up his cup and took a sip of his coffee, his pinky pointing up. "It's good to see someone eat everything on their plate these days. This whole new generation is so fickle about what they eat. But not me," he said as he patted his waistline, laughing out loud. Victor was a small man, but his joy of food was evident by the extra baggage he carried around his middle.

"Well, I was brought up to appreciate what was put in front of me. We were taught to adhere to the adage of eating to live, not living to eat," Emily said.

"Don't go there!" Victor said, pretending to challenge Emily about the motto.

"Yeah, unfortunately around here, or at least between the two of us, we live to eat," added Cindy as she placed her elbows on the table after retrieving the last roll in the bread basket.

Emily chuckled and then said, "I want to thank you both for inviting me to lunch and getting the chance to know you. You both seem like really nice people and I'm sure that our experience together will be a good one. I have so much to learn, and with the two of you to guide me through the process, well, I feel very lucky."

Cindy leaned back, her large masculine frame seemed to expand even more as she stretched her arms out in front of her, and then cracked her knuckles. "It's our pleasure," she said as she recoiled her arms to her side. "The meal is also paid for, compliments of the one and only, the honorable Dean Watson, that is if I don't forget the receipt. Lunch is just a part of a long list of 'getting to know you' activities that Dean Watson has put in place for the past ten years for the new instructors."

"I think it's been at least fifteen years," Victor interjected, carefully correcting his colleague.

"Whatever," Cindy snapped back in a terse, yet courteous manner. "The whole mentoring idea is a way for us to get to know our new instructors, as well as for people like you to have the opportunity to know us," she said as she chewed a small bit of the roll. "As mentors, we're the example of what happens to instructors who've been at this god forsaken place their whole adult lives," she added flippantly. "And now, we are now officially your mentoring team, so if you need anything let us know."

"How nice," Emily politely said. "I imagine that we will have a chance to meet on a regular basis, and I hope we can get together again very soon."

"Calendars!" Cindy and Victor yelled in unison as though they were imitating a rehearsed and passé version of the Valley Girls. They both reached into their briefcases stowed next to their chairs and pulled out their monthly planners. Cindy retrieved her drugstore readers from her pocket, resting them on the tip of her nose as she flipped the pages searching for the current month.

"How does Tuesday the 22nd work for everyone?" she asked while looking up over her wire-rimmed spectacles.

Victor was a step ahead of her. "That's the day after tomorrow. Works for me," he said as he took out his pen and marked the date. "Emily? How about you?"

Emily was a little stunned. She wanted to meet with them, but she hadn't anticipated another meeting quite so soon. She pulled out her iPhone, ran her fingers over the screen, scrolling up and down and giving it a few taps with her finger, then said, "Uh, yeah. Sure. Tuesday the 22nd. That will work for me as well."

"Then it's a date," said Victor as he closed his planner and carefully tucked it back in his briefcase. He felt a bit embarrassed that he and Cindy still relied on the old-fashioned paper calendar, while Emily was apparently tech savvy with the latest gadget. He hated her and envied her at the same time. Always quick to change the subject, he asked, "So, Emily, how's it feel to be newly hired at the community college?"

"Oh, I'm excited. This will be my first new job since graduation, and I just can't wait to walk in that classroom on the first day of the semester and face all those..." She paused, searching for the right word.

"Ungrateful degenerates?" Victor blurted out.

"No, I meant students," Emily said, confused with Victor's crude and blunt interruption. The seriousness in his response was sincere, but Emily was still trying to comprehend Victor's means of delivery with his words, inflections, and facial expressions. In the very short time in getting to know him, it was difficult for her to decipher when he was serious, funny, or just trying to be downright belligerent. There was very little difference in his mannerisms regardless of his opinion.

"I'm sorry," Victor said in a mockingly forgiving tone. "I shouldn't sound so jaded, and I don't want to put a damper on your enthusiasm. Your students will love you," he added as he tapped the table with his fingers.

"Thanks. I hope so," Emily responded, still not sure of how Victor really felt about the students at the community college.

Cindy was trying to be attentive as she pinched another piece from the roll, inserting it into her mouth. "Did you finish your scavenger hunt?"

"Ah, the scavenger hunt," Emily said, happy to switch the subject. "Yes, I have. Well, I think I did. I went to my final location just before I met you guys here," she said as she pulled a large tote bag up from under her chair and placed it on her lap.

Victor rolled his eyes in contempt. "Cindy, remember when Dean Watson came up with that idea to send new hires on a scavenger hunt just so they'd know their way around campus?"

"Hell yeah. How could I forget? It sounded like a great idea until he made all of us participate in one just so we'd know what our newbies would be going through when it was their time to go out on their own. As much as I loved the fantasy of walking through the men's locker room," she said turning her nose up in disgust, "do you know how embarrassing it was for me to actually go in there and steal a jockstrap?"

"Embarrassing for you," Victor exclaimed "but totally humiliating for me. I almost got beaten up trying to snatch one of those things out of a locker while the student who owned it was in the shower. The phys ed instructor saw me, called me a pervert, and then berated me in front of everyone. I pleaded with him that this was all Dean Watson's idea, you know, to help new instructors learn about the campus, and all these bare-chested Neanderthals just stood there behind their instructor, flexing their muscles, daring me to leave without going through the blockade they'd established with their bodies. I felt helpless and humiliated. No one was buying my story about a scavenger hunt." Victor began fanning himself with his left hand. "So there I stood, red faced, in front of all those half naked men barely covered up with their towels, with a funky jockstrap in my hand."

"What did you do?" Emily asked. She was torn between laughing and being seriously absorbed with Victor's story.

"He ran like hell," Cindy cracked.

Victor took a deep breath. "Yes, I ran like hell screaming like a woman about to get gang raped the whole time holding the jockstrap tightly in my hand. After what I'd been through, I wasn't going to come out of there without it. They slapped me with wet towels, grabbed my bottom, and hurled insults at me, but I made it past them and kept on running. Of course, rumors started after that, you know, that I was the perverted type; that I like to hang out in the men's locker room. It wasn't bad enough that I was the campus homosexual. Now I was perverted too. I tell you, I just don't know how I made it out of there alive."

Cindy put her hand on Victor's shoulder, trying to give him comfort by squeezing his thin muscles through his tweed jacket. "Well, that was a long time ago, Victor. Let it go."

"And people still think I'm perverted," he said, the look of defeat on his face.

"And you are...hell, we all are," his friend added. "So, Emily, whatcha got there?" Cindy asked.

Emily sat up straight, her arms folded over her tote. "Well, my scavenger hunt wasn't all that embarrassing, at least not compared to Victor's experience. I didn't have to steal anything, and I didn't have to end up in a locker room full of half naked men."

"Yeah, fortunate for you," Victor agreed.

Cindy sighed. "Yeah, now they have boxes with signs set inside the locations so you just get what you need and get out. Staff and security don't even care if you look suspicious these days."

"How convenient for the newbies," Victor chimed in.

Cindy looked at Victor. "Let it go, Victor," she said calmly. "Let it go."

"I did get the jockstrap from the phys ed department," Emily announced without wincing. "It's an odd thing to have on the scavenger hunt list. Do guys still wear these things?" she asked the couple as she lifted the male-genital supporter out of the bag.

"Oh my," the waiter gasped as he walked by the table with a tray of food, his eyes almost sparkling with excitement as he got a glimpse of the jockstrap. He stopped right in front of Emily and said, "Oh wait," as if he suddenly figured out why the young woman would be displaying the athletic supporter so openly. "You must be a new teacher or you've got some kind of really cool fetish thing going on," he said in a snarky manner, "or maybe both," he added as he winked and smiled, moving on to the next table.

Cindy lowered her voice as if she were about to deliver secret information to the new instructor. "Well, yes, it is odd to have a jockstrap on the list, and we've always thought that, but you need to know that Dean Watson is an odd man himself, and apparently, yes, they do still wear those funny little contraptions."

Emily widened her eyes in response. "Really? So, Dean Watson is odd?" she inquired.

"Yeah," Victor answered as he glanced around the café. "And we shouldn't say anything more. Just watch yourself around him."

"I will," Emily stated. She then reached into the bag pulling out the next object from the scavenger hunt. "And here's a microphone. I got it at the music department. There were four in the box, but this one just seemed a little more interesting than the others. I didn't know if I would need style points or not, but just in case, I took this one."

"Wait a minute," Cindy said abruptly. "I think that's the prop we used when we did that Forties show. Victor, Am I right? Isn't this the microphone we used for the show?"

Victor's eyes grew wider as though he had just uncovered a true relic from the past. "Oh my God, it is. Wow, that was five years ago, or maybe it was six."

"Whatever, it doesn't matter when it was," Cindy said emphatically.

Victor took the microphone, caressing it as he spoke, his demeanor changing. "Dean Watson requires the staff to do a fund raiser every December. It's one of those traditions that goes way back, you know, to raise money for...not sure where the money goes, we just always do it. And the show is always a Christmas show, and we create a period theme with it, and of course, as always, the dean is the star of the show. Dean Watson has to be up front and center for almost every number."

"And the man can't sing a lick," Cindy scoffed. "In fact, he's downright awful. And trust me when I say we've been tactful and merciful when we've tried to get him to stand in the back and just move his lips while the rest of us sing, but no, he insists on singing with us, and if there's a solo, and there always is, he has to be the one to sing it. Remember how he butchered "Oh Holy Night" four years ago?"

"Or was it three?" Victor asked.

"Whatever. However long ago, I still remember how bad it was," Cindy rebuffed.

"He ruins everything with his god-awful voice," Victor stated with sarcastic disappointment.

"Gosh, that microphone brings back special memories, doesn't it Victor?" Cindy asked as she held it up to her face. "Remember the duet we sang that year?"

"How can I forget? It was a song from *White Christmas*, and it was one of the worst experiences of my life."

"Oh, come on now, it was funny," Cindy said as she playfully nudged Victor with her elbow. "Emily, that evening our names were announced before we were to appear on stage, and I was anxious because Victor was supposed to be next to me but he was nowhere to be seen, and then the intro to the music started, and there I am all alone in the spotlight when the curtains opened. Still, no Victor. So, I went ahead and started singing all by myself. I was standing there in this gorgeous red chiffon dress that made me look like a dairy barn in Wisconsin, and by the time I finished singing the end of the first verse, all of a sudden the audience roared with laughter. Of course, I stopped singing and out of the side of my right eye I saw this 'thing' walking toward me. I turned and looked, and it was Victor."

"Yes, it was me in a flowing white strapless gown that was entirely too tight. Yes, me in a dress. Dean Watson made a last minute costume change for me. He threatened me, saying I'd lose my job if I didn't wear it. He said it would be hilarious; that it would surprise the audience."

"And it did. We couldn't hear a thing because the audience was laughing so hard and so loud," Cindy added.

"All I could do was try to hide my head behind that big 1940's something microphone, but to no avail. My head was too big, still is," he said as he took the microphone from Cindy and placed it in front of his face. "There was no escaping the moment. And once again, the rumors started around campus. Vicious rumors that I wore women's clothing. Like being a homosexual wasn't enough to deal with, but then I'm a homosexual wearing women's clothing. Imagine that."

"Let it go, Victor. Let it go. You're starting to lisp," Cindy said trying to comfort Victor. "Poor dear, when he gets all excited he starts to lisp really badly."

"Yeah, I revert to the stereotypical gay man when I get all

flustered. You know, nelly, excited, and effeminate. It took years of counseling to repress it, but occasionally, it still comes out and it's not pretty when it does."

"I say just be who you are," Emily said as she attempted to consol her mentor.

Cindy nodded her head in agreement. "I've been saying that as long as I've known the man, but I've learned to just listen and let it happen," she said. "And what else is in that bag?" she asked, once again attempting to change the conversation.

"I got my picture taken at Student Services for my ID badge," Emily proudly announced as she handed the ID card to Victor.

He glanced at the laminated card and said, "Nice photo, except for the deep shadows under your chin."

"Thanks, I think," Emily said apprehensively.

"Just trying to be myself," Victor retorted as he passed to card to Cindy.

"Here's a map of the campus," Emily continued. "And I grabbed this thing at the tech building. Not sure what it is, but it was in the box. Victor, do you have any idea what it might be?"

"Honey, I may be a man, but I don't know anything about anything mechanical."

Cindy cleared her throat and with polite authority said, "Victor, it's a carburetor part."

"And what's that supposed to mean to me?" he asked as he placed his hand on his hip, almost daring Cindy to give him a valid answer.

"Nothing, Victor. Nothing," Cindy replied, backing away from a confrontation. "What else is in there?"

"A rubber glove from Health Sciences," Emily said as she lifted it out of the bag as if it were contaminated with some unknown fungus or disease.

"Used, I'm sure," Victor quipped.

"And finally," Emily said as she took the last item out of the tote, "a book that I checked out at the library."

Victor paused for a moment, then with his best ill-tempered

voice he said, "That was too simple, Emily. When the library was on our scavenger hunt, I didn't have my reading glasses on at the time, and I thought the directions said to get an 'unchecked' book from the library. I mean there was no real challenge in checking out a book, right? And when I went into the library, there was a box of books next to the counter, so after some time browsing through the assortment of books, I took one. It was one of those lower-level kind like the Dick and Jane series, and I left with it. Tucked it into my coat. Simple as that. The bitch of a librarian screamed some profanities and came running after me, calling me a thief. She had already alerted security because, according to her, I 'looked suspicious.' Apparently, no one, and I mean the dean, told her or the security folks about the scavenger hunt, and no one informed me that the box of books was being donated to an afterschool program for needy children. Again, the rumors started that I was a thief. Yes, for awhile there, I was known as a homosexual who stole from needy children. How humiliating it is, you know, to be accused of stealing from poor little children, hampering with their ability to be educated and thus forcing them to live a life of poverty and welfare."

"Let it go, Victor. Let it go," Cindy said in a monotone, yet comforting whisper. She turned to the newbie. "So, Emily. Now what?"

"Well, after here, I'll go to the dean's office, turn over my bounty, and then I'm hanging out with my dad and my husband for the rest of the afternoon."

"How nice. I don't get to hang out with my husband much anymore," Cindy interjected. "He's so busy with his business. Victor has become my surrogate hubby."

"And my wife doesn't mind it one bit," Victor confided.

Emily looked a bit shocked. "Oh, Victor, you're married?" she asked.

"Yes, I'm married," Victor replied defensively. "Why does everyone have that same reaction when they find out I'm married?"

"I'm sorry. I didn't mean anything... I mean..." Emily apologetically stumbled with her words.

Cindy jokingly added, "It's okay, Emily. It's even more confusing when you see Victor and his wife together."

"Which is not very often," Victor interjected. "Yeah, she drives a big semi-truck for a living, and she wears these manly flannel shirts, no matter what the occasion is. I can't get her to wear anything else. The bright side is that she's easy to buy for. Yeah, one quick trip to Pro Bass Shop and she's a happy camper."

Emily was totally confused. "But I thought you were, a you know, a..."

"He is," Cindy calmly stated.

"I am?" Victor questioned.

"Yes, you are," Cindy said in a confirming manner, and then she turned to Emily. "So, Emily, let me give you one little bit of advice before you go to Dean Watson's office. How can I say this delicately? You see, Dean Watson has this small room in the back of his office, and there's a mattress in there. The son-of-a-bitch is notorious for hitting on staff, especially the new ones. I remember when he was going over my paperwork after he had hired me. I was young and naïve, a lot like you are now, and there I sat facing him, the desk between me and him. Right behind him to the left was that room, the door ajar, the mattress on the floor. He saw that I was staring at it, and he spun his chair around in a full turn. Then he looked at me and smiled that god-awful smile that he has."

"Oh Cindy," Victor said with nauseated expression. "Every time you tell this story, it gets more and more creepy. That asshole doesn't deserve his position."

"Well, nothing happened to me," Cindy continued, "but I know that over the years he's probably screwed at least half the staff."

Emily shot a glancing look at Victor. "Don't look at me," he said with assurance. "That would just be another rumor."

"Yes, Dean Watson is a sick man," Cindy stated. "A disgusting man. A filthy man." She leaned in closer to Emily. "Don't let him take advantage of you. Be strong, and whatever you do, don't look him straight into his eyes, because he'll jump on your young ass before you even know what's happened."

Emily pushed her chair back from the table, and began to put all the items back into her bag. With the loaded tote on her lap, she looked up and sternly said, "Well, Cindy, I appreciate your advice, and I am so glad that you shared all that information with me, but I must go now. And for your information, I've already been on a mattress with Dean Watson, I've looked him dead into his eyes more than once, and I've told him that I love him more times than I can count."

"Oh, you poor dear," Victor said, wincing at the thought of the young woman in front of him being taken and abused by the dean. "We're already too late," he said in shock.

"Yes, you are," Emily said. "You see, Dean Watson is my father."

"That's even more disturbing," Victor added, his eyebrows twitching as he spoke. "Erotic, yet delightfully disgusting. But wait." A moment of silence overcame the two mentors sitting at the table.

Cindy and Victor turned to each other, the look of doom on their faces. Victor put his hands to his mouth, the realization that his outspoken opinion of Dean Watson was heard by the wrong person. As usual, Cindy tried to come to the rescue, segueing the conversation into a different direction. She slapped her hand on the table, shook her head in affirmation, and announced, "Like I said, that Dean Watson is a fine outstanding man! He's done more for this college than anyone else I know. He's an upstanding citizen with a wonderful family and he has a fabulous daughter who will enjoy teaching." She stared down at the crumb littered tablecloth.

"Oh my yes, he's a fine man," Victor said nervously, slightly lisping.

Emily was obviously disturbed by the chain of events, and even more insulted by the inferences that her mentors had made regarding her father, the dean. She stood up, and glaring at the two said, "Thanks for inviting me to lunch. It's been…enlightening, to say the least." She turned around and without looking back, she walked out of the café.

In silence, Cindy took her hand and methodically gathered the bread crumbs into a short pile next to her napkin, and then with one stroke she brushed the crumbs off the edge of the table onto the floor. "Well, I think that went well, don't you?"

Victor leaned over and said with a gleam in his eyes, "It was your best performance yet. You're so good at scaring off these new instructors, and you get extra credit for totally disturbing the dean's daughter."

Cindy beamed with controlled pride. "And kudos to you, too, Victor. How could she think we wouldn't recognize her, especially after all these years of seeing photos from when she was a baby to even her wedding pictures? Dean Watson has her face plastered all over his office." She began to chuckle out loud. "I'd love to see his face when she tells him she heard about the office mattress that really isn't there. I mean, he'll tell her we're a couple of pranksters, that it was all a big joke, but there'll have to be a little bit of doubt in her mind about the whole thing, but then again, she's probably going to think that maybe it could be true. He'll deny it and she'll think he's lying. Victor, this is a good one and the best thing about it is that she thinks we're a pair of loonies and she'll never bother us with any trivial requests for help."

"Yes, another new instructor that we won't have to worry about. She can sink or swim on her own. Shall we do lunch again soon?"

In unison, the two shouted, "Calendars!" Again, they pulled out their monthly planners and turned the pages.

With her readers on, Cindy said in a very business-like manner, "Looks like Tuesday the 22nd is now open for just the two of us."

"Just you and me," Victor replied as he scratched Emily's name out of the little white square on the planner page. "Do you think we frequent this place too often? I mean, that's how rumors get started. You know, you an attractive straight woman dating a homosexual man. It could get confusing."

Cindy let out one of her usual bawdy laughs. "Victor, after all the rumors that have been started about you, why should you care about another one? I mean, people already think you're a book-thieving, jockstrap-stealing, dress-wearing pervert, not to mention someone who also has a flannel-shirt-wearing, truck-driving wife. Being known as a homosexual chasing a glamorous big bitch like me should be the least of your worries."

"You're absolutely right. Another day, another rumor. Bring it on," Victor said, smiling, his lisp repressed for the time being.

"Waiter! Check please!" Cindy hollered out. "Another free meal. Victor, don't you just love it?"

Watch Me Walk

Hal was slowly adjusting to his new life in the assisted living facility. It had been about six months since he first moved into his small one bedroom apartment, and he still missed his previous life as a retired military man, but with his failing health and aging knees, he required more attention than ever before. He was a loner and spent most of his day in solitude, resigned to watching game shows on television and reading short western novels. His one new friend, Robert, another resident who'd been living in the building for around five years, provided him with simple companionship a few hours a day. Each morning at eight, Hal would meet Robert in the commons area to read the paper together before breakfast and they'd have discussions regarding the latest news. Robert was outgoing and a bit gregarious, whereas Hal was a wallflower, speaking only when someone initiated the conversation.

"Good morning, Hal," Robert said as he walked into the room, his fast gait a bit out of step. Robert was a bit prissy, and even at his age, and despite a series of strokes, he still walked with confidence and purpose in making sure his strides were almost perfect. The left side of his body was a bit limp with delayed reflexes, but he made every effort to make sure no one could detect the lingering adverse effects of his strokes.

Hal looked up from his paper. "Good morning, Robert. How are you this morning?"

"Oh, just delightful," Robert answered.

"Delightful?"

"Yes, delightful. When I turned seventy I said that any day that I can wake up at my age and get out of bed is a delightful day," Robert said as he lifted a newspaper from the stack on the table before sitting down in the brown leather chair next to Hal.

"Yeah, you're the perky one this morning," Hal commented a bit sarcastically.

"I'm always the perky one, even without my first cup of coffee," Robert bantered back. "So what's up this morning? Any interesting news in the paper?"

"Well, the stock market is up, and the Reds won again last night," Hal answered in his usual manner.

"Come on, Hal. Every morning I ask you the same question and you always give me the same answer. It's always about the stock market or sports. Seriously, talk to me about something other than the market or sports."

Hal thought for a moment, then scanned the paper for an article that might interest Robert. "Well there's story about last week's serial killing in Alabama. But that's probably a bit of a downer for someone like you who just likes the good news."

"I've seen and heard enough horrible things in my life to last me awhile, thank you very much. And anyway, what's wrong with just hearing about the fun and uplifting events in life?" Robert asked as he opened his paper and began to peruse through it. For a few minutes, the two sat in silence as each one flipped through the first section of the newspaper as if they were students in class and had been assigned a project to research and then present their findings on some aspect of world events.

"Now here's a wonderful story," Robert announced. Hal kept browsing as if he hadn't heard Robert's statement. "Hal, listen to this," he said as he pushed Hal's paper down to get his full attention. "This is an article about America's first lesbian homecoming couple." Robert began to read the story as Hal sat quietly by, listening and taking in the event that was considered by the writer to be a milestone achievement. "And wait until you hear this, Hal," Robert continued, his excitement growing. "The young woman who was elected king, along with her girlfriend who was elected queen, posted this on her Facebook page for those who opposed their selection. She wrote, *'For all the girls who think tradition should be continued, go back to the kitchen, stop having sex before you're married, get out of school and job systems, don't have an opinion, don't own any property, give up the right to marry who you love, don't vote, and allow your husband to do whatever he pleases to you. Think about the meaning of tradition when you use it in your argument against us.'* Hal, isn't that incredible?"

"Yeah, I guess," Hal said, his eyes looking down, as though he was trying to avoid any further conversation about the topic. In his seventies, Hal was introverted and almost secretive regarding his past. Robert was pressed and curious to know more about his new friend. He had an intuition about Hal, and each morning he worked harder to delve into Hal's clandestineness.

"And Hal, do you remember me talking about that incredible story about a high school boy in Tennessee who was suspended for three days for wearing eye makeup on campus after school was out? And shortly after, the punishment for the young man was reversed, and now wearing makeup is not prohibited for anyone on campus. That kid was really brave."

"Or foolish," Hal interjected.

"Hal, why are you so uncomfortable when I read or discuss articles like this?" Robert asked.

"I'm not uncomfortable," Hal retorted with some amount of defiance.

"Yes, you are. I can see it in your face."

"Well, perhaps a little," Hal admitted.

"And why is that?"

"I don't know. I just do."

"Hal, I'm gay," Robert suddenly blurted out unexpectedly as he sat up straight, sitting on the edge of the chair. Robert was impulsive and sometimes things just came out of his mouth like rainwater out of a downspout, and though he wanted to share his own secrets with

Hal, he was hoping for the right moment to be open and frank. But there he sat, almost embarrassed that his announcement came out so unexpectedly.

Hal didn't blink an eye. "I knew that already," Hal responded with nonchalance.

"And so are you, right?" Robert asked. Again, his impulsiveness went rabid.

Hal looked around the room to see if anyone heard Robert's question. No one else was present except for Matilda, a ninety-year old woman who couldn't hear and spent most of the day staring out the window watching traffic go by. Hal lowered his head and mumbled in what appeared to be a shameful manner, "Yeah, I am."

Robert reached over and attempted to comfort Hal by taking his hand. Hal pulled back, embarrassment on his face.

"How did you know?" Hal asked.

"Gaydar I guess. And how did you know I was gay?" Robert inquired.

"Your walk."

"My walk?"

"Yeah, your walk," Hal said. Then after pausing for a moment he said, "You walk like a sissy."

"Well, now we're getting somewhere," Robert exclaimed.

"I shouldn't have said that. I'm sorry."

"No, Hal. Don't be sorry. I appreciate that you're being frank. And it's not like I haven't heard that before, but at my age, nothing really offends or surprises me. As a matter of fact, my grandfather once said to me that I walked like a girl. Of course, at six years old, I took no offense by his comment, but I didn't understand why the way I walked was such a big deal. With his stomach sucked in and his chest flexed, he demonstrated how a boy should walk, and then he proceeded to watch me sashay up and down the hall, the whole time shaking his head, and then he gave me critiques on how to man up my stride. Though I was a bit humiliated with the lesson, I just thought of it as a right of passage that all young boys probably went through. It was some years later that I realized that my grandfather was not attempting to change me; but instead, he was trying to protect me from the cruel elements of the outside world of the 1940's."

Hal sat motionless as Robert continued with his story. "He once told me that boys aren't supposed to cry as tears were streaming down my cheeks while we watched *Old Yeller* in the living room. As you know, in those days, only girls were allowed to let their emotions flow openly. Boys were to be strong and masculine, and any notion of displaying femininity was to be stifled and hidden. Like television, life was black and white back then, cut and dry. You were this or that, nothing in between, and everyone had to fit into the right tier of the societal structure to be normal. Yes, in those days, round pegs didn't fit into square holes. And it was apparent that I was a round peg living in a square world."

"I loved that movie, *Old Yeller*," Hal admitted.

"Did it make you cry when you saw it?"

"On the inside," Hal said as though he were drifting off reliving a painful emotion from the past.

Robert had waited months to have this conversation with Hal, to reveal something about himself that he wouldn't necessarily share with others. And he was hoping that Hal would open up too, and today was the closest that Hal had come to admitting who he was. Robert studied Hal's facial expressions as he waited for a few moments, and only when Hal made eye contact did he continue. "When I was growing up, I never recalled hearing words like 'faggot' or 'gay', and if I had, I don't think I would have been able to express what they meant, nor would I have had the ability to infer the implications of those labels. But there was one word that everyone knew. Yes, the word 'queer' was common, and it was used in the attempt to dehumanize anyone who was different. As a teenager, I occasionally dated girls, but I also had crushes on guys. I never played out my fantasies simply because I didn't know how, nor did I have the opportunity. I don't ever recall being called queer to my face, but a classmate referred to me as a hermaphrodite once in the ninth grade when I came out of the shower after gym class and he noticed

I had no pubic hair. At the time, I didn't know what a hermaphrodite was, but I knew the word was being used to demean me. I was a late bloomer, physically and mentally, and even without knowing the definition of a certain word, I was well aware when any verbiage addressed to me was used in a derogatory manner." Robert chuckled at himself. "One soon learns that verbal bullying also comes with the obvious body language. Looking back, I believe my developmental delay was nature's way of protecting me. I was always quick with a smile and a laugh, but my slow reaction to any kind of belittling comment kept me out of trouble and conflict. Though at times I felt different, I wasn't sure what that 'difference' really was."

Robert nestled his body back into the chair, crossing his legs. "Eventually, I made it through high school without any major incidents or shortcomings that would embarrass the family name, and shortly after graduation, I came out. It wasn't like an announcement, nor did I make some profound proclamation to the world. It was a gradual process filled with confusion and uncertainties. Some people know they're gay before they even have sex. I was having sex and contemplating the assumption that I might be gay. After about three months of mental anguish and a case of the crabs, I realized that I was gay, I always had been gay, and that I would forever be gay. Again, my delayed 'epiphany' was probably a good thing. If I had become sexually active and out during my high school years, I'm not sure I would have survived. I would have definitely been socially identified and condemned as a queer, and to this day, I don't know how I would have reacted to such a label at that time in my life."

"How did your family react?" Hal asked.

"Nobody was really surprised. I remember my grandmother's reaction when I told her. 'What's the big deal,' she said. 'They're on television all time.' It was a comforting response to my short catholic influenced confession of who I really was. I was expecting her to make me kneel and say a set of Hail Mary's to repent my ways and be cured of my sins. For a young man living in those days, there were no gay role models to look up to, no guidance or advice to be given by older gays, and definitely no consideration of normality or acceptance from society at large. The only visible people paving the way for us were 'funny' actors making appearances on late night television and daytime game shows. How about you, Hal? How did your family react to your coming out?"

"I never did," Hal calmly answered.

"You never came out?" Robert asked with perplexed awe.

"No, never did," Hal said, his eyes shifting back and forth, obviously uncomfortable, yet willing to divulge his secret. "I never admitted it to anyone in my family."

"I can't even imagine keeping a secret like that."

"No one in my family ever asked me. Maybe they were afraid to know."

"So, did you have a relationship with anyone?" Robert asked, still pushing Hal to be more revealing.

"No, not really. I mean I went to bars and the baths, always making up a different name so no one could trace me down or find out where I worked. And of course, I did have a crush or two," he said, his round face blushing. Robert paused as he watched his friend's facial expression begin to glow, a brief gleam in his eyes. "Yeah, there were a few of them, but nothing serious."

"No public displays of affection?" Robert asked.

"Of course not. I was too focused on my job, my career in the army to be caught doing anything like that. I thought it would be detrimental if anyone found out my secret. I mean I'd seen it so many times before, you know, people being let go because someone found out they were gay."

"I guess I was lucky. I lived an openly gay life, had a gay-friendly job, and I was surrounded by gay friends. I had nothing to hide, well," Robert said as he changed the course and tone of the conversation, "nothing but getting caught with somebody's lover. I had this knack for landing men in the sack who had lovers. I was considered the whore, though they were the real cheaters."

Hal laughed. "You are really funny."

"Yeah, a real riot," Robert said as he attempted to downplay the compliment.

"Looking back, I guess I should have been more open. I hear about the kids today and how expressive they are, and I'm amazed at their bravery."

"Yeah, their openness is astounding isn't it?" Robert stated. "Like we were afraid to be called gay, and these young people dare to label themselves as queer. I'm impressed with their openness, too. Why couldn't we have been that brave when we were younger?"

"Yeah, brave," Hal said as he stared off out the window. He turned to Robert, his eyes misting up. "Robert, I cried when DADT was repealed."

"Me, too," Robert responded. He reached for Hal's hand, and this time, Hal accepted the comfort of his friend.

"Thank you for being so kind," Hal said as he gripped Robert's hand.

"Thanks for opening up," Robert said as he smiled back at Hal. "Hey, I have an idea."

"A crazy one, I'm sure," Hal responded.

"You want to be my boyfriend?" Robert asked without hesitation.

"We're not sixteen," Hal said, totally surprised by the question.

"I'm aware of that, and to let you know, I was never into younger guys anyway."

"Well, I don't know. We have separate finances, and apartments, and..."

Robert interrupted, "Just a minute there. I didn't ask you to marry me. I just wanted to know if you wanted to be my boyfriend."

"And what exactly does that mean?" Hal asked, his hand still clinging to Robert's.

"It just means that we can hang out together, talk together, hold hands like this when we want to..."

"Go on a date?" Hal asked smiling.

"Yes, and possibly even more if you act right," Robert said playfully.

Hal thought for a moment then said, "I always heard it said that nobody loves an old queen. And I believed it to be true."

"I didn't say anything about love, but trust me Hal, it could happen. You're a great guy,"

"As are you. So, yes, what the heck. We'll be boyfriends!" Hal said as he reached for Robert's other outstretched hand. "I already feel twenty years younger," he added.

The cafeteria, adjacent to the commons area, had just opened for breakfast, and residents were filing in, some being pushed in wheelchairs by attendants, others in couples assisting each other walking down the hall and into the large room. The smell of coffee and crisp bacon permeated the facility.

"Well, are you ready for breakfast?" Robert asked.

"Yes, I'm really hungry this morning" Hal replied. He tried to raise himself out of the chair, but his weak knees didn't permit him to jump up as quickly as he could in his younger days. "So much for feeling younger," he laughed. Robert aided Hal in getting out of his chair.

"Hal, I have an idea," Robert said abruptly.

"You already had an idea a few minutes ago, and I said yes, remember?" Hal said.

"No, another idea," Robert replied. "It's time we manned up."

"And what do you mean by that?" Hal asked looking confused about Robert's request.

"I mean it's time we stood up, you know, like these young people are doing. Like being brave about who we are."

"Are you talking about being advocates or something?"

Robert became very serious. "You've never protested or stood up for anything have you?"

"Well, no, I don't recall that I have, except for my flag and my country."

"When I was in my twenties, I did my civic duty and proudly marched against Anita Bryant in Atlanta at the Southern Baptist Convention, chanting, 'What do we want? Equal Rights! When do we want it? Now!' I'm not sure what we really wanted, other than to not be harassed or arrested for being gay or gathering at a local bar. Those types of demonstrations didn't have the celebrated impact that made the Stonewall Inn in New York famous, but in the long run, being visible and loud served its intentions. Those times were definitely different, as the past usually is. No one talked about gay marriage, adoption, or serving openly in the military. However, even without specific issues to rally around, there was a pride in all of us in uniting for a cause as basic as the fundamental right to happiness."

"And?" Hal asked as though he needed more of an explanation, but still not sure which direction the conversation was leading.

"And," Robert said emphatically, "I've come to the point in my life that I don't bother about how I walk anymore, and I cross my legs whenever I feel like it. I even let the tears flow when I need to, though people say that my face doesn't look too appealing when I cry. Even the word 'queer' doesn't faze me as I have embraced it as a part of who I am. It would have been great if heroes had been there for us as role models when we were teens, but they weren't. My grandfather was my angel without wings and he was all I had to guide me through my formative years. I had a wonderful relationship with him and we even learned to cry together, unashamed, during his waning years. We never discussed my homosexuality; it was just understood. I know he did the best he could with me as he tried to teach me how to walk 'normal.' Looking back, how brave it would have been for me if I could have just turned to him and said, 'Grandpa, watch me walk, and then you do it like me.' What I'm trying to say is that I don't think I've done enough for this so called push for civil rights. And you obviously haven't either."

"So, what is it you propose we do to complete this civic duty that you say we need to fulfill?" Hal asked.

With elation, Robert said, "I want us to feel liberated. Me, and you. The two of us liberated." He paused then said, "I want our first kiss to be a kiss in public."

"Oh, I don't know about that," Hal quipped back, shaking his head in disapproval. "We just agreed a few minutes ago to date, and now you want to go smooching in public," he said as he turned to sit back down.

Robert held Hal's arm, not allowing him to retreat from the

conversation. "Quit being an old fart and stop acting your age," Robert demanded. He stared into Hal's eyes and asked, "You do want to kiss me, don't you?"

"Well, yes. Yes I do, but..." Hal stammered.

"Then let's do the brave thing, and hold my hand, and we'll walk into the cafeteria, and we'll have our first kiss, and not be ashamed to show our affection for each other."

Hal thought for a second, and realized how courageous Robert was being, and perhaps how foolish they would appear to the other residents if they were seen kissing in public. He gave Robert's hand a gentle squeeze, and said, "Okay, but don't be rubbing all over me."

"I promise I won't," Robert said, and then added, "unless you rub all over me first." The two walked hand in hand into the cafeteria, and Robert led Hal to the center of the room amid the small crowd of residents eating their breakfasts. He pulled Hal close, put his arms around his friend, and then kissed him right on the mouth. "That was nice," Robert said softly.

Hal, by nature, was a bit cautious, turning to look at the reaction of his fellow residents. There was no reaction. It was if no one even noticed, or perhaps they didn't even care.

"You've been living in fear all your life," Robert said to Hal, "and the reality is you never had to. You were very brave today."

Hal was at a loss for words, but the sense of euphoria was incredible. He felt proud, that even at his age and with the coaxing of a new friend, he could actually stand proud holding hands and at last feel the comfort of openly caring for another person. He and Robert walked over to the cafeteria line, placing their trays on the metal counter, discussing what they would eat that special morning.

"Good morning, Florence," Robert said to the cook behind the counter.

"Good morning to the both of you," she replied, a big smile beaming from her face. "That was quite a display of affection you two put on there."

"We were just trying to be brave," Robert said as he patted Hal on the back.

"And you were," Florence agreed. "Cost me five dollars though."

"What do you mean?" Hal asked, looking perplexed.

"We had a cafeteria pool and I said it would take two months before the two of you got together. Seems like Joanne won the pot. She said it would take six."

Hal seemed stunned at Florence's comments. "And how did you know that I was…"

"Gay?" she said, finishing his sentence. "By the way you walk. It's always in the walk."

"But I walk this way because I have bad knees," Hal retorted.

"Uh huh, if that's what you want to think, then go ahead and think it. Eggs and bacon?"

"Yeah, sure," Hal answered.

"Guess you walk like a sissy, too," Robert whispered into Hal's ear. "But you're a brave sissy, that's for sure."

Out of the Closet

By most standards, Erica and Greg were the perfect heterosexual couple, a matching set of wedded bliss dolls, one complimenting the other at all times to the point that they even dressed very similarly with matching colors or patterns. After ten years of marriage, the two still woke up every morning with bubbly "good mornings" for each other, warm smooches before heading off to work, and a subtle yet well rounded dinner every evening where they shared the day's events with each other. To say they were ideal would be an understatement, and because of their devout love and affection always on display, it was difficult for them to maintain relationships with other couples who found their behavior bordering on the sickening side. In fact, they only had one set of married friends, Dave and Joan, who were the complete opposite of Erica and Greg.

The two couples had dinner together on the first and third Thursdays of each month, taking turns hosting the night that usually ended with a nightcap together before the guest couple headed home. Erica almost always served Italian entrees on her night to cook. Though she was of Irish decent, she was an expert at a variety of ethnic cuisines, but especially Italian, and her secret-recipe meatballs always drew rave reviews, especially from Dave, whose wife viewed cooking as a chore.

"Great meal, Erica," Dave said as he pushed his empty plate away. Erica always made extraordinarily large meatballs and served them with a marinara sauce on top of al dente cooked spaghetti, and Dave acted as though he hadn't eaten in weeks by downing four of the savory, garlic-flavored balls of ground sirloin when most people would settle for just one or two.

"Thanks, Dave," Erica replied. As with any cook, Erica was enamored to get compliments on her cooking, and she was doubly pleased that Dave always left nothing on his plate.

"I suppose you're never gonna give me that recipe are you?" Dave asked.

"Now why would I do that? Why would I be giving you my recipe so that somebody," she said, nodding at Joan, "at your house will cook them and invite Greg and me over to eat my own dish when I could make it myself? Why?" Erica stood up and put her hands on her hips, then leaned over and jokingly said, "And anyway, between the two of you, who's gonna go to all that trouble to cook meatballs?"

"Are you making fun of my cooking?" Joan asked, rotating her head from side to side, mimicking a scorned woman with attitude.

"Of course not," Erica said smiling back. "Your baked dishes are wonderful..."

"But," Joan interjected. "I know you were going to put a 'but' in there, so 'but' what?"

Erica began picking up the utensils off the table, stalling for a second to carefully state her words so they wouldn't appear to be offensive to her good friend. "But," she said emphatically, "everyone knows it's so much easier to put things in a pot and throw it in the oven for an hour or so. You know, like your chicken or that incredible roast that you serve all the time."

"And all the time," Dave added.

"Hey," Joan said as she swatted Dave on the arm. "Those oven dishes are my specialties."

"And I truly appreciate eating your specialty dishes," Dave said as he rubbed Joan gently on the back. "Greg, help me out here."

"Sorry, Dave, this is your battle. I learned along time ago not to bite the hand that feeds me, right honey?"

"Yes, dear, you're right," Erica answered with a playful smirk on her face. "Joan, come on. Let's head to the kitchen and get this mess cleaned up and leave these two to talk about those primal things men like to talk about when the women aren't around."

"Yeah, the 'man' stuff," Joan said, flexing her arm muscle. "Dave, my darling macho man, hand me that plate, that is, if it's not too heavy for you."

"Joan, don't make fun of us," Greg stated as he leaned back in his chair. "It's not everyday that Dave and I get together to talk about 'man' stuff."

With her hands full, Erica turned as she reached the doorway. "Well, talk about it quick, because we'll be out of the kitchen in no time." Joan followed and the clatter of the plates and silverware could be heard as the women tidied up the kitchen. The two men started their after dinner conversation as they always did, by talking about how good dinner tasted, and then by conversing about the latest sports news and controversies.

"Great dinner, Greg. It was so good. You're lucky to have a woman like that who likes to cook, and who really cooks well," Dave said as he stretched his arms out, flexing his pecs.

"Glad you liked it. Yeah, Erica is an incredible cook, but I'm the one who has to cook the most around here. Of course, I don't mind, you know. With Erica's busy schedule I had to learn how to cook or I'd only be eating three meals a week."

"Yeah, I know what you mean. Joan stays pretty busy too, and when she's working late, I just order take out and bring it home, then I get it all fancied up with real plates, and when she arrives and sees the spread on the table, she assumes that I did all the cooking. I guess she'll catch on one day," Dave said as he cupped his hand around the side of his mouth as though he was telling some huge secret. "Hey, I never noticed that chair before," he said, pointing to an old piece of furniture that appeared to be a gaudy overstuffed red-velvet chair. With its high back and thick dark-brown wooden legs, it looked like something that would be better suited in a European medieval castle instead of Greg and Erica's modest two bedroom apartment in Nashville, Tennessee.

"We just put it out," Greg said almost apologetically. "Well, Erica just put it out. I've had it in the back of the closet for years, but she sort of 'rediscovered' it and said we should put it in the living room and show it off. Want a drink?"

"Sure. The usual… scotch, straight up." Dave followed Greg over to the small makeshift bar next to the sofa. "I bet she said she was cleaning out the closet and wanted to make better use of the space, right? Women like to claim house turf, even if it's some small menial place like a dark closet that no one ever even sees."

"You know, Dave, you're right," Greg agreed as he poured the Johnny Walker into a short glass, then handing it to Dave.

"Hell, I know I'm right. I can't tell you how many times Joan's cleaned out the closets at our house. Greg, I have no place to hide anything anymore. It's terrible."

"What is it about women and cleaning out closets?" Greg asked as he made a drink for himself.

"Beats me, but at least it keeps them busy." Dave took a sip of his cocktail, then stepped back, ogling the chair. "That's really an odd looking chair. Where did you get it?"

Greg tilted his head and grinned. "Well, it has an interesting history, or at least it's a colorful one."

"Really?"

"Yeah, my uncle gave it to me about ten years ago. He gave me a lot of things over the years. But the chair, well he had just purchased it and not long after he said it had to go… actually, his boyfriend at the time said it had to go."

Dave's eyes widened. "Oh, I didn't know you had an uncle who was… uh…"

"Gay?"

"Yeah, that," Dave said with some discomfort.

"My Uncle Jimmy. Really gay," Greg said as he flipped his wrist. "He was a great guy and very funny, and really gay. He passed away about two years ago. I was his only nephew and he left me a small bit of money. Thanks to Uncle Jimmy, Erica and I went on that Mediterranean cruise we'd always been dreaming about."

"So where did your uncle get the chair?"

"That's the fascinating thing about it," Greg said as he walked behind the bulky chair, resting his hand on the back, his fingers lightly brushing the red velvet fabric. "He said it once belonged to Paul Lynde."

"Paul Lynde?"

"Yeah, the weird guy on "Hollywood Squares" back in the Seventies who always had the funniest answers and he had that infectious laugh."

"That was before my time," Dave said shaking his head. "But I think I might have seen some of those shows on late night cable." He paused then snapped his fingers as he suddenly recalled seeing Paul Lynde on television. "Wasn't he the one in the center square?"

"Yeah, that was him, and he was in some other stuff too. He played Uncle Arthur on "Bewitched." Funny guy. Of course, I don't know if the chair really belonged to him or not, but my uncle said that he picked it up at an antique store in San Francisco, and the sales person told him it was one of a set of four that belonged to Paul Lynde. I got a little confused listening to the story, and especially with it being told to me so long ago. There was something about Paul Lynde buying Errol Flynn's old mansion in Hollywood and he did some renovations, but then my uncle said Paul bought several homes over the years, so I don't know if this piece was something he threw out or if he purchased it to go into one of his homes. I just don't know."

"So, you're saying there might be three others like this one somewhere out there in the world?"

"Yeah. Pretty ugly thought, isn't it?"

"A little. But it does have character," Dave said as he bent over, touching the overly plush fabric.

"And an interesting history," Greg added. "And who knows, it just might have really belonged to Paul Lynde and it might even be worth something some day."

"Enough for another cruise?"

"Yeah. Wouldn't that be great?"

"Can I sit in it or will it collapse when I put my weight on it?" Dave asked innocently. Dave was a rather large, but physically fit fellow well over six feet tall and he easily weighed over two hundred pounds.

Greg appeared startled that anyone would want to sit in the old relic. "We don't sit in it, and that was part of the reason for keeping it in the closet. Erica doesn't want anyone to sit in it."

"I promise I won't sue if I bust my ass," Dave said as he maneuvered himself in front of the chair, his knees bending, ready to recline.

"But, I really don't think you should..." Greg said, but just a bit too late. Dave put his bottom on the chair and nestled his body comfortably into the cushion. "I don't think you should sit in the chair," Greg said under his breath, restating and completing his last statement that went unheeded. "Not comfortable, is it?"

"Not really. But it's not too bad either. I mean, I wouldn't want to sit in it and watch a game. So, you've never sat in it?" Dave asked.

"No, never."

"Not even once?"

"Not once," Greg answered, a blank stare from on his face.

"Why not?"

"Well, you're probably not going to believe this, and you might want to call me superstitious or crazy, but..." Greg paused not sure if he should continue with the story.

"But what?"

"Well, another part of the chair's history is that my uncle said he was straight until the one night he sat in that chair, and the next thing he knew, he was acting sassy and craving man sex."

"What?" Dave asked as though he had just heard the most outlandish story ever.

"Please don't make me say it again," Greg half pleaded.

"No, I won't," Dave said. "I heard you, just not sure what to make of it."

"Yeah, he blamed that chair for his being gay."

"Greg, I don't think that's how it happens, you know...being gay."

"I know," Greg said, halfway agreeing with his friend, "but that's what he said."

Dave sat in silence for a few moments, took another sip of his scotch, and then asked, "So, you haven't sat in it because you fear you might 'turn' gay?"

"Well, yeah."

After another silent pause, Dave added. "And you let me sit in it?"

"I didn't just let you sit in it," Greg stated argumentatively. "You sat in it on your own free will. Like I said, call me superstitious and crazy, but I'm not taking any chances. I'm happy the way I am."

"I'm happy the way I am, too. And just to ease your mind, I don't feel any different. It's me, Dave. Heterosexual, Dave. In love with my wife, Dave."

"That's a good thing."

"Hey, what about the Packers last week? I think they're making a comeback this year," Dave said. The evening routine suddenly was back on course as the visit wouldn't be complete without talking sports.

Greg was relieved to switch the subject. He felt a little embarrassed about telling the story about the chair, but even more so about believing sitting in it could make someone gay. Perhaps the incident would dispel the myth and allow Greg and Erica to freely use the piece in their home, or at least sell it knowing there would be no adverse consequences, or at least having little guilt for passing it on to someone else. "Hell, we think that every year," he said as he sat down on the sofa, "and then they stumble down the stretch. It happens like that every season."

Still sitting in the red chair, Dave suddenly crossed his legs and said in a Paul Lynde voice, "Speaking of stretch, if those uniform pants get any tighter on those guys..." and then he slapped his leg with his hand, followed by that nervous infectious laugh that only Paul Lynde could deliver, well, with the exception of Alice Ghostly.

Greg looked surprised, as if a stranger had just walked into the room and traded places with Dave. "What?" he asked as though he needed to hear Dave again to confirm what he had just witnessed.

"I mean, those men are just poured into those britches, and there's nothing left for the imagination, if you know what I mean."

"Very funny, Dave. You can cut that out," Greg said. "It's a bit weird."

"Why, what do you mean?" Dave asked, continuing to sound and act like Paul Lynde.

Sam sat back, realizing that Dave was not acting his usual self. In fact, he knew that his friend didn't have the ability to act in any other way. "Dave, are you feeling alright? You're talking strange, like Paul Lynde."

"I've always talked like this. I just feel a little flushed right now. It must be the after dinner cocktail going to my head. I do feel a little light headed...kind of dizzy."

"Dizzy?" Greg asked.

"Did I say dizzy? I meant ditzy," Dave responded as he laughed and slapped his hand on his thigh again. "Yeah, ditzy like Mitzy!"

Greg became even more concerned as he watched Dave uncross his legs and reposition himself in the chair, only to cross his legs again and then delicately run his fingers over the pleat in his pant leg reinforcing the crease. Dave's mannerisms were becoming effeminate, the way his posture changed, as well as the way he held the glass in his hand.

"So," Dave asked as he flirtatiously batted his eyes, "can I ask you a personal question?"

"Sure. You always ask me personal questions."

Dave hesitated for a few seconds, and while stirring his drink with his forefinger, he asked, "Boxers or briefs?"

"What?" Greg replied, stunned that his good friend would ask that kind of question.

"So what is it, boxers or briefs?"

"Dave, we've been friends for a long time now, but I'm starting to feel a little uncomfortable with not only the way you're acting and the way you're looking at me, but also with the kind of question you're asking me," Greg said in a somewhat offensive tone.

"Uncomfortable?"

"Yeah, I feel like..."

"Like what, Greg?" Dave asked as he pushed the conversation

deeper into unchartered territory.

Greg looked down taking a breath and gathered the nerve to say, "Like how you're flirting with me."

Dave smiled and replied in a soft voice, "And what if I am?"

"Uh, well, Dave. I'm married and you're married, and our wives are in the kitchen…"

"Yes, and out of sight, and out of mind," Dave said as he raised his glass in the air.

Greg was at a loss for what to do or how to navigate the conversation. Though he first thought Dave was pulling off an incredible acting job, especially for someone not known to being able to lie his way out of a paper sack, Greg now believed the chair did possess some strange power. Either that, or Dave was having some off the wall reaction from drinking scotch, or maybe one meatball to many, or perhaps, Greg even thought, he was the one hallucinating and not Dave. In any case, he was alarmed with the situation and glanced at his watch. "Oh my god, look at the time. Erica! Joan!" he yelled at the top of his lungs. "It's getting late! We have to go to work in the morning!"

Seconds later, Erica walked into the room, Joan right behind her. "Oh, Greg," Erica said dismissing her husband's plea to cut the evening short. "Don't be a party pooper. It's only…" She came to a sudden stop as she noticed Dave in the chair. Under her breath she said to Greg, "Dave is sitting in the chair," as if Greg didn't already know it.

"Yes, I know. I didn't want him to, but…"

"Oh my god," Erica said raising her voice as though something was terribly wrong with the situation as she gazed at Dave sitting in the chair and acting like a drunken drag queen.

"Erica, what is it?" Joan asked.

"Oh, nothing," she said in a quick nonchalant tone, realizing she might have startled Joan. "It's just that no one has ever sat in that chair, except for Greg's uncle. It's kind of special."

Joan positioned herself in front of Erica to face Dave, and though she was only barely five feet tall, she took a pit bull stance and hollered, "Dave, get out of that chair right now before you break it."

Mocking his wife, Dave said, "Get out of that chair right now before you break it." He then glared at his wife, and still speaking with the Paul Lynde voice he said, "I'm a lot more gentle and delicate than what you give me credit for."

"Quit talking that way," Joan responded, confused with Dave's new voice and attitude. "You're a big lug and I love you, but you're too big to be sitting in that fragile chair."

Dave stood up, and with his shoulders drooping he asked, "Why would you make fun of my body type in front of our friends?"

"Your body type?"

"Yes, my body type... my figure."

"Your figure? What the hell has gotten into you all of a sudden?"

Erica and Greg were standing next to each other, both concerned with what was unfolding in their home. Erica leaned over and whispered, "Honey, are you going to tell her?"

Greg turned to Joan and calmly said, "I think the alcohol has gotten to him."

Joan became angry. "He promised he'd only have one drink, or did you guys sneak another one?"

"I'm not drunk," Dave stated as he held his head high.

"Then what is this all about?" his wife demanded.

"I'm... I'm..." Dave couldn't get the words out of his mouth.

"He's happy!" Greg blurted out.

Joan looked at Greg, not convinced with his short explanation. "Happy?" she asked, more befuddled than before.

"Yes, very happy," Greg replied, hoping Joan would accept his answer as an explanation for Dave's odd behavior.

"Yes, I'm happy... and I'm gay," Dave announced.

Joan had had enough as evident by the way she crunched her face and folded her arms as though she were ready to stand her ground for a major fight with her husband. Though she was petite and feminine, she was also feisty and not afraid of her husband's imposing size. "What did you say?" she asked as though she wasn't convinced with what Dave had just announced to her and her friends. When her husband didn't respond to her question, she raised her hand and shook her finger at her husband. "Okay, Dave. This charade has gone on long enough. It's not funny."

"Look at me, Joan. Look into my eyes when I say this. I'm gay."

Joan stared into Dave's eyes for a long moment, searching for some semblance of the truth. Her mouth opened wide as she gasped. "Oh my gosh. You're telling me the truth. I always know when you're lying, and you're telling me the truth," she declared. "But I don't understand how this... I need to sit for a minute," she said as her body went limp and she collapsed on the red velvet chair that her husband had vacated.

Erica reacted suddenly by saying, "Joan, please don't sit in that chair!"

Joan looked up at her best friend, and with a defeated expression on her face, she pleaded, "Just let me be for a minute. I need to sit and I promise I won't damage your precious little chair."

"Joan..." Dave began to speak, still sounding like Paul Lynde.

"Shut up, Dave!" Joan screamed. "There's a whole lot to take in here. I need a minute to try and understand how I could have been so blind. We've been married for eight years, and I would have never thought this about you. How could you have hidden this from me?" she demanded. "So, all that macho man stuff you were doing, was it just a façade? All those basketball games, all those football games?" She reached down and scratched her crotch, and suddenly her voice changed, and she too began to sound like Paul Lynde. "And how about those Packers this year? I think this just might be the year for them to go all the way. Whew! I'm feeling a bit warm. I could use a drink. A shot of scotch," she yelled out as she started to laugh uncontrollably.

Erica whispered to Greg, "Oh my. We've got two Paul Lyndes here in our living room." She then calmly said, "Greg, do what she says and get her a drink."

Dave interrupted, "But Joan, you never drink scotch. It'll give you indigestion."

"I want a damn shot of scotch and I want it now! Erica, you are my best friend. I know you will help me get through this, whatever it is that I'm going through."

"Of course, I will," Erica said as she approached Joan to comfort her.

Greg quickly returned from the bar with a glass of scotch, and wanting to stay out of the fray, he cautiously handed the glass to Erica. "One shot of scotch for the… uh, lady."

"Who the hell you calling a lady?" Joan snapped back.

Erica squatted down in front of her friend. "Here, Joan," she said. "Go on and take a sip. Perhaps it will make you feel better."

Joan took a sip of the scotch, and then wiped her mouth with the back of her hand. The two made eye contact. "God, woman, you've got beautiful eyes," Joan said romantically, her head jerking back and forth like a Paul Lynde bobble-head doll.

Stunned, but calm, Erica responded by simply saying, "Uh, thank you."

"And you've got a great body, too," Joan added as she scanned her friend before taking another sip of the scotch.

Meanwhile, Dave had moved to the other side of the room, almost oblivious to Joan's situation. "Greg, I'm over here thinking boxers, but I'm okay with briefs," he said as he winked at Greg, who was now at the point of feeling truly uncomfortable.

"Erica," Greg said in an authoritative tone, "this is way too over the edge. Okay, everybody. The party's over!" he announced. "It's time to go home and work out all the new issues that you're finding in your lives."

"But, Greg," Erica pleaded. "We can't just let them go like this. I mean look at them, and do you hear the way they're talking?"

"But we're letting them go like 'this' because there's nothing we can do about 'this,'" Greg said emphatically.

Dave sat his empty glass on the coffee table, and with the attitude of a diva he walked over to Joan and then reached down to assist her out of the chair. "Come on, Joan. Let's go home. I don't think we're welcomed here, and apparently, we have a lot to talk about."

Joan shunned Dave's gesture. "Get your hands off of me. The thought of a man touching me is just making me sick right now. Give me the keys to the car," she demanded.

Dave briefly resisted her request. "But, I usually drive when we go out."

"Not tonight, Cupcakes," Joan replied condescendingly, and then barked, "Now give me the keys before I whip your ass in front of our friends."

"Oh my, aren't you being the butch one," Dave said as his arrogant attitude quickly changed into one of admiration. "Here," he said, handing his wife the car keys.

"Oh, and one more thing," she said with her finger in Dave's face. "I know all about how you order take out dinners when I work late and pretend you fixed it yourself. You're gonna learn to cook or I'm leaving you for somebody who can."

Charmed by the challenge, an obedient "Yes, dear," was all Dave could muster up to say back to his wife.

Joan walked over to Erica, her arms outstretched, asking for a hug. The two embraced, and as Greg innocently stood by, he watched Joan plant a sensual kiss on his wife's mouth. "I love a woman who can cook like you do. I'll call soon," Joan said as she squeezed Erica's buttocks with her hands. She turned to Greg and said, "Later, dude," giving him the knuckle bump as she walked out the door, the car keys clanging in her hand.

Dave approached Erica, his hands in the air as though he was carrying an imaginary purse on his arm. "Erica, thank you so much for a wonderful evening. The dinner was just scrumptious and as always the meatballs were to die for. I did eat too much, so I'll probably be using Joan's Thigh Master all week just to work off those calories," he said as he nervously laughed out loud just as the real Paul Lynde would have done. "Let me know if you want to go shopping sometime next week. I know you're a tiny little thing, but Lane Bryant is probably having a sale and I sure could use some of your fashion advice for my new wardrobe. So maybe you'll come with me?"

"Of course. Sure, just call me," Erica answered as eerie visions of Dave in drag ran through her mind.

Then Dave turned to Erica's husband. "And Greg, as always, it was so good to see you tonight. And I'll be calling you too," he said winking his left eye. He leaned over and gave his friend a wet kiss on the cheek. Greg did not resist, but stood there in a state of confusion as he watched Dave scamper out the door trying to catch up with Joan.

The perfect couple stood in silence for a moment before Erica slowly walked to the front door and closed it. "My god, Greg. What just happened here?" she asked in total disbelief. Their life together was always orderly, with no drama or chaos. The evening was a challenge to comprehend for the both of them.

"The chair. I told you not to take it out of the closet," Greg said as he was searching for some kind of rationale for the outlandish display of zaniness the two had just witnessed.

"Dave and Joan are our best friends," Erica said, "and now they're our best 'gay' friends."

"They're our only gay friends," Greg added, still with no expression on his face.

"You're right," Erica said as though she had just discovered the positive aspect of a somewhat bizarre evening. "They are. You know, we needed gay friends in our lives. We have black friends, Italian friends..."

"And Hu, our Chinese friend," Greg interrupted. "And Martina, who's Puerto Rican," he said as he used his fingers to count, a smile of comfort on his face.

Erica enthusiastically joined in. "And Ed, who's Irish. Hey, Ed's overweight. Do we need to make a list of our fat friends?"

"No," Greg answered, "because then we'd have to categorize our skinny friends, and then our old friends, and then our not so old friends."

"Yeah, you're right. It would just go on forever, and what's the point?" There was a lull in the conversation as the two just gazed at the chair. "So what about the chair?" Erica asked, breaking the short silence.

"How about a sign on it? You know, one that says, 'Don't sit in the chair!'" Greg suggested.

"Or maybe we write a note that says, 'If you want to be gay, park your butt here.' But that's too many words for a sign," Erica admitted.

"Or how about we put it back in the closet and pile old clothes on it, you know, like we did before, just to be safe?"

"Well," Erica said, understanding that agreeing to her husband's solution would be admitting blame. "I hate that idea, especially after all that time it took to clean the closet out, but it's probably the right thing to do. But not tonight. I'm tired. I'll do it first thing in the morning," she agreed. "You know, I really think it'll be worth something someday," she said as she walked by it, touching the velvet fabric with both hands.

Greg walked over to Erica, placing his arm around her waist. "I bet it will," he said as they both made their way together toward the hallway. "Hey, wait a minute. I just had an idea. Think we can rent it out?"

"Rent it out?" Erica said as though the idea was farfetched.

"You know, for parties? Like bachelor and bachelorette parties. Or how about retirement parties? Wouldn't that be a blast?"

Always the entrepreneur, Erica lit up. "We could make a fortune! We might be back cruising on the Mediterranean before the year runs out. After ten years of sitting in the closet, this could be an unexpected blessing. Greg, I love the way you think."

"I know you do, Erica. I know you do," Greg said using his best Paul Lynde impersonation.

"Okay, okay. Cut that out. You're making me nervous doing that. You didn't sit in the chair, did you?" she said jokingly.

"Not yet, my dear. Not yet."

Virgil's Eulogy

The polite and quiet chatter ceased and a hush engulfed the church as the tall frail man in a black pinstriped suit made his way from the front pew to the coffin covered with a rainbow patchwork quilt. He took a moment, his hand caressing the fabric that separated him from his lifelong partner, with his other hand grasping a stack of index cards with his notes. He cleared his throat and then turned around holding his head high to deliver the eulogy.

"My name is James Downs, and Virgil was my partner," he said. The grief was apparent on his face, his eyes swollen from the tears he'd shed since Virgil's death. "Virgil made me promise a long time ago that when he died he didn't want people to see him laid out with makeup on his face, so that's why the coffin is closed. He was that way as most of you probably know. Unlike me, he hated the limelight," James said as he tried to laugh, but only grimaced. "The second thing he made me promise was that his funeral would not be sad. Of course, I made those promises to him not knowing that he would be the first to go. But now that he's gone, well, I must oblige his wishes." James took a deep breath and continued, "So the first thing I must do is apologize for this god awful quilt draping his coffin. This was Virgil's first quilt he ever sewed, and quite frankly, his worst. I used to hate it. He put it everywhere, on the bed, on the back of the sofa, took it with us when we had a picnic. I used to tell him all the time that it looked like a trailer-trash bedcover. But he paid me no attention. He said that each square represented one of his gay friends whether they had AIDS or not, and that at least he was paying tribute to those who wouldn't become famous, and for those who would lose their identities serving in the shadows of others. As you can see, there are many squares in this quilt, and he went on to sew many more. It's evident by your presence here today that he had many dear friends, and for that reason, I really do love this quilt, especially now."

James moved in front of the casket, clutching his hands. "Okay, let's keep it real. I know that most of you know me, you would if you knew Virgil at all, but I see some faces that appear new to me. I know what many of you are thinking as I stand here in front of you, my tweezed and arched eyebrows, the bit of blush on my cheeks, my effeminate mannerisms. Even after all these years I can't hide who and what I am. You're probably thinking that man had to be a drag queen sometime in his life. Am I right? Of course, that's what you're thinking, and you're absolutely correct. Yes, in another time, a more innocent time, I was a female impersonator, an illusionist, a drag queen. Please be patient with my indulgence, because you see, my journey has been Virgil's journey."

James cleared his throat and postured himself as though he were delivering a line from a Shakespearean play. "You might be asking yourselves, 'What's the difference between an impersonator, an illusionist, and a drag queen?' Well, my friends, very little. When it comes down to the basics, everyone puts on their pantyhose the same way, one arched foot at a time." Nervous chuckles rang out in the church as he delivered his one liner from the past. "As entertainers, we often don't want to be called drags, even though it's 'drag' that we're doing. To sound professional, 'female impersonator' is the preferred term, and if we are performing as some famous diva, say, like Liza Minnelli, Cher, Diana Ross, Madonna, or nowadays, Lady Gaga, then we are labeled 'illusionists.' It has an elitist sound to it, don't you think? Illusionist," he said again but with a more pronounced enunciation than before. "But the bottom line is that when we all stepped into drag for the first time, we would look into the mirror and think how the transformation was incredible. All of us are delusional to some extent, and regardless what we really looked like that very first time, in our minds we were beautiful, absolutely gorgeous! However, to those who either helped us or for those that just watched as we transformed from one gender to another, we were in 'booger' drag. Yes, booger drag. And of course, it would be our friends and witnesses to the event who would lie to our faces, telling us how glamorous we were. But, that's what we wanted to hear. No one wants to be told they're ugly."

James walked halfway up the aisle as though he were a professor delivering a lecture to students in a college auditorium. There was a sense that this would be his last performance, and of course, the most personal of his life. It was apparent that he would leave no details out of his oratory, and the array of people crammed into the church were giving all their attention to the over the hill performer. "How did the term 'booger drag' come into existence? Well, I'm no authority on ancient drag history, but it's easy to understand how the word booger can apply. I mean think of it. When you hear the word booger, you think of something nasty and well, downright disgusting. Most of us, and even myself, and no matter how gorgeous we think we are, were booger drags the first time we put on the makeup. The sad thing about the process is that some poor dears never get past that stage and are forever labeled as booger drags. And no matter how many times you yell at them as you pass them in the club, 'You're a booger drag!' they always just nod and smile, and act as if you're cruising them. I've come to the conclusion that most lifetime booger drags can't hear, and they don't read lips very well either. But they are with us, and we must not discriminate against them. Unfortunately, all of them are our sisters, and like all dysfunctional families, we must accept them as they are because they are not going to change, nor will they ever go away. They are booger drags forever, never to become impersonators or illusionists. Just a booger drag."

"My god!" someone yelled from the back of the church. "How much longer are you gonna stretch out this goddamn self-serving sermon?" Suddenly, there was a quiet sense of angst in the room.

"Who said that?" James asked in a defiant yet curious tone. No one answered. People in attendance looked around, even at each other, all with that "don't look at me, I didn't say it" look on their faces.

"Once again, who said that?" James demanded.

Slowly, a figure in the back row wearing a black dress accessorized with a wide-brimmed black hat and veil, raised from the sea of mourners. "It's me, James. It's me."

James scowled, his lips tightened. "Myrna Jean Campbell," he said with scorn. "I thought I recognized your 'fingernails on the blackboard' voice."

"Oh my god, it's Myrna Jean Campbell!" a lesbian at the front of the church screamed with excitement. Tracy, who worked at the homeless shelter for years, was a big drag fan from way back. James glared at her, prompting the woman to reluctantly sit back down next to Sammy, her young friend, who a year earlier was homeless and now made his living selling Avon beauty products to the local entertainers.

The person dressed in black lifted the veil, pulling it over the oversized hat, revealing a thin aging man wearing red lipstick, heavy black eyeliner, and perfect Joan Crawford eyebrows. He maneuvered his way to the aisle, then stood there striking a pose similar to the ones used by Hollywood vixens in the films from the Forties. "Yes, it's me, Myrna Jean Campbell, your old nemesis." Myrna Jean then addressed the crowd, "What James is not telling you is he was a shrewd and cutthroat diva who did anything he could to get what he wanted. That's all I'm saying," Myrna Jean said with a deep raspy voice. She then turned to James and said, "You stole that crown from me, and I will never forgive you for what you did."

James shrugged and said, "My dear Myrna Jean, that was so many years ago."

"Exactly forty-three years ago," Myrna Jean replied with pain in her voice. Gasps could be heard throughout the church as people were using their fingers to count the ages of the two former divas, and the word "old" reverberated throughout the room.

James' ninety-year-old mother, Irene, who had been in the front row snoozing through most of the funeral, stood up and in defense of her son said out loud to the man in the black dress, "Maybe you'd have won that damn pageant if you'd also slept with the judges!"

"Mother, please. I don't need your help," James snapped.

Irene had always been the perfect drag mother, accepting James for who he was, and adoring Virgil, well, because Virgil was more like the son she would have like to have had. "Whatever. I'm just saying..." she said, her voice fading as Gary and Victor, two very close friends of Virgil, forced her to sit back down in the pew.

Myrna Jean stayed stoic. "But I'm not here to get even with you at this moment, James. I'm here to pay my respect to Virgil, a fine man who didn't deserve you. I'm done," Myrna Jean said as she pulled the veil back over her face, and then turned to walk out the door.

"I love you Myrna Jean," Tracy hollered totally out of control. James snapped his head in her direction, again signaling for her to sit immediately, which she did.

When the door closed behind Myrna Jean, James composed himself as if nothing had disrupted his eulogy, and quickly browsed through the card on the top of the deck, finding the place where he left off. "Her timing was impeccable," he exclaimed with a smile on his face as if the whole scene with Myrna Jean had been staged. "That, my friends, was an example of a life-time booger drag." His snarky comment was well received by his supporters, especially local entertainers Ermina and Dante, all decked out in funeral drag that included an overabundance of black sequins and rhinestones, who lead the chorus of applause.

"For me," James said as he walked back to Virgil's coffin, "my drag career was an exceptionally good one, and unlike Myrna Jean Campbell, I made progress in refining my look through the years, from appearing glamorous as well as being sexy. I developed as an illusionist, performing my versions of Broadway hoofers and Hollywood movie stars. I learned to dance to improve my performances and enhance my stage presence. I even entered contests and pageants... ah, the contests and pageants. A performer was nothing without a tiara on her head. We all wanted to be the reigning queen. Gays love royalty. Whether it's fleeting royalty or not, gays are like the little bees in the hive, busy taking care of their queen, being loyal to her at all times, except when another queen comes along and they all follow the new one out of the hive, abandoning the first queen, who now can't fend for herself and is left to die, to become in some cases, a booger queen. A booger queen is nothing more than a booger drag with a crown on her head." There were chuckles from the pews. "Gays are fickle, aren't they?" James asked rhetorically. "Nobody said being royal was easy, but it is a status only a few can achieve." He paused for a moment, put the top card on the bottom of the stack in his hand, and continued with his oratory. "I ultimately won a few well recognized pageants, where all the contestants competed like women in a real contest, with evening gown, talent, and interview categories. With all the accolades I had received through my career, for some reason winning a crown was probably the pinnacle of my drag career."

James walked behind the coffin, carefully smoothing out a few lumps of batting as if he were finding real solace in feeling Virgil's spirit exuding from the stitches that held the fabric together. "However," he said as a smile came over his face, "in looking back, all the joy and gratification with the glory and fame that I achieved never exceeded the excitement and drama of when I was, and I will say it proudly, a booger drag. Yes, that short time before I became a legitimate and adored entertainer was the best time of my life."

"It was in the early Seventies when I performed my first number in a show at this little dive called the Cat's Meow. The bar was a place for people like me who were under-aged with dimwit minds. It's where you'd go to get a cheap drink, a quick trick, and of course, crabs and an assortment of venereal diseases. It was, as I liked to call it, the buffet of shame, and a disgusting place, but it was so much fun. Oddly, this was probably the most defining time of my life. This would be a time of 'finding' myself, but not just for me, but also for the new people in my life. We weren't necessarily trying to find our ways, but more so in creating a space that we could call our own. It was about losing our pasts and old identities and reinventing new ones. The exciting part of it all was that we had no idea of where we were going and how we would get there. There was no plan, just opportunity, though it would come with some pains. But our lives would also be filled with so much joy and humor. We were reckless with a sense of invincibility. We were young with no concept of time or ambition. We would live a day-to-day existence, with an innate desire to see who could last the longest in the subculture that we would be creating. One September afternoon..."

"James, dear," Irene hollered out.

"Mother, I'm in the middle of Virgil's eulogy."

"Yes, I know," she said almost apologetically, "but..."

"Then what is it?" James asked a bit perturbed by his mother's interruption.

"Could you speed it up? My catheter is feeling uncomfortable."

James was obviously aggravated, but the old woman was, after all, his mother, so he had to demonstrate some restraint in his response, especially in front of so many people. "Shift, mother. Shift," he instructed under his breath. And Irene shifted her position, tucking her skirt as she did so. "Better?" he asked rather tersely.

"Yes," she replied. "Thank you, dear, but hurry. I don't know how long it will last."

James tugged at his tie and continued with his tribute to Virgil. "So where were we?"

"Some September afternoon!" an anonymous mourner who sounded just like Paul Lynde shouted.

"Of course. Thank you. One September afternoon, I was at the park taking in the autumn sun, and just chatting with some friends and a few new acquaintances when I was approached by Virgil, another young guy our age. Said he'd seen me perform the week earlier. He was awkward looking, you know, short in stature, bulging brown eyes, and thin black hair. But there was something about him that I found charming. Soon, the two of us were in his blue Pinto, heading to his apartment, which was actually a room he rented in an old house in Midtown. Now keep in mind, I wasn't sure of what might happen when we got there, but to my surprise he pulled out a Dionne Warwick record, put it on the stereo, and played it really low as to not disturb the neighbors, and then he began to pantomime the song right in front of me. He was doing drag out of drag," he said, raising his voice as he became more demonstrative. "And he was awful! And when he asked me for an honest critique of his performance, well," he paused and smiled, "I told him it was good, very good. At that moment I had just created a real life booger drag." James shook his head. "I know I've told that story a hundred times over the years, but the image is one that I just can't get out of my head," he said laughing.

"When you're young and naive, making friends is an easy thing to do. It's a learning period for most, and for me and my new friends, it wasn't any different. In our short time together, we became a family of sorts, always watching out for each other. There were four of us, and of course, Virgil was the doting motherly type, the serious one always worried about how we'd survive, how we'd eat. Somehow, I persuaded Virgil and the other two to work in a show with me as backup performers. Being unemployed, and might I add, probably unemployable, they reluctantly agreed. The money we earned allowed us to rent an apartment. Our apartment on 12th Street was about a half a block away from the park and about two blocks away in the other direction from Main Street. It was basically a one-room basement apartment, the length of the entire building on one side. It wasn't much, but it was furnished, and freshly painted a mint green. Mint green was the rage for low-income folks back in those days. Even the pipes that hung from the ceiling seemed to add character to the place. Virgil seemed to think they would come in handy for hanging costumes and dresses, though most of our drag costumes were made of polyester and could be rolled up in a ball and they would never wrinkle. The rent was thirty-five dollars a week, paid on Mondays, which was perfect on both counts. Another plus was that two gay guys were our landlords, so we felt comfortable knowing that they would understand our new life style, though they might not agree with it."

"Psst. Psst." James stopped his speech when he realized the minister was standing next to him.

"Yes?" James asked.

"We have back-to-back funerals today," the minister whispered, "and we seem to be running a little behind," he added as he motioned at his watch.

"Of course, I understand. I'll speed it up," James said, and he did. He looked at his own watch, took a deep breath, and began to speak uncontrollably fast, but not missing a word from his notes. "We performed on Fridays and Saturdays, and half of what we made paid the rent for the week, and the rest went for food... none of us really knew what we were doing in the show... and the group just followed my lead... I was the only one interested in entertaining... Virgil and the others hated the being in the spotlight, and they never knew the words or the steps to the songs we performed, but what they did understand was that being a showgirl was paying the rent... at first we didn't know it, though it didn't take long to figure out, but our apartment was actually in a neighborhood that was a hotbed for prostitutes and drug activities, so it wasn't considered to be a safe area to be in, let alone live in." James paused, taking a few more deep breaths as he scanned the room noticing those in attendance were in a trance like state with eyes wide open. He knew he couldn't continue with the pastor's request so he purposely slowed the pace of his rhetoric. "Perhaps the metal door on our apartment should have been the first indicator. It was common to find used condoms and drug needles outside in the hallway."

"James!" Irene shouted as she stood up. "Stop it with that kind of talk about sex and drugs, especially here in church. We'll all be going to hell if you continue to talk that filth," she said, her voice cracking. A chorus of "amen's" filled the room. She turned to the pews and said, "I can only apologize to you all for his filthy mouth."

"Old woman, you're embarrassing yourself, and me as well," James scolded as if no one else was in the room.

"You're the embarrassment. You're the perfect example of why abortions should be an option. I love you son, but I had no choice in the matter." James was used to his mother's absurd outbursts. It seems that when she turned eighty, she began blurting out all kinds of things at any time of the day or place. By now, James wasn't even bothered about the comments, only that she had interrupted the ceremony once again. He demanded his mother have a seat, and in the corner of his eye he noticed the minister tapping on his watch, indicating to James that he needed to hurry up. He rotated his cards, and wiped the sweat off his brow with the back of his hand.

"None of us used drugs, and we simply dismissed our surroundings as just that, surroundings. Virgil was the most nervous of us all. It was his nature to be leery of anything new. But because we were young and wrapped up into our own little world, we were oblivious to the dangers of the streets, and found ourselves walking around them at all hours of the night, talking about our dreams, our worries, our hopes, a new song for the next show. We felt that if we looked confident and not scared, then the people of the night would fear us instead. This attitude permeated our daily and nightly lives. We began to fear no one. Of course, we weren't totally naïve to believe that something horrible couldn't or wouldn't happen, so each of us carried a paring knife on us, and when we were in drag, the knives would be tucked into the cup of our bras. Soon, as a group, we had a reputation as people not to mess with. Funny how all of us were kind and caring people, but we'd be eaten up alive if that was the first impression that people had of us. It was a shell of survival, an armor. It was attitude. Looking back, we must have been crazy as I think of how we danced in the dark shadows with the people of the night, eating and drinking side by side with the likes of the homeless and hustlers, the johns and junkies, and the predators and prey. At times it would be difficult to tell one from another."

James had just paused and started to recite his notes from the next card, "When Christmas rolled around, the times were bleak," when a man began wailing uncontrollably. "For god's sake!" James said in frustration, his eyes widening with ire. "This isn't even the sad part of the eulogy." He walked over to the area where the sobs were coming from. Fernando, his gardener, was in a fetal position crammed between the pews, his weeping face cradled in his hands.

"Fernando, please, control yourself!" James ordered, almost screaming.

"But I can't," Fernando responded, the sobs growing louder. "I'm so sad, and I can't quit crying."

James looked at the people surrounding his gardener and recognized local drag groupie Ricky who had worked with Virgil as a waiter at the restaurant, and the new man in Ricky's life who claimed to be a virgin. His name was David. "Can someone please help Fernando out of here so I might continue with the eulogy?" he asked, when suddenly, people in at least two full pews, including Ricky and David, stood up to assist Fernando out of the church. They figured it was their only way to escape the lengthy oration.

"Not so fast," James commanded as he snapped his fingers. "Only two may assist the man. The rest of you sit back down until I'm finished." Two Guatemalan men dressed in fiesta inspired ponchos gripped Fernando's arms and quickly led the young man down the aisle and through the doors. Referring to his notes, James once again returned to the eulogy.

"Our other roommates went home to be with their families. I couldn't afford to go home, so Virgil stayed with me. Because we didn't have any money, Virgil and I agreed to not give each other presents. Rent was still paid weekly, but we had less for food and any other necessities. We often ate one meal a day just to get by. Conveniently, we could attribute our thin girlish figures to our diet. According to all the gossip rags, that's what the top models were doing...not eating. To say the cupboards were bare would be an understatement. They were bare, alright. Virgil insisted on having a Christmas Eve dinner, and after searching through the cabinets, he found an onion under the sink next to the Comet cleanser, and he discovered a bag of all-purpose flour right behind the onion. Neither one of us remembered buying any of those things. We hardly ever cooked and we really never used the Comet cleanser. It wasn't long after that we were busy in the kitchen. Virgil fried the onions in some old Crisco and I baked biscuits with the flour and water. We made smiley faces on the dough. When they were ready, we took them out of the oven and Virgil prepared the plates. Oh, those biscuits looked so good, and the sautéed onions smelled so inviting. Well, the onions were delicious, but the biscuits were as hard as rocks and not at all edible. Virgil was so upset and I was so angry with Virgil for being upset. I put on my coat and ran out of the apartment. I walked down Main Street. It was dark and empty. I passed a gas station, and of course, being Christmas Eve, it was closed, but there was a vending machine out front, the kind that had knobs that you pulled. Oddly enough, I had a dime in my pocket, all the money we had until our next show. I approached the machine, pulled out the dime and put it into the slot. I heard a thud, not the usual clang. The coin was stuck. I walked away, but something told me to go back and try pulling the knob. I did. And I kept on pulling, until I had emptied the darn thing of all the Snickers bars. They were safely packed inside my coat. When I returned with the loot, Virgil, in all his holy glory, accused me of being a thief. But after a few minutes of reflection and giving thanks, he announced that the act of kindness had to be that of a Christmas angel looking out for us. And I couldn't disagree."

James took out his kerchief and dramatically wiped a few forced tears from his eyes. "Yes, looking back it was the best Christmas ever. And it was a lesson about life and surviving for Virgil and me. We knew that a certain amount of effort had to come from us if we wanted to eat and have a place to sleep. The Christmas angel couldn't be watching over us all the time, but low and behold, another unlikely angel came to our rescue. A few days later, we walked by the Blue Plate Cafeteria & Deli in Midtown and there was a sign in the window that said 'Now Hiring.' We walked in and met Sarah, the manager, and she offered Virgil and me jobs working there prepping and serving food to a mostly older clientele. Of course, it was a step down from my status as a star in my own little drag world, but Virgil was right at home in the culinary environment. The job tied us over between shows, and we were assured of at least one free meal per day. It was one of the perks of working there. We also got to take home any leftovers that couldn't be reused. By our standards, we were living high on the hog. Virgil was feeling a sense of security, and of course, I was too. But I still dreamed of being a real entertainer, of being famous, of being adored. However, I was still a booger drag, and working at the Blue Plate didn't improve that image very much. But I was now a believer in fate, and I believed that it was destiny that had brought me there to that place, to that time. I knew being a star would happen some day. I just didn't know when."

"James, can you hurry it up? I'm getting hungry," Irene said out loud.

"Yeah, is there a buffet reception after the funeral?" asked a man on the left side of the room. The man was Stella, a famous drag performer from Birmingham, Alabama. Seems Stella was notorious for booking shows in other towns to coincide with funerals of local gay celebrities.

"Mother, please quit talking out loud," and addressing the man's question, he added, "There will be a small get together at the American Legion Hall after the funeral."

Stella stood up and belted out, "There has to be a nearby steakhouse around here that has a really good buffet. A buffet is perfect for a wake!" he rudely suggested. James was not amused and glared with distain at the overweight out of drag entertainer.

"Of course, the American Legion Hall would be lovely," Stella said, cowering down to his seat, but before he could completely sit, he jumped back up and added, "But if I may, while I'm still standing, I would like to invite you all to my show tonight at 10:30 at the Rack, and if you mention Virgil's name at the front door, you'll get a dollar off the admission. Hope to see you all there." The brazen Stella sat down.

James stayed quiet for a few seconds, a bit outraged at Stella's solicitation, but he would not be deterred from finishing his eulogy. He stiffened up, and again took a deep breath, and after exhaling he said, "Yes, the past is the past, and anything I say about it will sound like another cliché that's already been written and spoken a thousand times over, but my early booger days were the best of days for me. They were, if you will, the formative days of my life."

"It wasn't long after that our roommates moved out, I

was discovered and became a featured entertainer, and Virgil continued to hone his skills at the deli, but other than work, we were inseparable. After being employed at the Blue Plate Cafeteria & Deli for two years, Sarah was fired for drinking on the job. Her coworkers never suspected that she was drunk the whole time she worked there. They just thought she was cranky and hard to get along with. It seems that one day Virgil mistakenly gave Sarah's spiked drink that was sitting next to the soda fountain to an old woman having a quick lunch. Virgil thought it was just a diet cola. The old woman drank the whole thing and got sick. Though it was an accident, Sarah blamed Virgil for getting fired. Of course, Virgil felt bad about the whole situation. That was just Virgil being Virgil. Sarah and her old man, who we never did meet, moved out of their apartment. We heard they went to Idaho to get away from all the crazy gay people living in the big city."

Just as most of the mourners in the church were lowering their heads as they fought off the nods of boredom, organ music blared at full volume throughout the church. Ruby, the organist, had fallen asleep, and she fell over, her head landing on the keyboard, and when she tried to raise herself up with her hands, more notes of discord rang out. Irene was the first to stand, and like all good Baptists who hear organ music in church, the mourners followed her lead and stood in unison ready to sing the next gospel inspired song. Realizing what had happened, the minister urged the crowd to sit back down. Ruby pulled herself together, publicly shamed that she had drifted off and consequently disrupting the eulogy.

More determined to complete his presentation, James shuffled his cards and continued. "Virgil finally found his perfect mate. It took him a few years to conquer the fool, but he didn't let up with his need to be celibate and wait for Mister Right. While I was out looking for anonymous sexual encounters, not wanting to be tied down to anything but my drag career, Virgil sat at home always waiting for my safe return. Yes, he was my best friend ever, and one isolated night, and I'll never forget that night, it suddenly dawned on me. Love was more than just sex, more than a total commitment.

It was about belonging, and that one night, I realized that I belonged with Virgil. That's right, I belonged with Virgil. When I told him of my feelings, he just looked me in the eyes and said, 'I know. I've known it since the first time you came over to my apartment and sat next to me. I knew it when you watched me practice my song, and even though I wasn't very good, you still told me that I was.' He also told me that I had been his Mister Right all that time."

James stepped back, wanting to take in the love he thought might be exuding from those in attendance. He glanced over at one of his old friends, Robert, who lived at the assisted living facility a few blocks away, and who was with his new boyfriend Hal, and said, "Please don't be sad. Virgil didn't want this to be a sad occasion."

Though James' comment was staged and intended to be rhetorical, Robert simply whispered back, "James, I'm not sad. Hal has to pee and I'm worried he can't hold it any longer."

James ignored his friend's response and then looked up and said, "Virgil went on to be the best sandwich maker ever, and eventually he opened his own deli. Later, he went to culinary school, where I did all the homework for him," he said laughing out loud, "and he became a master chef. We opened *Jamie Lee's*, an upscale restaurant, where he cooked and I played the host. After all, entertaining was, and still is, my specialty."

"While I was going through some of Virgil's things, his very private things, I found a note that he wrote a long time ago. Virgil had a way at looking at things, especially the details. He tried to attend most of my shows when he could, but when he didn't I'd fill him in on all the details. He was so attentive to every word I said. Somehow, he decided to write some of the things down that I had said that I never should have done in my life." James pulled the folded up white sheet of paper aged with time out of his jacket pocket. He slowly opened it up, and began to read out loud, "*Things Jamie Lee should never have done: Follow Tiffany Anthony's striptease act in a lesbian bar in San Antonio with a ballad.* Well, I shouldn't have followed that act with any kind of number," James added as a sidebar comment. "You see, she had implants and they were huge," he said holding his hands in front of his chest.

*"Perform top forty rock numbers in a Miami club filled with Cubans, while Natalie Green did the classic drag hits and the crowd sang along with her...*they looked at me," he stated sarcastically. "So the following night, I brought out the *Funny Girl* classics and they sang along with me, too. It was a language thing, I told myself. Next, *Perform in a new club in San Antonio only to find out they didn't use tapes, only albums.* I brought no albums, only cassette tapes...this was obviously before CD's. I had to go through the DJ's records and perform three songs that I didn't know. First was "Last Dance" (a disco remix) by Donna Summer. I don't remember what the other two were, but I wore ballad gowns to dance in. It was awful," he said as the audience began to encourage him with light applause hoping the end of the service was near.

Suddenly, the door to the church flew open with a bang, startling everyone. Fernando ran forth and announced, "James! James!" he yelled, pronouncing the J's like H's. "Myrna Jean is outside and she has a gun!" he screamed as loud as he could. To say that the crowd stampeded out of the church in every direction would be an understatement. Within thirty seconds, the room was empty except for James, Irene, and Virgil's quilt-draped coffin. Even Ruby outran the minister in seeking a safe place to hide.

"Mother, why are you still here? Aren't you afraid of being murdered?"

"Hell, as slow as I am, I'd be the first to be shot, so I might as well just sit here and wait for the bitch to come in and shoot me. Why waste the energy? And anyway, Myrna Jean's just bluffing. She's been bluffing for years now."

"Yes, she has. And knowing that, I have an obligation to finish this eulogy," James said holding his head up high. "And so without any further ado," he said looking at the empty pews as though they were still full, "I will continue."

"Good lord, Myrna Jean," Irene mumbled. "Get in here and put me out of my misery."

James cleared his throat then continued. *"Have a hairdresser in*

San Antonio agree to do my hair. With just five minutes before I was to perform, the queen declared that there was nothing she could do with it, threw her hands in the air and walked out. I never looked good in flat hair, even in San Antonio."

"*Agree to do the duet, "You Don't Bring Me Flowers" by Barbra Streisand and Neil Diamond with a local birthday drag favorite.* I did the Diamond part out of drag, but got confused and tore into the Streisand lines. Again, another faux pas in San Antonio. *Perform "There's Got to be a Morning After" from the "Poseidon Adventure" dressed like a drunken hooker.* I thought it would be funny. I should have been wet with a fish stuck in my mouth instead. *Embarrass a former Miss Gay United States who was trying to hit on me in Nashville, Tennessee.* She thought I was hot trade. When she told me she was a former Miss Gay United States, I told her I was too! Ah, the look on her face. *Try to help an ugly queen out in a contest by giving her a few makeup hints as I passed through the dressing room.* Later, while in the audience, I was a caught off guard when I heard my name announced on stage as one of her sponsors. That was so embarrassing," he added.

James looked at the page in front of him. He folded the note and put it back into his pocket, then walked behind the coffin. Without referring to any notes, James began speaking on a more personal level, his voice softened and weak, his emoting to the pews over. "I'm trying to keep it funny Virgil, but it's hard. It's hard," he said again. "There are many more things you wrote down, but the last thing on the list of things I should have never done, well, I know what you wrote. You wrote, *He should have picked somebody else to love because he could do so much better than me.*" James became overcome with grief, a grief so painful to understand. "It was me who could have never done better than you," he said as he wiped his eyes with his kerchief.

"We spent over forty years together, forty wonderful years, and now you're gone. Yes, you're gone now, a heart attack after eating so much bacon and pastrami. I told you it would kill you one day," James said trying to laugh his way through the sadness. "I will miss you so. The quiet walks, the one-sided conversations, and yes, even those bulging, bloodshot brown eyes." James once again began to run his hands over the quilt. "Virgil, you had a unique perspective on life. It was the little things, you would say, that are the important parts of life. And you were right. In the scheme of my life's plans, and when I look back, so much of life that I thought was important was not even meaningful. What is really significant after all these years is that our souls touched and we will be tied together for eternity. And in that, I can say, I have been so lucky and so blessed." James gently leaned on the coffin, clutching the quilt, pulling it to him like a scared child holding its favorite blanket close as to seek comfort and safety.

He paused for a moment, and with more thespian flair than what Vivien Leigh used in the scene from *Gone With the Wind* where Scarlett O'Hara swears she'll "never go hungry again," James raised his head and declared, "So now, when someone asks me why I performed in drag for all those years, I can now tell them that it was my destiny, my fate at one time to be guided by a Christmas angel, and to one day meet and then love a man named Virgil, the love of my life." And just like any dramatic sequence in a theater staging, James finally ended his eulogy to Virgil by providing a full-body collapse onto the coffin. Of course, the response in the church was quiet, unlike when James had rehearsed the speech, envisioning a standing ovation from those who would come and pay their respects to Virgil and also be entertained with a memorable eulogy.

Amid the tears, James could feel the emptiness in the church. Other than his mother sitting in the first pew waiting to be shot down by Myrna Jean, no one was left to hear his final words. He closed his eyes and began a silent prayer, his last prayer before the coffin and Virgil would be taken to the crematorium.

James' eyes opened wide when he heard three knocks coming from the casket, three sounds like that of knuckles rapping from the inside. "My god! Virgil's alive!" he screamed with excitement. "Mother," he yelled, "we've got to get him out of here!"

Irene didn't say a word, but pointed back to the end of the coffin.

Standing behind James was the minister who had quietly walked back into the church, tiptoeing as to not disturb James in his moment of private prayer.

"I'm sorry, James. I didn't mean to startle you. I just knocked on the coffin to get your attention," he said in his best minister's tone. "We're ready to take Virgil now. We have another funeral due to start in the next five minutes."

"Of course," James said as he tried to compose himself. He took the quilt, gently folding it and placing it under his arm, then asked his mother to leave with him. They slowly walked down the aisle, the pews empty, no one to comfort them, just the two of them.

"You have to give Myrna Jean a lot of credit," Irene said to her son. "After all these years she still knows how to steal the show."

"Perhaps, but she's no Rachel Wells," he responded, his eyes looking forward.

"Who the hell is Rachel Wells?" the elderly woman asked.

James didn't answer his mother's question, but he did quietly scowl and then squeezed her arm tighter as he guided her down the aisle. "Shut up old woman," he said out of the side of his mouth, "and just walk."

Acknowledgments

This book is dedicated to the love of my life, Jack Shelman, to all the fans of Rachel Wells, and to all those misfits out there who are confused about their sexual orientation, gender identity, or creative abilities, and who also dare to challenge the norms of society that restrict their development and growth as individuals.

About the Author

In the 1970's, J.R. Greenwell was a premiere headliner for many years at the Sweet Gum Head in Atlanta, GA, and performed as a female illusionist across the country. He later earned a Masters of Education at the University of Louisville, and now devotes his time as a queer writer creating plays and prose at his home in central Kentucky.